# BLACK PHOENIX

# GEORGE BERNAU
# BLACK PHOENIX

**WARNER BOOKS**

A Time Warner Company

Warner Books, Inc., 1271 Avenue of the Americas, New York, NY 10020

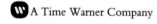 A Time Warner Company

Printed in the United States of America

First Printing: April 1994

10  9  8  7  6  5  4  3  2  1

Library of Congress Cataloging-in-Publication Data

Bernau, George.
    Black phoenix / George Bernau.
        p.    cm.
    ISBN 0-446-51610-4
    1. World War, 1939–1945—Fiction. I. Title.
PS3552.E7277B47 1994
813'.54—dc20                                                                 91-51170
                                                                                    CIP

Book design by H. Roberts

Laurie and Erin
for their courage.

The following message was found partially burned in a grate in the garden area immediately adjacent to the Fuehrer Bunker by Allied intelligence officers on May 2, 1945.

*My dearest, let nothing deter you from the execution of our plans. What you have not been told is for your own safety, but know that nothing will be as it appears. The beginning will masquerade as the end, and triumph as defeat. In the end, however, final victory will rise from the ashes.*

The note was in a code used by only the very top members of the Third Reich's High Command. Its meaning and importance have never been fully explained. This note fragment and several other tantalizing clues and leads left behind in the ashes of postwar Berlin form the basis for this story.

# PART
# ONE

# PROLOGUE

*Germany, somewhere west of the Elbe, April 25, 1945*

A new war was beginning. Major Thomas Sheridan of the American Army's Counter Intelligence Corps stood at the side of an untraveled mountain road in northwest Germany. His dark blue eyes squinted against the sun as he strained to make out the details in the river valley that lay beneath him. A new war, he thought, in which for the first time, the enemy had a weapon with a truly unlimited potential for destruction. And a war against an enemy that was actually capable of using that terrible weapon, no matter what its ultimate consequences might be. How in God's name, Sheridan asked himself, could such a war, against such an enemy, ever be won?

Sheridan was barely thirty-five years old, but in many ways he looked older. There were only traces left now of the freckles that once had been sprinkled across the bridge of his nose and

3

along his straight, hard-boned cheeks. There were deeply cut lines now too that fanned out from the corners of his eyes. And there were already touches of silver sprinkled through his short-cut, sandy brown hair and even in the neatly trimmed moustache that he'd grown over the last few months as he'd waited in London for this assignment to be set in motion. War did that to you, he'd told himself without much concern when he had first begun to notice it happening to him. It was a small price compared to what others were paying.

That morning Sheridan's tall, loosely built frame was dressed in olive-drab fatigues, but over his Army uniform he wore a canvas protective suit. The bulky suit had thick rubber feet that covered his combat boots and a long, one-piece canvas body that stretched from his ankles to his shoulders. It was topped off by a rubber hood that for the moment hung unused down his back. At his hip the American major wore a side arm, and below that a pack containing a gas mask and long rubber gloves.

The jeep's driver wore similar protective gear. At a moment's notice both men could be covered entirely by rubber and canvas, but whether they would be safe was something that Sheridan, knowing what he did, was far from certain.

The American intelligence officer checked the map that lay on the jeep's dashboard. It was a German map and it showed the mountainous terrain of the remote region with precision. Sheridan found the spot on the map that was his final destination, a small stretch of river valley buried deep in the rocky terrain called by the locals "the Resting Place," an obscure location, but the spot that Command needed an Allied intelligence officer to inspect and to photograph in detail as soon as possible. Sheridan had been selected for the job, as he had been for more than half a dozen of Command's toughest assignments over the last three years.

There was already one other confirmed location for Phoenix in a remote area of southeast France. Sheridan had seen the pictures of the location taken by British intelligence. He had no desire to see anything like it in person, but he knew that he had to, and he could feel his insides tighten as he realized how close he was to it now.

Sheridan tossed the map back on the jeep's dashboard. The breeze had picked up slightly and the foul sweetish smell that he had caught only a hint of a few moments earlier was thick in the air. Sheridan unsnapped the pack on his hip and removed the protective rubber mask inside. Gesturing for his driver to do the same, Sheridan removed his steel helmet and fitted the mask on over his face, tightening its straps down into place. Then he snapped the top two buttons on his canvas bodysuit, drew the rubber hood up over his head, and tied the hood tightly into place.

When he was finished, he looked at his driver. The young man seemed hesitant. Sheridan reached over and straightened the shoulders of the other man's canvas suit and then drew the rubber hood up tightly around the sides of his protective mask, being very certain that no part of the other man's body was exposed to the open air. The driver nodded a thank-you, but his eyes behind the mask's gray plastic lenses still looked confused. This was not the kind of a war that he had signed up to fight, the young man's expression seemed to say.

There was no reason that both of them needed to go down into that valley anyway, Sheridan decided. He'd walk in from here by himself. And he slid his long legs covered in the thick protective gear out of the side of the jeep.

"An hour," Sheridan said. Command had been very clear not to stay any longer than that. He reached into the rear of the vehicle for the rubber bag that contained his camera equipment and the detailed map of the lower region of the valley that London had provided for him.

"Be careful," Sheridan called out in a muffled voice from inside his protective mask, and then patted the side arm that he wore on his hip. His driver nodded back and reached for his rifle and placed it across his lap. Both men knew that there was a good possibility of German soldiers still being in the area, mostly deserters from units that had been left behind in their army's retreat back toward Berlin. He almost looks grateful, though, Sheridan thought as he took a final glance at his driver, for a chance to fight a real enemy, one that he could see and understand.

Sheridan slung the rubber bag over his shoulder and started across the few feet of open space between the road and the hillside that led down into the deserted valley.

The thick plastic eyepieces of his protective mask distorted his vision, blurring the outline of shapes and turning the landscape faintly gray. It would make the going slow and Sheridan wanted to remove it, but he knew now that he didn't dare. It had been the intensely powerful smell in the mountain air a few moments before that had finally convinced him that what Command said lay at the base of the hill really existed. He had never smelled anything remotely like its strength or its foulness. He wondered then what part the sickening decaying odor played in the overall process, but he knew that he wasn't really qualified to think about that and he let it go. He was neither a scientist nor a career intelligence officer. He was just a volunteer soldier out here in this very frightening place a long way from home, because for some reason that he didn't even begin to understand, the world had temporarily gone mad. And just when he had begun to believe that all the insanity was ending, this final outbreak of madness that the enemy called "Phoenix" had begun.

# CHAPTER ONE

*Berlin, April 29, 1945*

Reichminister Joseph Goebbels felt a deep shiver of anticipation pass through him as the door to the secret underground chamber beneath the Berlin bunker opened and the stooped and bent figure of the Fuehrer entered the room.

He certainly wasn't the man that he once had been, Goebbels thought as he watched Hitler cross the chamber and sit at the head of the long oak conference table. The Fuehrer's hands shook and his face was worn and aged.

Why had he called this final meeting? Every part of Phoenix was solidly in place. There wasn't even the slightest detail remaining to be discussed. All that was required now was action. And why here like this, buried deep beneath the city? The Fuehrer's penchant for secrecy and darkness had truly reached bizarre proportions.

The only light in the underground room came from a collection of black wax candles that flickered erratically from the center of the table, and in their light Goebbels looked around at the faces of the other men seated with him that night. Hard-faced, determined men, mostly military, a few political, but the true believers, the most committed men remaining in the Reich and all men of true action, not words. These were not the famous faces or those that had been included in the Fuehrer's recent public statements. There were no soft fat men like Goering, no cowards like Doenitz. This was the true secret inner circle of Phoenix. But why had they been assembled now, with the barbarians at the gates of the city? Even buried deep within the catacombs of Berlin, the rumble of the Russian artillery could be heard in the distance. There was one possible answer, and as he considered the possibility, Goebbels felt a renewed sense of hope and expectation.

Goebbels' gaze returned to the door of the secret underground chamber as a second man entered the room and followed behind the Fuehrer. It was Morell, Hitler's private physician. And the fat, sloppily dressed man held tightly to his small black physician's bag even now as he crossed the room and seated himself at the table on the Fuehrer's right hand.

Morell was a man of less than medium height, but of enormous girth. He was squatly built with a protruding belly that pushed out at the confines of an ill-fitting gray suit.

Goebbels felt anger and revulsion pour through him at the other man's presence at such a moment. There had been a blood oath among the others in the room never to disclose a whisper of Phoenix to anyone and here was this outsider, this fat weak doctor, being allowed to participate. But Goebbels knew the power of the contents of Dr. Morell's black bag. Inside that bag were syringes and needles and vials of a murky gray liquid that now gave Morell influence and control over the Fuehrer beyond that of everyone else in that room. But knowing the source and intensity of his power only made Goebbels hate the fat man even more.

"The Fuehrer welcomes you," Morell said, speaking for the leader, as he had more and more over the last few months. But as he continued the prepared opening words, slowly the Fuehrer himself leaned forward, letting the erratic flicker of light and shadow from the candlelit table move across his face until finally Morell stopped talking and a tense expectant hush filled the room. The silence and the tension seemed to stretch into a dark infinity. Then the Fuehrer spoke.

"I have decided to die," he said in a hoarse broken voice.

He had been right, Goebbels realized, and he was filled with horror, but at the same time with the sense of deep anticipation that he had felt earlier. He had devoted himself to the Fuehrer with all of his body and soul, but he knew that the Adolf Hitler he had known for so many years no longer existed, that the war and pursuit by his enemies had worn him down, made him less than a shadow of his former self, and that Phoenix' success could only be ensured by placing it in fresher and more competent hands. His own! Goebbels wanted to shout the words into the maddening darkness of the underground chamber. His own! But what would the Fuehrer's decision be?

The hush in the room reached a level of intensity that Goebbels had never experienced before, as each man in it strained to hear the Fuehrer's words, and each syllable, every nuance, became of monumental importance.

"Die!" the Fuehrer said again, his voice so thick and hoarse with emotion and tension that Goebbels could barely recognize it.

Slowly then and with every eye in the room on him, Hitler removed a small silver box from the pocket of his tunic.

"My work is done," he said as with his shaking, almost palsied hands he opened the small box. Inside lay a ring hammered out of gold with its crest showing a great winged bird, the

Phoenix of legend, rising from a field of fire and destruction, while its claws held a large black reverse Aryan cross, the swastika of the Third Reich. This crested ring, Goebbels understood in a flash, was to Hitler the symbol of the entire great operation. The Fuehrer had worn it at these meetings from the very beginning of Phoenix months before, and now one of the men at this final secret meeting was going to receive it, as a symbol of the Fuehrer's true successor.

"My work is over, but yours has just begun," Hitler said, and stood on shaking legs and began his way down the long table. Goebbels looked at the other tense faces gathered with him that night, realizing as he did that each man believed that he alone would receive the Fuehrer's final prize, but Goebbels focused all of his energy on the ring and its meaning, using the entire power of his own will like a hypnotic force to draw the great symbol of power and glory to him, and slowly, with a broken, tentative step, the Fuehrer circled the table to place the golden ring before Goebbels, symbolizing the passage of power of the Third Reich and the glorious future of Phoenix from one man to the other.

"I give you ultimate victory," the Fuehrer said, and Goebbels repeated back to him the remainder of the phrase that had become the watchword of Phoenix. "Total victory," Goebbels whispered, "or total annihilation."

*　★　*

*London, April 30, 1945*

Sheridan snapped suddenly awake. He wanted to scream, but the sound stuck in his throat. Instead, he shook his head trying to wipe from his mind the nightmarish images that had filled his dreams. The room was cold, but he reached up and mopped a thick coating of sweat from his forehead. He knew where he was now—London. And he knew what had happened to him. The sight, the sounds, even the smells of what he had found on his last mission had returned to him in his sleep. The fifth night in a row that he had awakened like this, the exact number of nights since he had gone into that river valley in northwest Germany.

Sheridan looked out the window of his little third-floor flat. It was still dark and it was raining, but probably not hard enough to cancel his dawn flight, he decided as he watched the big drops of water slap against the window glass.

Debra was already up and out of bed. He marveled at her seemingly endless supply of energy. She had such a beautiful body, lean and hard like a dancer's, he thought as he watched her short lithe figure move in silhouette among the kitchen things at the other end of the apartment. And then he felt his body growing excited again. He laughed at himself. They had made love until late the night before. He had never known that he was capable of such excesses of desire. But then, he'd never known anyone with the capacities that Debra had either, capacities not only for lovemaking but for so damn many things. He wondered if she had always been that way, or if the intensity of her passions had been born from the extremes of the experiences that she had been forced to survive over the last few years.

She began her way across the room toward him, carrying a steaming cup of tea in each hand. "I left one for Peabody on the windowsill," she said, her voice low and throaty, and powerfully disarming for such a physically small woman. Then smiling, she set the cups down on the nightstand next to the bed. "Peabody" was their name for the agent that had turned up outside Sheridan's apartment on the second night that Debra had spent with him. Love affairs were forbidden between CIC agents and members of British intelligence, particularly when both participants were members of the same operation, and there were few secrets within the

Phoenix counteroperation, but so far their superiors had said nothing. The flat was probably bugged though, Sheridan thought, and someone at headquarters might very well be spending his mornings listening to the recorded sounds of their lovemaking. They might as well give the bastard his money's worth, he thought. Debra had removed her robe and she stood for a moment in front of him, naked. Her body was small but beautifully proportioned, with strong smooth legs and tight, round, deeply curving hips and thighs. The full globes of her breasts were large for such a slender woman and their firm dark nipples were erect in her excitement.

Sheridan opened the bedcovers to her, and the cold of the room poured in below the blankets, but she remained for a moment in front of him, teasing him, with the dark red display of the pubic hair between her legs only inches from his face. She placed herself on top of him then, seated facing him, with her shapely legs spread open, positioned so that he could slide himself deep inside of her. Debra's face was small and very pretty. It always pleased him to look at her. The small pixielike features, the shoulder-length, dark red hair, her bright green eyes, everything about her pleased him. She moved tantalizingly on top of him, rocking her body skillfully up and back. She stopped for a moment then and smiled, her green eyes filling with light. Sheridan laughed in return. Wherever she had learned to make love, it was beyond his experience, although he would never admit that to her, he thought as he felt the deep thrills from being inside of her pass through his body in slowly spreading waves of intense pleasure. Sheridan knew from the talk around headquarters that he was not the first to be with her—far from it—and that thought, which could trouble him at other times, only gave him a rush of desire now, as he watched her body once again begin making love to his, and then he could feel his passion reaching a breaking point. He reached up and pulled her down to lie next to him on the bed. Then he rolled himself on top of her and entered her again with all the force of his own powerful body.

They kissed long and passionately and it was Sheridan who said that he loved her as their mouths parted and then rejoined. He wished immediately that he hadn't, but then she breathed the words back to him and their bodies joined deeper and closer. He could feel her climaxing and he pressed himself even harder into her, holding her close to him with his strong arms, while her body spasmed in excitement and then relaxed. He withdrew himself from her and let himself reach his own climax by pushing himself hard several times against her small round belly.

He collapsed down next to her then. His muscles were slack and his skin wild with sensation, but she held him firmly and her touch felt warm and reassuring. If there was such a thing as a special chemical attraction reserved only for one person, they had it with each other, or perhaps she made love to everyone like that. Sheridan didn't know which way it was and he didn't want to find out. He was happy for the moment to just lie next to her and listen to the rain on the room's single window. Finally he looked over at the clock on the bed stand. It was past time to leave. And one thing that he could be certain of was that the 8th Air Force was not going to wait.

Reading his mind, Debra slipped from the bed, showing Sheridan the lightly freckled skin of her back, with her dark red hair falling just below her shoulders. "We're very lucky, you know," she said, turning back to him, her powerful green eyes looking deep into his.

Sheridan said nothing. And she crossed the room to the closet that held her clothes. Sheridan felt vaguely angry as he watched her walk away. He knew that she wanted him to respond, to confirm the very special thing that had just happened between them in their lovemaking. But he didn't. It was better for both of them if he said nothing, he decided.

She had to stand on tiptoes to see her reflection in the mirror that hung over Sheridan's dresser. His flat was difficult for her to deal with in many ways, he thought as he watched her. There were many differences between them, and some of them a hell of a lot more important than their height. But there was something so damn powerful between them as well. If it weren't for the war . . . But there *was* the war and it changed everything, he reminded himself angrily, and then cut his thoughts off.

When she had finished dressing, she turned back to him for a moment, smoothing the skirt of her dark blue uniform down in front. The dark blue wool of His Majesty's Navy looked as if it had been designed with her in mind. The skirt fit neatly to her trim figure, displaying her fine legs beneath it, and the over-blouse hugged her shapely upper body in an alluring but still somehow proper and military way. She looked as if she'd been born to be a British naval officer, but, of course, Sheridan thought as he looked at her standing in front of him, nothing could be further from the truth. Maybe that was really what kept him from truly committing to her. Who she was. Where she'd come from. Things that he understood so damn little about. Maybe, he admitted to himself, but he hoped that wasn't true. That he wasn't like that.

He turned his gaze away from her. The rain had let up, only a faint drizzle streaking the window glass. He couldn't delay any longer. The reconnaissance flight that he had arranged to take would be leaving Coventry at dawn. "We should be going," he said.

"I'll bring the car around," she called back to him as she started for the door. Sheridan nodded. He had been unable to talk her out of taking him to the airfield. She had borrowed a car and she insisted on driving it herself.

He pulled on his shorts and T-shirt and then went to the sink to shave. He washed and then dressed quickly in his uniform before going downstairs.

14

BLACK PHOENIX

Debra was waiting for him in front of the flat. The car that she had borrowed was a British Army Land-Rover, painted olive drab and open on the sides, except for a flap of canvas that barely overhung the roofline. The drive from Chelsea to the Allied field at Coventry took nearly two hours on rain-slick roads, and by the time they reached it, Sheridan's trench coat was dark with rainwater.

Debra began to guide the Rover off the highway and down a dirt road that led to the airfield's guarded front gate. Sheridan moved his gaze back to the wet windscreen. He could feel the wind and the rain blowing in on him through the vehicle's open side panel. Neither of them had said very much during the long drive, but he wanted to say something to her now, although he still wasn't sure what it should be. He almost welcomed the dangerous mission that lay in front of him. In some ways it was less complicated than his life, he thought as he moved his gaze out into the darkness.

The Rover's headlights picked up the outline of a security gate, manned by a single guard. Behind the gate stood a parked jeep. The jeep had a full canvas stretched across its top and buckled down around its sides, covering the interior. Sheridan could make out the figure of the jeep's driver, slouched in the vehicle's front seat. It was Hearn. The young dark-haired pilot was leaning back, casually smoking a cigarette, one foot propped up and resting on the jeep's dash.

Debra pulled the Rover to a stop in front of the gate and showed the guard her ID as Sheridan leaned forward and displayed his CIC card. The guard saluted and Debra pulled the Rover past him and then stopped it a few feet from Hearn's jeep. Sheridan could sense her hesitation. Below the cool surface, she was anxious and frightened. He put his hand out and she reached over and held it. "Just another mission," he said. Through their clasped hands, Sheridan could feel her reaction to his lie. God, there really was something special between them, he thought

15

then. He had never had so much with any woman. She cut the car engine off and he leaned over and kissed her full, sensuous mouth.

Sheridan opened the door on his side and stretched a long leg out onto the mud of the road. He stepped from the side of the Rover out into the rain and then reached into the back for his gear.

Debra jumped from the driver's seat and moved quickly around to the front of the vehicle to block his way. The soldier watched from the guard hut, but he did nothing. This was a place for dramatic good-byes, Sheridan thought, and the guard had probably seen his fill. And if Hearn was watching from his jeep, there was no indication, just the faint glow of his cigarette from the dark interior. Debra ran to Sheridan and stood close to him, making him look directly at her. The rain had matted her hair and darkened it. Some of the color on her face had caught the rain too and was beginning to run down her cheek. She paused for a long moment as if she were collecting her courage before she spoke. "I want you to know that I love you," she said, her voice intimate and throaty.

Sheridan felt the words thump hard against him. They weren't supposed to say that to each other. It was one of their un-spoken rules. Not because it wasn't true—who the hell knew at a time like this what was true—but because it was stupid, and impossible, and he was damned if he was going to torture himself with anything like that now. Damn it, though, he thought, if it wasn't love that he felt when he looked at her at times like this, what the hell was it? But how could he let her know that? In a world like the one they lived in, every time they walked away from each other, there was a very real chance that they would never see each other again.

"Easy," he said, smiling and making light of both their feel-ings, and then he took the collar of her trench coat in both of his big hands and pulled her toward him. "There's another time for this," he said, still smiling and motioning over at the fogbound air base where only a few hundred meters away an aircraft waited to fly him on a mission over an enemy city. A mission from which he might never come back. He couldn't say things or even let himself feel things that could only end up hurting her. She was too damn important to him to do that to her. He couldn't let Debra feel the pain of losing another loved one. Later maybe he could tell her how he felt. It would all be different after the war. "Not now," he whispered.

Debra shook her head no. "How we feel about each other is all we've got to fight this with," Debra said. "Don't let them take that from us too."

Sheridan stood looking down at her. He felt confused. All jumbled up inside, as he looked down at her pretty pixielike face. It seemed so easy to him. First the war, then their lives. It had to be that way, but Debra could never see it.

"I love you too," he said, finally giving in, but he could tell from her eyes that she knew in that moment he didn't really mean it, that he was just saying the words because she had said them and he cared for her enough that he wouldn't leave her like that, without saying something. He kissed her and held her close, but whatever it was that they had felt earlier that morning wasn't there any longer.

He broke the embrace and turned away from her. He just wanted to find Hearn, he told himself. Hearn, the graceful, quiet, Irish schoolteacher, who just happened to fly an airplane with more style and skill and daring than anyone Sheridan had ever known. Together they would fly right into Berlin, right into the heart of the Third Reich, and do their part to end this new war, this damn Black Phoenix of a war.

# CHAPTER TWO

*Berlin, April 30, 1945*

There was an explosion, a small popping sound, quite different from the larger blasts of the air raid that were rocking the walls of the heavily fortified cement bunker, deep beneath the streets of Berlin, but close and terrifying in its intimacy. As soon as Goebbels heard it, he moved immediately into action, and he made his way through the crowd gathered in the corridor in front of the Fuehrer's suite of underground rooms and used his key to unlock the heavy outer door.

Goebbels was a short man. He had narrow sloping shoulders and slim hips. He walked with a slight limp, caused by a clubfoot he had developed as a child that had never been totally corrected, but that limp hardly seemed noticeable as he hurried inside the bunker suite.

He was dressed that afternoon in a full military uniform. The formal gray tunic was trimmed in the black and red insignia of the elite SS officer corps, and though he had never served a day in the field, several rows of decorations of red, green, and gold adorned the front of his uniform. And beneath his uniform tunic now he felt the reassuring weight of the gold-crested ring of Phoenix, which he secretly wore on a ribbon around his neck.

He passed quickly through the suite's empty waiting area, pausing only imperceptibly at the door that led to its sitting room, his heart beating hard in his chest, and pushed his way into the room. Slumped on the red velvet settee were two bodies, a man and a woman's. It was all just as he had expected it to be, Goebbels thought.

"The Fuehrer," Goebbels said, as he knelt and inspected the uniformed body of the man that lay with his head snapped back, his eyes gazing at the low ceiling. A stream of crimson ran from a wound in the man's forehead, obscuring the features of his face. Next to him lay the Fuehrer's wife of less than twenty-four hours, the former Eva Braun. She wore a blue silk dress, her head pitched forward, strands of blond hair covering her closed eyes. A small crystal vase with a single pink flower lay smashed on the carpet beneath her. There was the smell of gunpowder in the room, and on a small table in front of her lay a wineglass and the remnants of several plastic capsules. A smoking pistol was lying on the floor beneath the two dead bodies. Goebbels felt a confusing rush of feelings, sadness and pain mixed with an uncontrollable excitement.

He heard a commotion behind him then and the thick gray-suited figure of Dr. Morell moved authoritatively through the crowd that was beginning to form in the open doorway and entered the suite. He bent over both bodies, feeling for a pulse on each of the lifeless figures. Then he looked at Goebbels. "The

Fuehrer is dead," Morell announced decisively, and a tense hush filled the room.

"But everything is not as the Fuehrer would wish it to be," Morell said, beginning to wipe blood from the face of the corpse, and then he looked back at Goebbels.

The Reichminister nodded his head, understanding. "Clear the room," he announced, and pointed at a nearby guard.

And the black-uniformed SS officer did as he was told, moving the crowd of onlookers back into the corridor, leaving only Goebbels and Morell alone in the room with the two motionless figures on the red velvet couch. "You have only a moment," Goebbels said, and then left the room himself, moving as quickly as he could on his deformed leg. He returned through the suite of underground rooms to the small exterior waiting area and then opened the door to the outer corridor.

"The Fuehrer is dead," Goebbels announced, and listened as the crowd of horrified onlookers reacted to the news. Then he held up his black-gloved hand for silence. "His final words were to ask me to thank you for him," Goebbels continued. "To thank you and to ask you to continue on with his great work."

Goebbels heard Morell behind him then, stepping from the bunker room into the corridor, and he turned back to the doctor. "We are ready," Morell announced, and then pointed at two black-uniformed guards standing in the hallway with the other onlookers. "Help us," he commanded. "Arrangements have been made in the garden."

The guards moved into the suite, going to the blanket-draped body of the uniformed man and lifting it onto their shoulders. Then they quickly carried the body into the crowded corridor and followed Goebbels up the several sets of switchback metal stairs that led to the bunker's top floor. Behind them, another guard, assisted by Dr. Morell, carried the woman's body.

21

Sad and fear-filled faces appeared at the doors along the narrow, dimly lit passageways—common soldiers, high-ranking officers, secretaries, servants, lowly office workers and high government officials. And as they moved to the top floors of the bunker, the crowd grew larger and more vocal until finally when they reached the bunker's ground-floor corridor, it was completely blocked with bodies. Goebbels had to push forward through the crowd the final few feet to stand in front of the guard post that protected the cement steps that led up to the Chancellery garden. As he approached the final checkpoint, two sentries sprang to attention, one on either side of the exit.

Goebbels moved past the guards and mounted the stairs without a backward glance. He started up the cement steps to the heavy metal door at the top and passed outside into the gloom of the Berlin afternoon. The soldiers bearing the blanket-draped corpses followed only a few steps behind him.

Aboveground the late afternoon sky was dark and the air was filled with smoke from the fires burning throughout the city. Big gray ashes blew across the barren landscape like dried autumn leaves in a fall storm. Goebbels paused at the top of the staircase.

"There," Goebbels said, pointing toward the spot at the edge of the garden protected on one side by a short brick wall where soldiers, earlier in the day under his direction, had dug shallow twin graves, side by side. The graves were marked with a tower of metal gallon cans filled with gasoline, a dozen in all, just as he had requested. Then without hesitating any longer, Goebbels walked with his head up, his narrow shoulders squared, through the smoke and blowing ashes, to the open graves.

He watched carefully as the bodies were lowered into the shallow holes and the large military gas cans were emptied onto the two blanketed bodies, washing them with the brownish liquid. Goebbels knelt and used his silver lighter, a gift from the

Fuehrer himself in less chaotic times, and touched its flame directly to the corpse's gasoline-soaked tunic. The bodies roared into flames.

Goebbels stood then, watching the wind blow the flames in erratic patterns above the shallow graves and the thick black gasoline smoke blow off into the dirty gray air of the late afternoon.

The full power of Phoenix, he thought, finally letting his true feelings rise to the surface of his consciousness, belonged now to him alone.

★   ★   ★

Berlin was in flames. From the navigator's seat of Hearn's DeHavilland Mosquito, Sheridan could see up the Wilhelmstrasse to where the buildings surrounding the Adler Hotel were burning out of control. Farther up the broad boulevard flames leapt from the remains of the Reich Chancellery and the rooftop of the Propaganda Ministry onto other nearby rooftops. Soon the entire Wilhemsplatz, at the very core of the Reich, would be engulfed in flames.

As he looked down at the destruction, Sheridan thought that he could almost hear, above the thunder of the exploding bombs and insistent ground artillery, the crescendo of Wagnerian music that should accompany such a moment. Perhaps someday, he thought, he would write such a piece himself.

They had timed their arrival to correspond with the Russian daylight bombing run. The vast formation of Russian planes had approached the city from the northeast, arriving at its outskirts around midafternoon. And Hearn had brought the Mosquito in across the North Sea and had arrived over Berlin minutes after the Russian planes had begun their attack. Below their aircraft, Sheridan had looked down at miles of lakes and thick evergreen forests. There had seemed to be no way to orient the aircraft above all the miles of thick forest, but Hearn had followed British and American bombing runs into the city on escort and reconnaissance missions dozens of times before and had taken the highly maneuverable little Mosquito down low, and soon they were skimming across the treetops toward the very heart of the capital by keeping the great wide artery known as the East-West Axis in view out their port window. Sheridan knew all about the Axis. It was one of the seemingly endless details that he had been force-fed back in London in preparation for his mission. The Reich had built the road in 1938. It had been the march route of their great victory parade two years later after their conquest of France. And the grand avenue cut a straight line through the thick evergreen forests directly to the Brandenburg Gate itself.

The decision to follow the bombers into the heart of Berlin was a dangerous one, Sheridan thought as he looked around at the flak-filled sky. Despite the Allies' control of the air and the massive destruction being poured on the city, there was still considerable ground fire coming from below, and dense clouds of black smoke curled up around the aircraft, obscuring the view of the city. But Sheridan could still see above him the Russian daylight bombers protected by their long-range fighter escorts as they swooped in as low as they dared and delivered their bombs.

Sheridan could see too the German shells exploding around the Mosquito, some of them so close that the little fighter would temporarily rock out of Hearn's control. Then suddenly in the distance a Russian fighter plunged from the sky in flames. Sheridan waited for the white flash of a parachute to escape from it, but there was nothing, only the flaming aircraft disappearing into the thick layer of smoke that covered much of the ground below him.

"Should I head back?" Hearn called out.

Yeah, take it back to London, to the States, to the goddamned other side of the world, for all I care, Sheridan thought.
I can't stand even another moment of this, but, "No, not yet,"
was all he said out loud, pointing ahead to where the antiaircraft
flak from the ground was even thicker. "Get as close to the damn
thing as you can."

Then suddenly below him, emerging out of a wash of gray
smoke, Sheridan could see the marble columns of the Brandenburg Gate. Rubble surrounded the base of the great monument.
They were at the very heart of the Reich now.

Sheridan strained to see down into the narrow strip of land
between the powerful marble columns of the Gate and the dark
meandering line of what he knew to be the Spree River at the
very center of the city. Finally he began to make out the large,
isolated square building, the Reichstag, the German Parliament
building that had been gutted by Nazi fires twelve years before.
And now once again it was in the process of being destroyed,
Sheridan thought as he squinted down into the inferno of smoke
and flames.

Sheridan tried to remember the details of the intelligence
photographs that he had studied for the last several weeks, and
match them in his mind to the chaos that he could see on the
ground. He could see behind the Reichstag the roofline of the
badly bombed-out house in the Wilhelmstrasse garden that
British intelligence suspected to have once been the hiding place
of Goebbels himself. God, how he would like to come face-to-
face with that bastard, Sheridan thought.

Sheridan traced with his eye across the wreckage of the garden to the point where the primary entrance was supposed to be
to the heavily fortified underground bunker that headquarters
believed now held what was left of the Nazi High Command.

"There it is, Major." Sheridan's pilot had spotted the garden and the entrance to the bunker too. "It must be taking a hell of a beating," the young pilot added.

Sheridan nodded. This was their destination. Sheridan's job was to go into Berlin with the first American ground troops, probably within the next day or so, and join in the questioning of the highest leaders of the Reich and learn everything he could about Phoenix. Intelligence believed that most of the top leaders were in the bunker now, and Sheridan had wanted to know what the current situation was on the ground, after the devastating bombing of the last few days.

He was skeptical now though. Had he come all this way just to see this, a smoke-filled courtyard piled high with rubble? The chance of anything of real value being left down there was damn near impossible, he thought. Even if there ever were bunkers under the city that had held the Nazi hierarchy, they'd certainly had plenty of warning to leave Berlin. The reports that the Nazi leaders had moved south to Berchtesgaden, Hitler's Bavarian retreat high in the German Alps, seemed far more likely.

As Sheridan looked down at the rear of the Wilhemsplatz, there was more gunfire from somewhere on the ground, angry white puffs of smoke, exploding around the low-flying aircraft. Suddenly a shell exploded very close, rocking the little craft from side to side. Someone had spotted them and was bracketing them with artillery fire. "Had enough?" Hearn called to him over the sound of the guns.

All right, Sheridan decided. This was no place to delay. He'd seen what he'd come for and it didn't answer very much. He would have to wait until Bradley and his troops crossed the Elbe and took the city to find out for certain where the Nazi leaders were now. He would go down into the bunker itself then or anywhere else the trail led. He just hoped to God that he could get to them before the Russians.

Sheridan raised his thumb in the air and smoothly, neatly, the little Mosquito began its way back up into the gray cloud-filled sky. Sheridan couldn't help admiring Hearn's skills. Despite the explosions, the young pilot was flying the little fighter as gracefully as if they were in an air ballet on a Sunday afternoon in some safe corner of southern Ireland. Sheridan almost began to enjoy the feeling of soaring through space as he took one last look down through the clouds of thick smoke to the bright orange flames leaping from the buildings that surrounded the Wilhemsplatz.

The curving dark line of the river was just in front of them now and past that the outline of the Tiergarten, the great public park that extended along both sides of the East-West Axis that would lead them back to the Elbe.

Suddenly he heard a thumping sound and he felt the impact against the side of the aircraft. Something heavy had struck the wing on his side.

The Mosquito began to rock out of control, and then its nose dropped and the plane began to dive toward the ground. Sheridan looked down at the fires and smoke and the onrushing sea of destruction that lay below him.

It took all of his willpower to force himself to finally turn away from the twisting picture of flames and smoke and look over at his pilot. Hearn's face and eyes were totally focused, concentrating on the job of bringing the violently rattling wheel in his hands under control. Sheridan felt an even greater admiration for the calmness and control of the young pilot than he had before. But then there was barely time for Sheridan to think even that brief thought, but only to act.

The intelligence officer reached up and began sliding the cockpit's canopy top back. He knew from his training that if he could slide it far enough, it would blow off the opening and leave the exit clear for both him and Hearn to parachute to safety.

Sheridan's parachute was strapped to his back, as it had been since they'd crossed the Elbe. And so was Hearn's, basic procedure when flying over enemy territory. As Sheridan continued wrestling with the canopy, slowly the cover began to slide toward the rear of the aircraft. But then it stopped halfway, jammed shut in its metal runners by the force of the explosion.

Suddenly the front end of the small plane dipped at an even more violent angle. Hearn had lost his battle with the controls. The Mosquito began twisting in the air, spinning wildly in a mad corkscrew pattern as it began to plummet toward the ground.

Sheridan could see Hearn gesturing at him with a gloved hand. The aircraft was on fire and the cabin was rapidly filling with smoke, obscuring Hearn's face and hands, but the pilot continued gesturing, even more urgently. Through the cloud of thick dark smoke, Sheridan could make out now that Hearn was pointing up toward the shattered cockpit canopy above them. The pilot was telling him that despite the jammed opening, he should try and climb the hell out. The opening was only a few feet in width, but it might be large enough to fit through. If they both were going to make it, though, he had to act now, Sheridan realized in a flash as he felt the small aircraft dropping at an even greater speed.

There was no time to communicate anything back to the young pilot. There was only time for Sheridan to stand and then to use all of his strength to burst through the opening. He lay flat on the top of the descending aircraft, his hands grasping the top edge of the cockpit. The air was rushing at him at an incredible speed, and he had to struggle with all his strength to maintain his hold on the outer edge and then to reach his free hand back in for Hearn. But the pilot had already returned to the wheel, trying to steady the aircraft so that Sheridan could jump free. The hell with that, Sheridan thought angrily. This was a trip that they were both taking. But he could see the ground rushing up below them even faster now. He had only seconds left.

He grasped the shoulder of Hearn's flight jacket and lifted him off his feet, moving his body toward the smashed-out opening. There was more firing then, and machine-gun bullets ripped into the exterior skin of the plane. Sheridan continued to pull with an angry fury at the body of his pilot, and finally he was able to move Hearn's head and neck up through the opening. The pilot was helping now, his hands free of the wheel, the Mosquito free-falling through space. More bullets ripped at the small plane. Sheridan knew then that the shooting couldn't be ground fire. It was too well directed, too consistent. There was a Nazi plane somewhere close. And if they managed to pull free of the hurtling plane, they would be easy targets for the German fighter as they hung helplessly from their chutes and fluttered slowly toward the ground. But still they would have to make the jump, Sheridan realized. There was no other choice.

Sheridan extended his body outward in one final thrust, holding Hearn tightly by the shoulder of his flight jacket as he did. There was another rain of machine-gun bullets and then Sheridan felt Hearn's body crack through the opening. Thank God, Sheridan thought in the brief moment before he and Hearn tumbled away from the flaming Mosquito. He could hear yet another burst of machine-gun bullets following them into the smoke-filled air and then he could feel himself beginning to lose his concentration in the powerful downward movement of the spinning dive through space. Sheridan's hand fumbled with the metal ring attached to the front of his parachute. His ears filled with the roar of the wildly rushing air. In what seemed like the far distance he could hear the tearing sounds of enemy machine-gun bullets ripping through the wind. Sheridan knew that the bullets were far closer than they seemed. He could see the ground now, just a dark brown smoke-covered blur rushing up at him, faster and faster, until it filled his entire field of vision, but still he knew that he didn't dare open his chute, not yet. Drifting from a wide, slow umbrella of white silk would make him too good a target for the Messerschmitts or whatever they were that were up in those clouds with him.

There was a dense patch of dark smoke blowing toward him. He would wait, he decided in the flash of a second that he had to make up his mind, until he fell inside that patch of smoke. Only then would he open his chute. But the ground was so damn close. If he waited even another fraction of a second, would he have enough time? Pull the cord now! he heard his fear-filled brain screaming. Slow the fall! The hell with the fire from the Nazi fighter. Sheridan's hand tightened on the metal ring, but somehow he managed to restrain himself from pulling it. White silk billowed out, filling the sky near him. Hearn. Hearn had opened his chute. Orange flames leapt across the sky. Sheridan strained to look, but before he could see anything more, black clouds of smoke fell in around him. Sheridan pulled hard at his rip cord.

# CHAPTER THREE

The children had gone first, easily in their sleep. At least that was what his wife had told him, but Goebbels had seen enough death that he knew that it was never that simple. Even with Morell's morphine to make them sleep, there had to have been pain for his little ones, his dear ones, but he couldn't let himself think about that. Time was of the utmost urgency now. It was imperative that nothing be altered: the plans and their timing were all too precise to withstand even the slightest deviation.

If only Magda could see it as clearly as he could, he thought angrily as he looked over at his wife. Her eyes were full of sorrow, her head lowered, letting her long, thick brownish-blond hair fall down and cover the sides of her face. She was standing across from him in one of the small chambers reserved for leaders of the

31

Reich, on the lowest floor of the concrete bunker built beneath the Chancellery garden.

The room had become their bedroom over the last few months, and it was filled with the last of the treasures that they had moved from their home on the Wilhelmstrasse, rich, ornate furniture, too large for the narrow, low-ceilinged room, great oil paintings with enormous gold and lacquered wood frames crowded in along the gray cement walls, thick Oriental rugs of deep maroons and dark blues that greatly overfilled the limited floor space. The effect of such opulence in the small grim cement-block room was grotesque, almost comical, Goebbels thought, but his wife had insisted, cramming the small space with precious expensive items, until there was barely room for either of them to move.

Goebbels could hear shells bursting overhead, and occasionally even the thick concrete walls of the bunker shook with the tremendous force of destruction that was occurring above them on the streets of Berlin. The explosions seemed very close now, and even more violent than they had just a few minutes before. He must hurry, he thought, or the Russians would be on top of them and everything that he had worked so hard for would be in ruins.

"So, it has been done?" he said, his voice, he thought, just the right mixture of authority and regret.

Magda nodded her head in desperation and then let her big soft body sink down onto the garish purple couch that stood pushed in tightly against one short wall of the gray cement room. He had married her for that body, Goebbels thought as he watched it sag into the plush sofa, the wide, powerful, Nordic shoulders, the lush breasts and curving full hips, but soon after their marriage its succulence had turned to fat and the mysteries of her body had been lost with the too-easy intimacies of marriage, and as he looked at her now, she seemed covered with rolls of ugly flesh, and he realized that with very little effort he could find himself hating her, just as he had in some ways, he admitted, hated the thick-waisted, pampered, peasantlike children that she had given birth to. He was disgusted with her, but he couldn't let that disgust show now, he warned himself. The next few minutes must go like clockwork. It was the key to everything.

"And the Fuehrer?" Her voice trembled as she asked the question, and she looked up with weary red-scarred eyes at her husband's face. She had been crying, Goebbels realized then. Did that mean that she would not go through with it? The possible alternatives if she refused swept through his mind. None of them were good. They all radically endangered the overall execution of his plans, but he would choose one of them, if he was compelled to, he decided grimly.

All that was being done was necessary, he told himself as he looked into her tear-stained face and eyes. There can be no sorrow when duty is involved, but that was something that women seemed never to understand. "The Fuehrer has done his final duty. As has Eva," Goebbels said. "And now we must do ours," he added a moment later. He extended the container of pills. And as he watched, she chose the capsule resting on the black velvet interior of the silver pillbox that was closest to her. What if she had taken the other one—the one intended for him? But, of course, that would have been impossible, Goebbels thought. Not choosing the capsule positioned closest to her would have shown disrespect for her husband, and even at such a moment she was incapable of that.

The wine was already poured into the twin antique silver goblets that they had used on their wedding day. Goebbels had prepared them while she had been with the children. He reached out and handed her one of the goblets, his heart beating fast.

With nervous frightened fingers she took the goblet, all the time staring down at the dark gray capsule that still rested in the palm of her hand. Then quickly she took it and swallowed it with a small, ladylike drink of the wine from the silver cup.

Goebbels, playing his part to the very end, removed the second capsule from the black velvet case, and then with one swift and dramatic move, he threw the capsule into the very back of his mouth and then drank several long swallows of the wine.

She looked up at him suddenly, studying his face, an expression of doubt and puzzlement on her own broad, peasant features.

Did she know? Goebbels felt a shiver of fear pass through him. But then it mattered no longer.

She slumped forward with all the great weight of her fleshy body. The silver wedding cup spilled from her hand, its contents running bloodred against the gray floor.

Goebbels watched her fall and he heard a hard thump as her skull cracked against the heavy walnut table. He set his own glass down hurriedly with shaking fingers. Why the trembling? he asked himself, more fear shooting through him. He hadn't expected to feel anything, but as he looked down at his wife's long blond hair, falling across the tabletop, he remembered for a brief moment when he had first seen her. It had been in a reception at Nuremberg. She had been dancing with an officer in the air corps and her long blond hair had swung gracefully behind her as she whirled to the music. She had been beautiful then. He had wanted her desperately. He was one of the most important men in the Reich. How could he be denied anything? And in the rear seat of his limousine that night as his driver had taken them home through the rain-slick streets of the city, she had seated herself on him and raised her dress and Goebbels had made love to her. He had thought that night that she was the most beautiful woman that he had ever seen and now, not that many years later, she lay dead in front of him. Who would have ever thought that it would lead to this? he asked himself, looking down at the long blond hair spread out across the walnut table. But he couldn't afford even another moment of sentimentality. And he stood and went to the ornate chest of drawers at the back of the room and moved a lever built into its metal underside. As the lever moved, the wall behind the desk opened slowly, revealing a big man with a large misshapen face. The man wore a knee-length, black leather jacket. A shiny leather holster strapped to his side held a black-handled Luger pistol. The man was Herbert Gruening. He once had been the Fuehrer's most trusted and feared private bodyguard. But now the man's fierce and highly valuable loyalty belonged to him, Goebbels thought triumphantly.

In his arms Gruening held an object wrapped in a rough gray blanket. He carried it past Goebbels into the bunker room.

Behind Gruening stood Morell. The two men's eyes locked in mutual appraisal. "What do you think of my little replica?" Morell said finally, gesturing past Goebbels to the chair next to Frau Goebbels' body, where Gruening had deposited the package wrapped in the rough gray blanket.

As Goebbels turned to look, the blanket dropped away, and Goebbels felt the pit of his stomach tighten and his body fill with a strange emotion. He was looking at his own corpse, or at least a nearly perfect duplicate of it. The body was of a small man dressed in a gray uniform tunic with rows of green, gold, and scarlet medals splashed across his chest. Whatever differences between Goebbels' own and the corpse's features had been obscured by the damage done by a large bullet hole in the other man's forehead, and the splatter of dark red, drying blood that had burst from it.

"We will see to the rest," Morell said, and Goebbels managed to tear his eyes away from the corpse that wore his face, and carefully then, he moved through the opening in the wall and hurried on into the darkness of the underground tunnels that connected the bunker with several other parts of the city.

The world would believe what he told it to believe, Goebbels thought as he moved off down the dark tunnel. And for now he wanted it to believe that he too was dead. There would be a time soon for the truth, though, a time for the world to know that he was not only still alive but that he was to become its absolute master.

★   ★   ★

Flames leapt from the shallow graves dug in the rough soil of the Chancellery garden while high above, on the very top floor of the Chancellery building itself, a woman stood at a balcony window and watched.

The woman was in her late twenties and very beautiful, with long, flowing, light blond hair. She wore only a dressing gown of shimmering emerald-green silk.

Geli, as her friends called her, had a well-deserved reputation for courage and coolness based on her dangerous and highly publicized contribution to the Reich's war effort. Angelique Von Stahl was said to be one of the best pilots, male or female, in all of Europe. Before the war, she had been famous throughout Germany for her daredevil aerobatic flying, but more recently she had become a real heroine of the Reich for her work with the German military as a test pilot with some of the world's most advanced aircraft. But as she stood looking down at the leaping flames, her anxiety was apparent. She lit and then nervously smoked a cigarette and then another as she stared at the eerie scene being played out below her. She had known what the strange ceremony that she had witnessed had meant well before the announcement of the Fuehrer's death had been made on the radio. There was only one grave that Reichminister Joseph Goebbels would have stood guard over at a time like this. Goebbels had left the grave several minutes earlier, but still Geli stood on the Chancellery balcony and watched the last of the flames.

She took another anxious taste of her cigarette. She was worried about time, but she didn't need a watch. She knew from the faltering afternoon light and the sounds of the exploding artillery shells that the hour was growing late. These days the Russian artillery and the Allied planes sounded the time of day with as much precision as the finest church bells in the finest cathedral in Germany, she thought.

Behind her, she could hear people calling out, asking her to join the party that was in progress in the adjoining suite of rooms, but she stood for another moment and looked out at the wind blowing the flames in an erratic pattern above the twin graves. There were parties everywhere now, she thought. This was the response to the end of the Reich from its great leaders. The Chancellery had filled with wild revelers each evening for weeks now. Guards and secretaries, women from the street seeking shelter from the bombing, willing to trade their bodies for a few hours, perhaps a night, of safety. And now, Geli thought as she listened to the sounds coming from the room behind her, at the news of the Fuehrer's death, the last of his followers in the city had broken into drinking and fornication. The Chancellery and the great cement bunker that lay beneath its rear courtyard had become one enormous lust-filled brothel, Geli thought contemptuously.

She looked out at the streets of the city beyond the walls of the Chancellery. There were fires and destruction everywhere. She slowly turned her gaze to the building's nearby windows and balconies. Was someone watching her? She'd felt as if there had been someone out there in the shadows for several moments. Her eyes swept the nearby buildings, and then she searched the garden below her, looking for who it might be. But it was growing dark, and the courtyard was filled with smoke, and she could see no one. Just her nerves, no one was there, she told herself as she tossed the cigarette away. It would be impossible not to feel anxious on a day like this.

There was a loud knocking behind her then, and she left the balcony and returned to her dressing room. The door that led from the dressing area into the suite's grand salon stood open. She went to the doorway and looked out into the intimate gathering in progress in her rooms. The heavy curtains had been drawn and the salon was dark. The only light came from a few burning candles and an occasional flash of an exploding artillery shell from the streets below.

And in the room's shadowy darkness, couples danced tightly, most of the women in various stages of nakedness. The music playing on the Victrola was a low, sensual, female voice singing a German tune reminiscent of Berlin in an earlier time before the war. The room smelled heavily of alcohol and burning tobacco and hashish smoke mingling with the harsh woodsmoke seeping into the room from the street fires.

One of the couples near Geli made love as they danced slowly to the music of the Victrola. Others were engaged in the sex games being played on the room's couches or the arrangements of pillows that lay on the floor. The candlelit room was filled with the sights and sounds and the smells of unrestrained debauchery. And the men in the room were waiting for her to join them, like the predators they were, she thought as she looked around at some of their hungry, expectant faces. She looked then at the great four-poster bed that she had slept in for the last several nights. It held other couples now intertwined in their own complicated lovemaking. The high-ranking politician that had permitted her to seek shelter with him for the last several days had left Berlin only a few hours before. He had begged her to go with him, bragging of the enormous fortune that he had hidden away in some remote corner of Germany, but she had turned him down, as she had so many similar offers over the last few months. She had suspected that it was her well-publicized ability to fly an airplane that he and at least some of the others had coveted as much as the delights of her company. Good pilots were in far more demand in Berlin these days than simply beautiful and desirable women.

In front of her, she could see a very young officer, a second lieutenant, tall and blond with wide shoulders and a simple boyish face, his uniform chest bare of campaign ribbons and his sleeves of service marks. His fresh innocent face looked to be no older than seventeen. He had been one of the people calling for her to join the party, and he smiled, beckoning to her again. A very strong part of her yearned to corrupt the young fresh-faced boy. On a different evening she might very well have chosen him to be the first of the men in the room to make love to her. She would very much enjoy ruining this young man for any other woman, she thought, looking hard and unsmiling into his clear blue eyes. She could do things that would make him hunger after her forever. And leave him aching for the special kinds of pleasures that only she could give him. But not tonight, she reminded herself, turning away from him scornfully, not with the fires still burning in the shallow graves in the courtyard, and the entire Russian Army less than a day's march from the front steps of the Chancellery.

She started back for her dressing room, but as she did, she felt a man's powerful hand caressing her between her legs. She looked up into the cruel eyes and lean, deeply lined face of General Rausch. The general's expression was cold, contemptuous, betraying nothing of what he really felt, Geli thought, returning his angry, reproachful look. He had made love to her before, as had many of the other men in the room, and at that moment, despite the coldness of his expression, Geli had no doubt that she could make this powerful man debase himself in front of her. She also knew precisely what he wanted now. He wanted to make love to her openly and in public, with all of the people in the room watching them. They had spoken of it often in their private lovemaking. It would be a perfect opportunity to humiliate and degrade this seemingly proud and powerful man, and the idea appealed to her enormously.

Geli felt herself beginning to give in to him and to the sounds of encouragement coming from some of the others, but then she laughed and spun away from his touch. She rushed inside the dressing room, quickly closing and locking the door behind her. She stood leaning back against the tall, ornately decorated door, breathing deeply and attempting to regain her composure, while shudders of desire moved through her body.

She slid off the silk bathrobe, letting it drop to the floor, leaving her naked at the center of the grand, high-ceilinged room. She stepped to the set of tall mirrors that filled the entire far wall of the dressing room. There was a long crack caused by the bombing and the crack ran at an angle across the image of her face and upper body, but Geli was still very pleased with what she could see of her reflection.

She was tall, slightly over six feet, with wide powerful shoulders and a long, straight, slim body, with tight, shapely hips and hard, thrusting breasts crowned with round, light pink nipples. Her hair was long and straight, and so blond that when she removed it from the tight roll at the back of her neck that she'd worn it in that day and let it fall down her back, it appeared almost golden. A perfect Aryan type, the pride of the Reich, and she laughed as she thought of the phrases that the magazines and the newspapers and all the rest had used to describe her as she'd risen to become a true celebrity within the Nazi world.

Satisfied, she replaced her dressing gown and then sat down at her dressing table and began to apply her makeup, accentuating the startlingly beautiful but disturbingly cold sapphire blue of her eyes.

Suddenly she thought that she felt someone's eyes on her again, this time from the open door to the balcony. She walked to the door that led to the balcony and peered out into the descending darkness. As she started outside, a man stepped from the shadows. She wanted to scream, but something stopped her. She would be safe, she told herself. She had learned long ago how to use men. They loved her beauty, her notoriety, her wild sexuality. This man would be no different, but what was it that he wanted? She took a step toward him. He was wearing the ceremonial black uniform of the SS. And at closer inspection, his face was not as young as it had appeared in the shadows of the balcony. It was lined and hard, with cruel, dark brown eyes.

"Angelique Von Stahl," the black-uniformed officer said.

Geli nodded her head. The man held out a small envelope. Geli took it and opened it immediately. Her heart leapt with excitement and expectation, as she read the words of the message inside it. It was a summons to come at once to the bunker built beneath the Chancellery garden. And the letter was signed by and carried the personal seal of the Füehrer's own physician, Dr. Ernst Morell.

"One moment," she said, and returned quickly to her dressing room. She could still hear the sounds of the party in progress in her room as she dressed quickly into tight-fitting khaki slacks and a uniform shirt. She completed her outfit with knee-high black boots and a brown leather flying jacket.

She hurried back to the balcony then and followed the officer across the rear of the Chancellery, climbing from one balcony to the other and down a darkened rear staircase to the garden. They crossed the windswept courtyard, passing within only a few meters of the still-smoldering double grave that Geli had discovered less than an hour before.

They crossed to the entrance of the underground bunker then. There was a guard at the entrance, but he was seated on the floor drinking from a bottle of schnapps, a half-naked whore lying next to him.

And all along the corridors of the bunker it was the same, more drunken parties, more debauchery. It, like the Chancellery, seemed to be just one lust-filled brothel.

They arrived at the lowest level of the bunker and Geli followed the officer to the final door in the narrow corridor. The officer knocked on the door and then opened it with a large heavy key. The black-uniformed officer moved inside. She paused for a moment, summoning her courage, and then followed.

There was no one in the small bunker room, but the officer moved quickly to the far wall, knelt next to a metal field desk, and pushed at an unseen lever built into the gray cement wall. As he did, the wall itself began to slide open.

Geli hesitated only for a moment before stepping past the officer and into the dark corridor that lay behind the opening.

The officer followed after her, closing the opening carefully. He hurried down the dark corridor with Geli only a few meters behind. They descended deep below the city. Geli could smell the stink of the nearby sewers. And once or twice she could even hear the rhythmic tap of the boots of soldiers passing on the streets above.

They proceeded along a maze of interconnecting, rock-lined passageways, the beam of the officer's flashlight their only guide. The cavern behind them remained silent, and finally the interconnection of tunnels stopped against what appeared to be a wall of solid rock, but once again the officer knelt and uncovered a steel lever that protruded from the floor of the tunnel. He pushed hard against the lever, moving it on some unseen axis, until the wall began to move slowly inward, sweeping dirt and rock in front of it. Soon there was an opening large enough to slip through. The officer looked back at Geli, warning her to be cautious. He withdrew a pistol from the black leather holster at his hip and held it out in front of him as they moved slowly through the opening and into the dark underground room that lay on the other side of it.

The moment that she entered into the basement room Geli could sense that something was wrong. She let the officer's broad-shouldered figure move in front of her, clearing the way. Only darkness and silence stretched in front of them.

The officer flashed on his light. The beam searched the basement room. Rough cement floors, heavy wooden beams holding the low ceiling in place, firewood stacked in a corner, and the cold damp smell of a million German basements. Why was this one so different? Full of so much foreboding? A smell? A shape? Something terribly out of place, but what? Then the officer's light found it. First just the heavy black boots protruding from behind the stacks of firewood. Then the officer moved cautiously forward with his light revealing the rest. Attached to the boots was a man's body. The body was dressed in the gray and black uniform of the Luftwaffe, the Nazi elite flying corps. And Geli knew the man's identity even before the officer used his foot to turn the body over to reveal the dead man's smashed and bloody face. It was Kline, the personal pilot to only the very highest leaders of the Reich. He was dead—murdered within the last few hours, Geli saw from a quick inspection of the prominent bullet wound in the middle of his chest and the drying blood on the floor beneath him.

"I thought you should see this," a voice said. And then a man stepped from the shadows of the room. "It will help you to understand why you were brought here tonight." Geli looked again at the body of the pilot.

"I am Dr. Ernst Morell," continued the man who stood in the corner of the basement room. "I believe that you know of me."

"Of course," Geli said.

Morell nodded. Then he lifted a hand, and when Geli turned, the SS officer that had been her escort had disappeared back into the secret passageways that led below the city.

"There are plans for certain high-ranking officials of the Reich to be flown to safety outside the city tonight," Morell said. "But as you can see, these plans have apparently been discovered by someone who wishes to stop us." Geli moved her gaze back to the body of the pilot, lying on the basement floor beneath her. "That makes the request that we have for you now very dangerous," Morell added, and then waited for an answer.

Geli didn't hesitate. "It will be an honor to serve you in any manner you request," she said, her voice confident and determined.

"Good," Morell said. "A plane will be leaving Berlin in a few hours, a flight of truly historic consequence. You will be the pilot of that flight."

A second figure stepped from the shadows then and stood next to Morell. "I will be one of your passengers," Morell said. "And the new Fuehrer of the Reich will be the other."

Geli looked across the basement room at the man standing next to Morell. It was Dr. Joseph Goebbels.

# CHAPTER
# FOUR

P hoenix" was what the Nazi High Command called the operation. That was one of the few things that they knew for certain, Debra Marks thought. She kept staring down at the photographs that Sheridan had taken in the river valley in northwest Germany as she listened to the rain falling heavily against the window of her office at the War Ministry in London.

*Phoenix.* The name sent a chill of fear through her whenever she thought of its meaning. The Phoenix was a legendary bird that had ruled the earth, until it burned itself to death on a great funeral pyre and then rose youthfully alive and even more powerful from the ashes to rule over the world once again.

Some of her colleagues at CIC headquarters in London had begun jokingly to call both the Nazi plan and the Allies' counteroperation mounted to defeat it—"Black Phoenix." Very British—Debra smiled to herself as she thought about it—very understated. But it also troubled her. The name reflected the sense of disbelief and lack of urgent attention that her superiors were giving to the Nazi operation. But Phoenix was far more real and far more dangerous than anyone wanted to believe, Debra decided as she continued studying the reports and photographs on her desktop. She understood how stretched Command's resources were and that almost all of its attention was focused on the final push into Berlin, but this was her chance to dispel the lack of urgency and understanding for Phoenix. It was her job that night to synthesize all the current information that they had about the Nazi operation into a single coherent report for Command. The report would then be used to develop an overall strategy against it. The job was the type of thing that Debra usually did very well, but for some reason that night, she had not been able to even begin her work and a clean sheet of paper still lay rolled around the typewriter on her desk.

Why couldn't she get started? she asked herself angrily as she stared down at the photographs and reports, trying to find any possible way to cut into the mountain of difficult material.

The photographs showed that both Phoenix locations that they had discovered so far had been totally devastated. Some as yet unknown amount of the Phoenix material had by either accident or design been left behind in both areas, and within a few days vast stretches of once rich fertile land were reduced to a fine black-gray ash; not an insect, not a blade of grass, remained. And as she looked at the photographs, Debra felt that she could almost smell the destruction, the foul sweet smell of decay, that everyone who had actually come in contact with Phoenix and its devastating results had reported.

The Allies had discovered both locations as the Nazi Army had retreated back across Europe to Berlin. Hitler had bragged of his scientists having discovered at least one superweapon for months now. The V-2 rockets that he had set loose on London had been the first. Was Phoenix to be next?

Both of the Phoenix sites were approximately two to three miles in diameter, with the destruction radiating out from a central point. The center of the destruction appeared to be the sole dispersal point of the Phoenix material. One crucial fact that they didn't yet know was just how much of the material had been used at these sites to begin each process. Several tons, perhaps. Certainly it would require a great deal of any poisonous material to cause the kind of large-scale destruction that they had found at the Phoenix locations. And it was the matter of quantity and supply that gave Command its greatest feelings of confidence of ultimately defeating Phoenix, Debra reminded herself. Command was convinced that the Third Reich couldn't possibly have had the capacity to manufacture sufficient quantities of the material to mount a major threat to the Allies. Debra wasn't quite as certain. She had learned long ago that it was never wise to underestimate this particular enemy. But there were important limitations and possible defenses to Phoenix, Debra thought. A countermeasure or counteragent was the most obvious. If Allied scientists could find a way to combat its effects with some kind of a procedure or chemical or biological antidote, its threat could be neutralized, but work on that area had just begun.

And then there was the question of leadership. The other key, Debra thought, as far as Allied Command was concerned, was Hitler himself. Only a true madman could ever dream of actually using a weapon like Phoenix. And now he was dead and so was Goebbels and most of the remainder of Hitler's top staff. That was what Clarendon was picking up from Berlin radio. Without Hitler, there would be no one left alive capable of actually using something as monstrous as Phoenix. At least if the news was true. And that was where Sheridan came in. He should be moving with Bradley's army across the Elbe into Berlin itself, maybe as early as tomorrow morning, to confirm the deaths or to help interrogate whoever was left alive of the Nazi leadership. But where was Sheridan tonight? Debra thought angrily. Perhaps that was why she wasn't thinking clearly and she couldn't seem to get anywhere with her report. She was too damn worried about him and his safety.

Debra walked over to the door to her office and looked down the hall to the message center. The plan had been for Sheridan to meet up with Bradley's troops well before sunset. It would have been standard procedure to radio in then. She wasn't particularly close to any of the girls in the center, but they all knew that she was waiting for word from him and one of them would have told her, if he'd reported, but she'd heard nothing all night.

It was probably all right, she told herself, turning back into her office. If there ever was a night to break procedure, this was certainly it. Sheridan was probably drinking to the news of Hitler's death on the banks of the Elbe in some temporary officers' club, if they had such things, or maybe just in some field tent with the boys from the Ninth. Of course, there were other possibilities, but she didn't want to think about them.

She thought, instead, of her morning parting from Sheridan. Its awkwardness had hurt her deeply. Certainly he knew that she was waiting for word now. He wouldn't just begin celebrating without letting her know that he was all right, she thought, her anger toward him building. He would have called for her benefit, wouldn't he? Or maybe this was his way of finally driving home the point that he seemed to have been trying to make to her for the last few weeks, that he couldn't let them fall in love now, not here, out here in the middle of all this. He didn't want to risk hurting her. But he was so damn wrong, she thought. If only she could make him see it. He couldn't protect her from the world and its pain, no matter how much he wanted to try. And, in the end, she wouldn't really want him to. He couldn't tell her when

to love and when to feel loss and sadness. Whatever there was between them, she wanted to feel all of it, for however short or even
how ultimately tragic it might be. But telling Sheridan to stop trying to protect her from the world was like telling him to stop
being who he was. He was a warrior, Debra thought. She had always known that about him and loved him for it. And warriors
defended the people and things that they loved, whatever the
costs.

"Report in, damn it," she found herself whispering down a
dark empty hallway, and then, not wanting to think about the
complications of their relationship any longer, she walked quickly
back to the single window of her office. Through the double
glass panes, she could see the wind blowing the rain around
under the lights of the embankment and then farther down the
river, the outline of Waterloo Bridge enclosed in rain. The city
was lit up too, not to its prewar splendor, but more brightly than
she had seen it in years. There would be no blackout tonight, she
thought as she watched the stream of joyous people moving
along under the diffused yellow light of the lamps mounted along
the embankment wall. The people were waving and calling out
to each other in celebration. She could hear cars honking and in
the distance somewhere from the fogbound harbor, the sounds of
ship horns. That was very un-British, Debra thought. They were
a strange people. Whenever she believed that she had grown to
know something about them, it seemed that they did something
to surprise her. She hoped they were right, though. They had just
fought a long, deeply exhausting war and it wouldn't be fair if
now, as they reached what they believed to be a great victory, the
worst still lay ahead.

Did she dare write that? she asked herself, looking back at
the stack of empty white typing paper lying on the edge of her
desk, next to her typewriter. She believed Phoenix could truly be
that great a threat, but how could she tell that to Command?

That was the other reason that she was having so much difficulty with the report, she realized then. Not just Sheridan, but her knowledge that if she wrote what she really believed, it would only help to reinforce the fears that she knew most of her superiors and fellow workers had about her anyway—that as a female and a foreigner, and all the rest of it, she could not really be trusted, that her work was too emotional, too dramatic. But she knew that she had to say it. Her instincts told her that Phoenix was far more serious than Command yet realized. And it was her job to tell them, no matter what the consequences were to her personally.

She returned to her desk and the thoughts began to tumble out of her and onto the paper. After a few minutes, she stopped and reread her opening paragraph:

> The findings from the laboratory at Hillborn confirm that the enemy, more precisely elements in the Third Reich's High Command, have developed and utilized effectively in the field a superweapon of extraordinary capabilities, a synthetic biological substance. This biological agent appears to have the capacity to destroy every form of vegetation, including trees, grass, plant life, farm crops, and also many forms of animal life— birds, insects, wildlife, and even domestic and farm animals—in essence all living things in which it comes in contact. However, to this date, the areas of its use have been remote and uninhabited; and therefore, its direct effect on human beings still remains a mystery.

She stopped then and thought about how to continue. The report still didn't feel right to her. Was she still holding back something of what she really believed?

Suddenly Debra stopped her work and turned to the open doorway of her office. Two women and a man, all wearing the dark blue wool uniform with the gold trim of British Naval Intelligence, were making their way down the dimly lit hallway from the message center. Sheridan had finally reported in, she thought, but then she could see the face of the first uniformed woman. It was a girl named Jill that she knew slightly. Their eyes met and Jill shook her head, indicating that there was still nothing.

Behind Jill was Bob Lowry, a slimly attractive British intelligence officer. "Come have a drink," Lowry called out to her, but Debra could sense the uneasiness in his voice. Was there anything more uncomfortable than two former lovers? Debra asked herself as she called back "No" to the invitation. Lowry seemed to relax a little then, and Debra thought for a brief moment of their time together. And as she did, her hand went to the vacant place at her neck where she had once worn a golden Star of David, a final gift from her parents before she had left home. It had been Lowry and his very British family that had subtly shamed her into no longer wearing the gold medallion. And it lay now in a plain white box in the drawer of her desk, rather than around her neck where it once had been. Not that removing it had mattered at all in the end in their relationship. They had just been too many worlds apart. He had never really understood her. None of the men that she had known in London had. But maybe Sheridan was different. She'd thought so at first, although lately she wasn't as certain.

She looked up to see Lowry still standing awkwardly in the hallway outside her office. She guessed that in his own way he was trying to come to terms with what had happened between them and what this war and her job here really meant to her. The poor bastard, she said to herself. He thought that by sitting in London reading the reports, listening to the briefings, somehow he knew about the enemy, understood something of its evil, but he had no real sense of it. Debra could feel anger and revulsion rising up inside of her again. She had to stop herself from thinking about it, or it would consume her. And so she just waved a second "no" at their request and turned away. She couldn't blame Lowry or any of the others for not appreciating what they had never experienced themselves. She never would be one of them, she thought then. She might never really be able to prove herself. But she would do her best now with her only weapons, her typewriter and the truth and the decision she'd made long before to do her job as well as she knew how, no matter what anyone thought of her for it. She would tell Command precisely what she believed, she decided: that with Phoenix the Third Reich potentially had the ability to do what they had been unable to do over all these long years of war. They could use it to conquer the world, conquer or destroy it.

★   ★   ★

Geli stood for a moment in the dark basement, looking into the face and eyes of Joseph Goebbels. In the distance she could hear the roar of the Russian artillery.

Suddenly there was a sound in the alley behind the house. Geli's strained nerve endings fired off an alarm as she turned to it.

She went to the cellar's single window. It looked out at the alley behind the house. The glass was filthy and the daylight was almost gone, but there was a streetlamp casting dim rays from the end of the alley, and under it Geli could see a long dark sedan. A single figure got out of the driver's side of the vehicle, but the darkness and the low angle of vision prevented Geli from being able to see the identity of the new arrival.

She looked over at Goebbels and then at Morell, but both men had moved back into the dark corner of the room, hidden again in shadows.

Geli went to the body of the German pilot and removed his Luger pistol. She could hear steps in the house above. They crossed to the door of the cellar. She raised the pistol toward the sounds. The door opened. A large man wearing a knee-length, black leather coat stood filling the doorway. She recognized the man as Gruening, the Fuehrer's private bodyguard.

Goebbels and Morell stepped from the shadows and crossed the basement to the staircase. Geli tucked the Luger into the pocket of her jacket and followed them up the stairs and through the charred remnants of the bombed-out house that lay above the cellar and into the alley where a long, dark Mercedes staff car waited. Gruening went immediately to the driver's side of the Mercedes and got in. The big man reached over then and threw open the passenger side door, motioning to Geli to step inside, while Goebbels and Morell entered the vehicle's rear compartment.

Within seconds the Mercedes began its way down the dark back alley. The car sped down deserted side streets toward the outskirts of the city. Geli sat tensely in its deep leather seat. She could guess their destination now. Tempelhoff or one of the major airports could have been impossible to reach, but planes had been taking off from smaller makeshift airstrips around the outskirts of the city, some of them no more than abandoned fields and empty lots. The one they were headed for now was just northeast of the city. It was dangerously close to the edge of the advancing Russian troops, but with any luck they would arrive ahead of them. Would there be a plane, though, waiting for them when they arrived? Geli asked herself. Nothing could be certain on a night like this.

The staff car passed rows and rows of burned and bombed-out shops and houses, the wreckage left behind by months of bombing.

As the Mercedes approached the end of a long, dark side street, Geli could see flames leaping from the buildings surrounding the street's central square. A small ragged-looking crowd had formed at the end of the street watching the flames.

When the crowd saw the long, black staff car coming into the square they started toward it. Refugees, Geli realized. The city was filled with tens of thousands of her countrymen fleeing in front of the Russian troops advancing from the east.

But Gruening accelerated the Mercedes past them. Stones battered the side of the vehicle. The Mercedes sped forward down a back alley as Gruening jammed his boot to the gas pedal and accelerated the car ahead into the darkness, leaving the burning square and the throng of angry refugees behind.

Then the Mercedes moved along an interconnection of increasingly less-populated side streets, until finally its headlights found the outline of the temporary guard post established at the perimeter of a makeshift airstrip located at the edge of the city. Geli looked over at Gruening as he began to slow the vehicle. He had removed a pistol from his coat pocket and placed it on his lap beneath the folds of his black leather coat. Everyone, even German soldiers, was an enemy to them this night, Geli realized as Gruening brought the Mercedes to a stop in front of the guard post's wooden crossing bar. The inside of the car filled with light as one of the guards at the barrier directed a spotlight at them.

A second guard walked to the side of the Mercedes and bent down. "Identification," the guard commanded.

The guard looked at Geli then, ignoring for the moment the letter of authority that Gruening handed him.

Geli could see only a few hundred meters ahead on the other side of the guard post the shape of a lone aircraft outlined against the light from the flames coming from the city, a Junker-52. She had flown one many times. It would take them far from the city. It was less than five hundred meters away, but there were several jeeps parked behind the guard post and several guards standing nearby. What was going to happen? The guard looked past Geli now to the glass panel that separated the front of the staff car from the rear seat. Slowly Gruening's hand tightened on the pistol under his jacket.

The guard started for the rear of the Mercedes. As he knelt to look inside, Gruening raised his pistol and fired. The guard fell backward onto the side of the road and Gruening immediately accelerated the staff car through the crossing bar, splintering it into pieces, and then the Mercedes raced toward the parked aircraft.

Within moments there was the sound of car engines starting up behind them and the wide arcs of searchlights sweeping the dark airfield. Geli turned back to see several sets of headlights bouncing over the uneven ground after them, with two sets of single headlights in the lead. Motorcycles, Geli guessed, and at least two jeeps.

The searchlight found the Mercedes and within seconds a bullet struck the staff car's rear windshield, spraying glass into the interior of the vehicle. There was another volley of shots from their pursuers. Gruening moved the Mercedes' steering wheel sharply to the right, out of the range of the searchlight, sending the car leaping off the road and across the darkened airfield toward the cargo plane in the distance. Suddenly the darkness above the field was lit by an explosion of light. The night bombing had begun, Geli realized as she looked up into the sky. The flash of light from the first incendiary bomb had faded away, but she could see more shadowy shapes beginning to emerge through the night clouds. It was the first of what she knew to be hundreds of Russian bombers with their fighter escorts that each night filled the air above Berlin. And she knew that the first incendiary bombs would be followed by a host of much more deadly concussion bombs from the British planes. She was going to have to fly the Junker into a sky filled with enemy aircraft. She would be caught between the enemy planes and the massive return ground fire from the city. But there was no other choice. She glanced behind at the burned-out shell of the city she was leaving and the lights of the oncoming vehicles. There was nothing to return to now but destruction and death. And the moment the staff car spun to a stop in front of the transport, Geli leapt from the vehicle's front seat and started across the runway. She grasped the Luger tightly in her right hand, and when she turned to look behind her she could see that the first of the army motorcycles had closed to within only a few meters of the Mercedes. Gruening leapt from the vehicle, his pistol blazing at the first of the soldiers mounted on the speeding cycles. At least one of the bullets found its mark and the soldier's cycle flew out from under him, leaving his body to bump hard across the surface of the airstrip, as the bike skidded into the side of the staff car and burst into flames.

The second cyclist was right behind the first and the two jeeps filled with soldiers less than a hundred meters behind him, but Gruening held his ground, firing off an angry series of rounds until the hammer of his revolver clicked on an empty chamber.

The soldier on the second cycle held an automatic pistol in one hand and fired it as he raced across the airfield. One of the shots grazed the shoulder of Gruening's black leather coat.

Geli could hear the gunfire erupting on the runway behind her. The cyclist was closing even faster now, his pistol moving to point at Geli. There was a flurry of shots. The cyclist's pistol burst in flashes of light and the bullets sailed through the night, barely missing Geli's head and shoulders. There were more shots then, but this time they came from behind Geli, and the cycle erupted into a cloud of bright orange flames when a round hit its gas tank, and the cycle continued on across the airfield, its flaming rider outlined against the night sky.

Geli looked back to where the shots had come from. Goebbels had emerged from the rear seat of the burning Mercedes. Smoke still curled from the pistol in his hand.

The first of the jeeps slid to a stop and soldiers began jumping out of it and running across the field toward her, and she knew that there was no longer time to think, but only to react. She turned and ran to the aircraft's metal staircase and leapt on board.

She strode quickly through the plane's interior to the front of the aircraft and strapped herself into the pilot's seat. She began her preparation for takeoff. She pulled the small lever to the right of the wheel and the propellers began kicking into action, slowly at first and then more powerfully. She looked out the side window of the cockpit at the runway.

The second of the pursuing jeeps had slid to a stop and more soldiers were spilling out of it, firing as they ran toward the aircraft. Goebbels was moving quickly up the exterior steps of the plane now, and behind him Morell and Gruening. Bullets were flying around them as they quickly mounted the staircase. A second later Geli could hear the staircase being pushed away from the side of the aircraft and the bulkhead door slamming closed.

She reached down then and released the aircraft's ground brake, and immediately the Junker began moving ahead over the surface of the airfield.

The transport began picking up speed. Geli could see the first of the Allied concussion bombs explode on the runway in front of her, lighting the path of the accelerating aircraft with bursts of orange-yellow fire and rocking it from side to side. But Geli remained determined, her hands steady on the wheel, as she accelerated the aircraft even faster down the airstrip directly into the path of the exploding bombs. Then she felt the transport leave the ground and lift off into the danger-filled sky. Ahead of her were lines of orange tracers, just the start of the heavy return fire from the ground that would not be able to detect the difference between her aircraft and the enemy's. And above them the sky was filled with Allied planes.

She forced the aircraft straight through the bursts of smoke and fire that exploded around her. She pushed the plane at a hard sharp angle, until it seemed that it would blow apart, or at the very least its wings would explode away into the night, but somehow the aircraft held together, and soon Geli could see the city of Berlin beneath her, lit bright with flames.

Immediately around the aircraft, the explosions had subsided and Geli could see only an occasional line of the deadly orange tracer fire.

They were going to make it, Geli realized then. They were going to rise above the holocaust on the ground, fly up and out of the smoke and flames to safety.

She glanced behind into the interior of the cabin. Suddenly there was a flash of light from the city below and Geli could see Goebbels' face in stern profile against the great panorama of fire and destruction coming from the burning city—the new Fuehrer of the Reich, she thought, and she felt a thrill of hope pass through her. And as she did, she was reminded of the words that she had heard him speak at a torchlit rally in Nuremberg many years before. If Europe had to be destroyed, he had said, even all of the earth and everything in it as well, so that it could be reborn again in perfect purity, then that destruction must be begun.

# PART
# TWO

# CHAPTER
# FIVE

Sheridan regained his consciousness to the sounds of distant explosions. When he opened his eyes, he slowly began to make out the olive-drab canvas ceiling of a temporary field hospital.

Sheridan looked at the man lying next to him. The man's face was frozen in pain, his eyes open, but staring at nothing. He wore the olive-gray wool of the German winter uniform. Surrounding him was a sea of men, each wearing similar German uniforms. Some of the men were crying out in anguish, others were deadly silent. The rows of wounded and dying men seemed to go on forever in every direction and Sheridan knew that he was looking at the end of the once awesomely powerful German Army.

He felt a flash of memory. He had been drifting through the sky. His pilot, Hearn, had been with him. They had followed a

Russian bombing run into Berlin, but they had caught some flak
and they had been forced to bail out over the city. There had been
danger everywhere, bombs and gunfire and enemy planes. Sheridan wanted to cut the memory off but he couldn't. It kept forcing itself on him. A round or a random piece of shrapnel,
something deadly, had struck Hearn, and the young, dark-haired
boy had drifted through the sky next to him for several minutes,
blood pouring from his wound onto his flight suit. Then his
chute had drifted away from Sheridan out of sight and Sheridan
had known that he would never see him again.

Sheridan let himself feel the pain of the loss, as he had
taught himself earlier in the war, let it fill him, waited for it to
lessen a little, and then remembered the rest of it.

After Hearn had gone, he had landed on a rooftop, slamming into it and, unable to break his fall, he had slid to the
ground. He had hit with a pretty good jolt, enough to knock
him out, and then he guessed the Germans had found him and
brought him to this field hospital.

He could hear artillery fire being exchanged nearby. The
sounds brought him back to the present, but he didn't understand. Were American forces finally advancing on Berlin? The
last he had heard they had been ordered not to cross the Elbe and
enter the city, but the orders could have been changed. If they
had, he should try and join up with them, but first he had to get
out of this place, he thought, and raised himself up onto his el-
bows.

The first-aid station was little more than a series of olive-
drab tents strung together in a series of disorderly rows. In the
distance he could see a few attendants in white coats, and the
ones that he could see had their backs turned to him. The large
tent that he was in was open on one side, and across the rows and
rows of wounded men Sheridan could see an opening with the
start of a ragged pine forest just beyond, less than a hundred me-

ters from where he lay. There could be guards at the perimeter. But if they hadn't arrested him when he came in or at least separated him from the German wounded, the enemy was probably in total disarray. If he could get to the woods, maybe he would have a chance.

How badly hurt was he? That was the first thing that he had to know. He raised himself to a sitting position. His shoulder hurt and his side. Nothing bad enough that it could stop him from trying for the tree line, he decided.

He stood and started his way toward the end of the tent. His spine was stiff and it hurt badly when he moved, but his body responded. The pain was severe, though, on his left ankle, as his weight came down on it against the cold, hard ground—a break or a sprain, it was impossible to know. He could feel the severe cuts on his shoulder now too, running from his calf up to his shoulder. He looked at his uniform. It was badly torn and he could see a line of dried-blood stains from his leg to his armpit. He must have caught a tree limb or something coming down. He watched as the rows of bodies danced around his eyes and then began a full gyrating roll. He bent his head and closed his eyes and let the sensation pass. Too soon, he realized. He was trying this too quickly, but he kept going, reeling like a drunken man toward the dark opening at the end of the tent.

He heard a sound behind him and he turned to look. A guard or an orderly, a figure of some kind, was making its way down the long line of wounded men toward him.

Sheridan didn't stop. He heard a voice calling out in German to halt. He turned back again. The figure was almost on top of him. It was one of the orderlies, and the squatly built man had a pistol strapped to his side over a blood-smeared apron.

Then there were other voices. The wounded men in his path were calling out to him, and one made a try for his leg, but Sheridan shook it off.

The opening was almost in front of him. He could hear the attendant behind him, louder and closer, calling out again for him to stop, then the report of a pistol firing. A round sailed past his shoulder, but Sheridan kept running, darting through the last of the field of wounded men at a sharp angle, his head bowed, trying to present less of a target, but knowing that the orderly was unlikely to miss again at such close range.

Suddenly the sky above him cracked open with a bright shower of flames followed by an explosion that flung Sheridan to the ground with its force. He clutched the earth hard as shrapnel whirred in the air above him.

This wasn't the distant noise of the rain of the bombs falling on the center of the city, he realized as he lay facedown in the dirt at the edge of the forest. This was something closer and far more threatening. Sheridan finally dared to lift his head a few inches. The white-aproned orderly lay bleeding only a few meters away. There was more gunfire. Sheridan stood and ran toward the woods.

Then in a flash, the darkness that had surrounded him was lit bright as day. There were explosions everywhere. And out of the woods came soldiers firing rifles. At first, Sheridan could see only a few dozen, then hundreds more. Then the entire first-aid station was being overrun by masses of soldiers in dark gray uniforms. Sheridan was frightened and disoriented. The muzzles of a dozen rifles seemed pointed directly at him.

One soldier emerged from the woods and stood only a few feet from him. The soldier raised his rifle, its barrel pointed at Sheridan's chest. There was rifle and small-arms fire exploding on every side. Sheridan reluctantly began to raise his arms into the air, in an act of surrender. The soldier across from him hesitated, his finger on the trigger of his weapon.

Sheridan could see that the soldier that faced him was old, a veteran, with a stubble of gray beard and a deeply weathered face.

The older man hesitated. Sheridan stared at the man's face and uniform intently. And then he understood.

The man across from him holding the rifle was a Russian, a soldier of the USSR, and around him on every side his comrades were overrunning the nearly unprotected first-aid station just as easily as they were capturing all the rest of Berlin that morning in an overwhelming dawn attack.

★ ★ ★

The secret of Camp 19 was about to be revealed to the world, Goebbels thought as his Focke-Achgelis-1000 hovered above the heavily wooded valley that held the mysterious compound.

Explosions and fires were sweeping the camp's grounds, and cries of anguish and machine-gun fire came from behind the main barracks street, but it was all just as he'd ordered it, he decided as he studied the locations of the fires and the burst of destruction that were erupting below him.

The airstrip was ringed by fires, but the Focke set down neatly at the center of the field that lay just above the camp and then taxied to the edge of the road and came to rest only a few meters from the waiting staff car. What a remarkable piece of equipment, Goebbels thought. It was one of only two flyable models of a highly experimental design that had been kept secret throughout the war. It had capabilities that far surpassed anything that his enemies would ever conceive. And the woman had flown it brilliantly. Once she had managed to bring the Junker transport safely out of Berlin, she had landed at a nearly isolated airstrip north of the city and exchanged the transport for the Focke. Angelique Von Stahl, what a beautiful and clever woman, a woman fit even for the master of the world, but now was no time for entanglements, however seductive, Goebbels thought as he watched her stand from the controls and approach him across the interior of the aircraft.

"I congratulate you," Goebbels said as he looked up into the tall blonde woman's ice-blue eyes.

"I am at your service," Geli said in a low sensual voice that filled her simple words with layers of meaning and invitation.

"Good," Goebbels said. "There are more challenges ahead." He pointed through the open exit door down the landing field to where a second Focke-1000 stood, waiting for takeoff.

"Dr. Morell will give you your instructions and he and one other passenger will accompany you to your next destination," Goebbels said briskly, and then turned to Morell, giving Geli no time to reply.

"You will see to the prisoner that you will be transporting, and then you and Miss Von Stahl will continue your flight. And we will meet again soon," Goebbels said.

"In final victory," Morell said.

Only then did Goebbels smile. "Yes, in final victory," he answered, and then turned to the exit, Gruening following closely behind him.

As he departed from the aircraft, Goebbels could see two men waiting for him at the edge of the landing strip. The taller man, with stooped shoulders and thin frame, was General Hollenitz, commanding officer of Camp 19. The other man was his executive officer, Lieutenant Schuman. Goebbels was struck by how bad both men looked. Hollenitz' tall frame was shrunken, his chest caved deeply inward, his face a sallow yellow color. Even Schuman, the younger man, who had only come to the camp a few months before, was beginning to show signs of deterioration. There were black circles beginning around the young man's eyes and a slackening in his face and body that had not been there when he had served in Berlin. A deadly place, Camp 19, a deadly and powerful place, Goebbels thought as the two men greeted him.

In the open air the smell of the camp was overpowering Goebbels' eyes began to pour out moisture and his stomach began to move in revulsion, but when Lieutenant Schuman offered him a gas mask, he refused, choosing instead to use only his own handkerchief to cover his nose and mouth. Gruening, standing behind him, did the same.

A large JU-52 transport had already reached the head of the runway. It was fully loaded and ready for takeoff. Goebbels turned to watch it lift off.

"How many?" he asked, his eyes on the large aircraft.

"This is number nine," the general said, and then the noise of the transport roaring down the runway and into the night sky made any further discussion impossible.

The large silver plane began to have difficulty moments after its liftoff, but it struggled on into the night, gaining altitude. Goebbels watched it until it was nearly out of sight. Suddenly it burst into flames and dove from the sky. A moment later the rumble of an explosion reached his ears.

Goebbels' eyes scanned the night sky, pretending to be looking for an intruder, but, of course, there was none. "It must have developed internal problems," he said, turning to Hollenitz, but then looking past him to Schuman. The young officer had done his job well. The ninth transport had contained an explosive device, one placed in it by Schuman, but no one else, not even General Hollenitz, knew that. A dramatic way to accomplish their purpose, Goebbels thought as he watched the flames in the distance, but a very effective one. The crash would bring Allied reconnaissance, and probably very soon. By then, his business would be completed here, and he would be safely miles away. He looked over at the others. They seemed to be held spellbound for the moment, staring off at the spot above the crash where a

trail of smoke and flames still leapt into the darkness. Goebbels
returned them all to action, gesturing with his swagger stick toward the staff car that waited at the edge of the runway. "You
have the prisoner?"

"Yes, Herr Minister," General Hollenitz said.

"Dr. Morell will attend to him. I will see the camp now,"
Goebbels snapped.

"Yes, Herr Minister," General Hollenitz said again. "I must
take care of this." He pointed toward the spot in the distance,
where a trail of smoke and flames was now leaping into the sky
from the crash site.

"That will not be necessary," Goebbels said. "One plane
more or less means nothing. Leave it and continue with the mission," he added sharply, pointing with his swagger stick to the
line of remaining aircraft waiting to depart.

"Yes, Herr Minister," Hollenitz said, breathing hard and
managing the words only with some difficulty. It was clear that
he was a very sick man, Goebbels thought, and led the group
quickly across the runway to the waiting staff car. He was eager
to have his business at this hellhole quickly over with for more
than one reason. No one knew for certain how much time here
was too long; even a few hours might turn out to be fatally dam-
aging.

A few moments later the limousine moved from the edge of
the airfield and passed by a series of warehouse buildings. The
first few buildings were empty, and as Goebbels watched they
were being set on fire while crews of men unloaded long, coffinlike gray metal boxes from the other buildings, loading them
onto trucks that took them up the hill to the airstrip and the remaining transport planes.

The staff car descended even deeper into the pine-shrouded
valley that lay beneath the airstrip until it reached the main camp
street. Most of the buildings that lined the narrow muddy road

were on fire. And those that weren't soon would be, Goebbels thought as he watched soldiers leading men and women wearing gray-and-white-striped uniforms from the inside of the huts and into the woods that stood at the rear of the rows of barracks. Then when each hut was empty, it was lit on fire.

In the distance Goebbels could hear the sounds of screams and gunfire. He knew that in the woods great holes had been dug in the ground. The soldiers themselves would learn too late why so many holes had been dug and of such size, far more than would simply be required for the prisoners alone. The final operation of Camp 19 was proceeding, just as it had been planned.

From the safety of the rear of the staff car, Goebbels observed the condition of the prisoners being led from the barracks. They moved slowly, hobbling on withered legs. Their heads were shaven, and even from a distance Goebbels could see the blotches of blackened skin erupting on their exposed flesh that were the first outward symptoms of Phoenix.

Goebbels nodded approvingly toward Hollenitz, but the aging general did not respond. He only kept his deeply sunken eyes focused ahead of him into the darkness, not looking directly at the carnage around him.

"That will do," Goebbels said forcefully, and he pointed back toward the airfield. The Mercedes stopped then and returned back up the main camp street.

Goebbels said nothing as he continued looking out at the fire and destruction. He noticed an aircraft hovering above the valley. He smiled as he craned his neck to see the small reconnaissance plane through the vehicle's side window. An Allied spotter plane, Goebbels guessed from its shape and speed. He had planned that the fires and then the crash of the transport would bring the enemy sooner or later, but this was far quicker than even he had expected. He wasn't concerned. Everything that needed to be done here could easily be accomplished long before the enemy could do anything to stop it. And when the enemy came to Camp 19, Goebbels thought, they would learn the true power of Phoenix and that knowledge would breed a fear and perhaps even a sense of panic in the Allies that would move the operation one step closer to ultimate success.

"Herr Minister." Hollenitz' voice was uncertain. Goebbels turned to him. He could smell brandy on the general's breath and he could see a wavering of purpose in his light gray eyes. Hollenitz was far from being the man he had selected for the post only six short months before, but that was not to be helped, Goebbels thought. War meant death, usually sudden, quick endings, but the kind of war that they were fighting now, the war of the future, meant a slower death. General Hollenitz, as brave as he had been in the other kind of war, was a coward in this new type of warfare.

"Herr Minister," Hollenitz began again. "With all that has happened in Berlin in the last few days, I must ask"—he paused, letting his uncertainty show—"if there has been any change in plans."

In the distance the volleys of shots and screams of agony continued. Then, Goebbels spoke in a low hiss. "There will be no changes," he whispered. "The final orders are to be carried out with total precision," he said, sweeping his hand out toward the streets of the camp.

Suddenly one of the prisoners twisted away from his guards and began running toward the staff car. The guard aimed his rifle and fired, but his first shot only ripped the dirt behind the prisoner and the man surged forward and pressed himself against the rear window of the staff car, clawing against the glass.

Goebbels removed the Luger from his holster and pointed it at the man, but before he could pull the trigger, he looked closely at the man's face. The prisoner's eyes were sunken dark holes lost in deep, lifeless sockets. And his face had become almost a single mask of blistered skin with spreading black sores. The horrible black sores had spread over the top of his head as well, and even down his neck and shoulders, disappearing below his striped uniform shirt.

The hideous-looking man stared at Goebbels for a long moment before Goebbels fired his pistol through the glass at the man's face and the grotesque head exploded in a torrent of black-red blood against the glass surface of the window.

"Get out of here," Goebbels screamed at the driver as the man's body fell motionless into the dirt of the road. "Now! Drive!" The staff car accelerated down the narrow camp street.

Goebbels felt his stomach churn in disgust and revulsion. The hideous smell of Phoenix seemed to hang even more heavily in the air of the car now and he wanted desperately to be on his plane and leave the camp immediately and never return, but he knew that he must show no emotion, no reaction of any kind in the presence of General Hollenitz.

The staff car continued on to the top of the hill and the landing field. The slickly elegant Focke-1000 was serviced and refueled and its new pilot waiting for Goebbels at the edge of the runway.

"I leave you to your duty, General," Goebbels said as he stepped out of the rear of the staff car, being careful not to let a trace of the prisoner's dark blood that had exploded against the side of the vehicle adhere to his hands or uniform.

Above the landing field, the enemy reconnaissance aircraft was still circling slowly. Yes, that was good, Goebbels thought, continuing to force himself not to think about the highly unpleasant scene that he had just participated in, as he crossed the landing field toward his own waiting aircraft. Despite the single ugly moment with the prisoner, the destruction and ultimate discovery of Camp 19 was working out almost precisely as he'd planned it. If only the remainder of the master plan would go this well, he thought. Then truly he would see Dr. Morell again soon in final victory.

# CHAPTER
# SIX

History was laid out before him, Sheridan thought as he stood on the balcony of the suite of rooms on the top floor of the Adlon Hotel. The Adlon was practically right on the Wilhelmstrasse, and from the windows and balconies of its west side, its occupants could see from above the broad boulevard where the Red Army was marching in celebration through the streets of the German capital.

Loud brass bands were playing on the street below the hotel and the German crowds had turned out to line the boulevard, if not to celebrate the conquering heroes, at least to begin to satisfy their curiosity about them.

It was a tense scene, though, conqueror and conquered. If the band stopped playing for even a moment, Sheridan thought, the sounds of gunfire from the last few pockets of Nazi resisters could be heard.

Behind Sheridan in the hotel's top-floor conference room, a group of British, French, and American generals, including his own boss, General Harkins from Eisenhower's staff of Supreme Command in London, were in conference with some of the Soviets' highest ranking generals and officers.

Sheridan waited nervously on the balcony along with a few other Allied officers watching the historic parade in progress and wondering what lay ahead. One of General Harkins' aides had woken him early that morning at the billet just outside the grounds of Tempelhoff Airport in the southern section of the city that the Soviets had given him and transported him across town to the Adlon. Harkins wanted to meet with him. For all Sheridan knew, Harkins could be sending him back to London on the next flight. Stranger things than that were happening in the highly charged political atmosphere of occupied Berlin.

And the strangest of all, as far as Sheridan was concerned, was the American Ninth Army. It had stopped its advance into Germany at the Elbe River less than ninety miles southwest of Berlin. All that separated it from the German capital was a nearly empty Autobahn and a few thoroughly beaten German soldiers waiting for someone other than the Russians to surrender to, and yet it still didn't receive orders to move. The answers, of course, were all political, Sheridan thought, and were all being made in smoky conference rooms like the one behind him on the top floor of the Adlon.

American generals were pouring into Tempelhoff on the air force's C-47s, and the French and the British higher-ups were arriving on their own flights. Meetings were being held all over the city, each attempting to focus on the many issues of occupation, but for all of the seemingly endless meetings, one overwhelming fact remained supreme above all others—that without an American advance into the city the Soviets controlled Berlin. It was their troops that marched in the Wilhelmstrasse. It was Red

Army soldiers that ringed the airports, guarded the checkpoints at the major roads, controlled the jails that were rapidly filling with political prisoners, while for whatever reason the American troops remained camped west of the Elbe.

Sheridan listened to the brassy martial music of the Soviet Army as it passed below the balcony. He could feel the thrill of being in the middle of history radiate through his body. He couldn't go back to London now, he thought. He had to convince the generals to let him complete his mission.

Sheridan would never have believed that was possible when it had begun, but in some way the war had actually given him a feeling of accomplishment and personal pride that he'd never achieved in peacetime. Two years of college in his native Wyoming and then nearly four years of traveling, trying to write and play his music, had led nowhere, but surprisingly he was good at being a CIC agent, and he wanted more than anything else to succeed this one final time. He wanted desperately to crack through to the heart of Phoenix, not for glory, not even just for his country, but for himself.

Suddenly Sheridan felt a hand on his shoulder. He turned back into the tense face of General Harkins' aide, Lieutenant Dwyer. Dwyer was a handsome, serious young man from Chicago with very fine pale brown skin and a small pencil moustache. He had a slender build and moved quietly and gracefully. Sheridan had never even heard him coming. It had been Dwyer who had pulled Sheridan out of his bivouac that morning well before dawn and driven him across the city to the Adlon.

"Major Sheridan," Dwyer said with the barest hint of a Midwest twang.

Sheridan didn't need anything further. He turned and followed Dwyer from the hotel balcony and through the adjoining room to the hallway. As Sheridan passed, he noticed that the doors to the large conference room were closed, the meeting still in session.

"The general can give you just a moment," Dwyer said.

He led Sheridan down the ornately designed if somewhat frayed-looking hotel corridor toward a door that stood ajar at the end of the hall.

When they reached the door, Dwyer opened it and stood aside. Sheridan started forward and then stopped. His uncertainty was greeted with a hearty laugh and a cloud of thick cigar smoke.

The room was a maid's closet full of linen and cleaning supplies. General Harkins, smoking a long black cigar, was at the rear of the closet seated on a pile of folded sheets. The small room was filled with smoke.

"Major, it's good to see you," the stockily built general said, gesturing for his aide to close the door behind Sheridan. They were alone then in the dark linen closet. Harkins waited for a moment while Sheridan's eyes adjusted to the darkness. Then the general laughed deeply. "I've been havin' meetings in here for the last two days," he said, extending a packet of cigars toward Sheridan.

Sheridan took one but didn't light it, twirling it between his fingers as he awaited Harkins' orders.

Harkins was a red-faced, roundly built, and nearly bald officer whose sloppy appearance and squat physique stood out dramatically within Eisenhower's handpicked Supreme Command, which was known for its trim, well-tailored look. General Harkins held the position that he did, not for how he looked, but because of his skills. Harkins was one of the best officers Sheridan had worked with in three long years of warfare.

"Ever'body's doin' just about the same thing," Harkins continued in his East Texas mountain-country drawl. "There's a meetin' in every coat closet, bathroom, fire escape, and elevator shaft in this buildin'. We got ourselves a prime spot," he said, replacing his packet of cigars into his chest pocket and slapping the stack of linens that supported his portly body.

"The rooms are bugged," Harkins explained, "even the goddamn privies. But everybody's got to talk to their people. This city's up for the takin', and so's the whole goddamn country. So we've all got to maneuver. Can't do it in our rooms, though, or the bar or any of the normal places, so we do it in the coat closets." He laughed and spewed cigar smoke again. "The French've got the public bathroom, the British the fire escape. Leaves me with the storage closet. Suits me fine." Harkins beamed broadly and poured out more smoke. "I kin do business anywhere. Probably why Ike sent me here."

Harkins paused and looked Sheridan over carefully. "Damn good to see you, Major," he said. "I could use about a hundred good men that I know I can trust about now. There's a hell of a lot to do." He paused again, still inspecting Sheridan carefully. "How are you?" he asked finally.

"Good," Sheridan said. "I saw the medical people yesterday. They say I'm ready to go." That wasn't quite the truth, Sheridan thought, but it was close enough and he sure as hell didn't want to get sent back to London for a sprained ankle and some cuts and bruises.

"Okay," Harkins said, getting down to business, "it's like this. I don't know how you got into Berlin ahead of just about everybody else, and I'm not going to ask. I'm just damn glad that I've got you. Your—" Harkins dropped his voice and looked around the small enclosed space as he continued. "Your Phoenix team has been sent to a spot north of here. We found some pretty ugly things up there at a place called Camp 19 that we want them to take a closer look at. Dwyer will brief you on that." Harkins waved his cigar toward the door outside which his aide waited. "They're nearly in place already and they don't need you for what they're doing, but I do need you here. I'll have you back with them in a few days, though, that's a promise. In the meantime, the Soviets have something they want to show us. I'm not certain what it is, but I know it's something big and if it's what I think it is, it's directly tied to Phoenix and your team's mission. They asked for a liaison with my top intelligence officer. For the moment"—Harkins smiled—"that's you. You speak good German and Russian, but more important to me is the fact that I know you, Major. I trust you. I've pinned half those ribbons for bravery that you're wearing on your chest myself and you deserved every damn one of them. I don't know exactly what the Reds are up to, but I don't trust them and that's why I want you in on it, whatever the hell it is. I'd go myself, but"—he blew out a big puff of exasperated cigar smoke—"I can't get out of here. So I'm going to tell them that you're my man, unless, of course, they got this place bugged too and they already know."

Sheridan nodded. He felt relieved. He was eager and ready to get back into action.

"They're to know nothin' about Phoenix," Harkins said. "That's from Command. And be careful of them, Tom." Harkins became almost fatherly as he began to finish with the younger officer. "The Reds are supposed to be our friends, but they've got their own agenda in Berlin and if you get in their way . . . " The general paused for a moment. "Well, from what I've seen of them, they can be a goddamned brutal people. And they won't give a damn what they do to you."

★   ★   ★

Debra could see the miles of blackened devastation from above, and near its center, the twisted wreckage of a Nazi cargo plane, its burned and twisted tail sticking up from the dark earth. She could even feel the impact of the devastation on the ground inside her own body, leaving a sick, dead feeling in her stomach and chest. She had never dreamed that her return to Germany would be like this. First Berlin, then the scorched, dark, dead earth below her now. Was the entire country just one mass of destruction?

She had tried for months to be one of the first Allied intelligence agents into her native country, but when the orders had finally come, they had surprised her with their speed and urgency. She had been ordered to leave London and proceed with the rest of the Phoenix team to Berlin immediately. Their mission called for them to establish a liaison in the German capital with the head of Allied intelligence in Berlin, General Harkins. But once they had arrived in the German capital, Captain Lowry and the newest member of the Phoenix team, an elderly Scottish scientist from the Allied Advanced Scientific Laboratories in Clarendon named Stevenson, had been instructed to continue on to the northwest of the city. Debra's orders to join them had come less than twelve hours later.

She hadn't even had time to find Sheridan. Communications in Berlin were a muddle. All she discovered in the last few hours that she'd had was that there were a few Americans in the city, but that they were scattered and no one seemed to have much of an idea yet who they were or where they were located. Debra knew that she shouldn't, but she was finding herself beginning to really worry about him. Her thoughts of Sheridan and Berlin were suddenly cut off, though, as Lowry directed the pilot of the L-5 down lower to give them a better view of the crash site. "I want you to see everything," the British captain called out to her.

Debra could feel her own sense of revulsion growing even more intense as the L-5 began to approach the area of blackened desolation around the crash site. But it was her job to report back to Harkins and the others in Berlin everything that they'd found out here, and no matter how much it hurt, she was going to see it all and report it accurately, she told herself as she reached for her field glasses and began studying the wreckage.

"We've only had one chance to fly over this site ourselves," Lowry said. "There's so damn much else to do back at the camp. Tell Harkins or whoever you're able to report to that we need some help out here badly. Personnel. It would be best if they had some biological or chemical training, but at this point we'll take anybody. And equipment. I've got a list that Dr. Stevenson prepared."

Debra turned her attention briefly to the latest member of the Phoenix team. Stevenson was a stern-faced old Scotsman, the kind that the English always imagined lived in the farthest, wildest reaches of northern Scotland. His long, thin face was a sour yellow color against his thinning, reddish-brown hair. His cheeks were sunken and hollowed, his lips thin and straight. He was one of the most brilliant biologists in Great Britain. So brilliant that Command believed that he and the other scientists that had been working with him would be able to break through to the secrets of Phoenix and discover some kind of a counteragent that could destroy the deadly microbe and neutralize its threat to the Allies. Debra hoped to God they were right.

The L-5 circled the site again and Debra looked down at a ring of dead land several miles in diameter, spread out in roughly a circle, with the crash site at its center. She was actually seeing the results of the monstrous stuff now, seeing firsthand for the first time the devastation that it caused. Within the vast circle were only dead or dying things—blackened trees, dead grassland, the corpses of decaying birds and wildlife. Seeds of death, Debra thought as she continued moving her gaze across the face of the landscape. The final legacy of the Third Reich. Where would it end?

"How much material did it take to do this?" Debra asked.

"There's no way to know yet," Stevenson said. "There are tests we can run, though, and we need to inspect the crash site more closely. We'll have a pretty good idea in a few days. For the moment, we're guessing—quite a bit. I mean, look at all this." The scientist's hand swept the vast destruction laid out beneath them.

"American aerial reconnaissance found the crash site three days ago," Lowry said. "There were reports of planes like this one leaving from a location less than ten miles south of here, the same night as the crash."

"Planes?" Debra said, feeling a flood of alarm. "How many?"

Lowry's answer came reluctantly. "We think a dozen, maybe more. The reports are that they're all the same size as the one down there." He pointed toward the crash site.

Debra shook her head in disbelief.

"I know," Lowry said. "It was almost impossible to imagine that they could mount an operation of that size at this stage of the war. They must have planned it for months."

A dozen planes, good God, Debra thought, looking down at the size of the tail section pointing up from the wreckage. What did that mean? If they were filled with the Phoenix microbes, how much destruction could they do?

She would have to wait for the answers to Stevenson's tests before she could answer that question with any certainty, but it could be one hell of a lot, just from this one storage facility. And, of course, there could be even more of it stored in other locations.

"Seen enough?" Lowry asked, looking first at Stevenson and then at Debra. The words were a terrible understatement. She had seen far more than she had ever really desired to see in her entire life, but she knew that it was necessary for her to take it all in and that what lay ahead of her now was likely to be much worse.

"There's one more stop, I'm afraid," Lowry said. "They flew this stuff out of a highly secret installation, just a few miles from here. We've barely had a look at it, but what we've found is pretty bad. Command needs a firsthand report and I'm afraid that means you."

"Yes, I know," Debra said, her fingers anxiously going to the empty place at her throat beneath her uniform blouse.

"You're not going to like what you see," Lowry said, fixing Debra with his clear blue eyes. "The Nazis called the place 'Camp 19.' "

# CHAPTER SEVEN

The Soviet jeep slid to a stop in front of Sheridan. And a figure stepped from its passenger seat onto the curb.

"Colonel Dimitri Ivanov," the figure said, and Sheridan looked over at what at first appeared to be a thickly cut slab of granite packed into a Soviet officer's uniform.

"Colonel," he said, saluting the superior officer.

The two men shook hands. Ivanov's grip was punishing, and Sheridan was forced to look into a pair of intense steel-gray eyes set in a hard square-jawed face, topped by a stiff, dark brown brush cut.

The colonel was still dressed in the Soviet gray-and-red winter uniform. The uniform was clean and freshly pressed, but badly frayed and worn. Sheridan read the crimson-colored insignia of Ivanov's brigade on the overcoat's collar. He knew that it had been in some of the worst fighting of the war. It had been under siege in Leningrad for an entire long and bloody winter and then had broken out and fought its way to Berlin. Sheridan felt instant respect for the hardened Russian officer.

The two men settled into the jeep, and its Soviet driver drove it away from Tempelhoff as a dusky orange sun crept slowly across the gray Berlin sky.

The short trip from Tempelhoff to the Brandenburg Gate could have been more easily taken by a Sherman tank, Sheridan thought as he looked out at the desolate bombed-out landscape. The only road that was cleared for vehicular traffic was a labyrinth of rubble. Chunks of buildings as big as boulders lay blocking the streets and sidewalks. Signs and an occasional Soviet soldier directed traffic away from impassable streets. Around him, Sheridan could see a seemingly endless row of burned-out buildings, their exteriors charred black, their windows blown out, their roofs and upper stories collapsed.

He looked out at the nearly apocalyptic panorama of destruction that most of the great city of Berlin had become. The streets and the buildings were no longer smoldering, but a pall of powdery yellow dust lay over everything and hung in the air like a malignant fog.

Occasionally the jeep would pass a single refugee stumbling down the ravaged streets, or they would pass a small band of frightened ghostlike figures, picking among the rubble.

Sheridan looked over at Ivanov. The Russian's tensely muscled face was set hard and grim, showing no emotion of any kind. He had probably seen even worse where he'd been, Sheridan thought.

Finally the jeep broke into the heart of the city. The battered Brandenburg Gate appeared in front of them, and Sheridan could see signs of people beginning to rebuild their lives. He had heard stories of the start of a black market at the center of the city and now he could see it in front of him, the first stirrings of a renewed Germany. Already, lean-faced, hungry-looking house-wives, refugees, Soviet soldiers, and local tradesmen were making the first stirrings of a renewed life and enterprise. Sheridan wondered how long it would take before it made any real difference to the new nation.

The jeep pulled slowly by the Reichstag, the old German Parliament building. The bombed-out building was surrounded by generals, both Soviet and their Allied guests. Groups of Russian officers were being led by Soviet guides around the ruins of the gutted and bombed-out Parliament building.

The driver then turned back toward the Brandenburg Gate and then angled off onto the Wilhelmstrasse. As they drove, Sheridan sat looking out at the ruined buildings and the grand houses on the boulevard, now all fire-gutted, and covered with the awful yellow powder of destruction that lay everywhere.

The jeep finally stopped at the entrance to the new Reich Chancellery. The building that the Nazis had built to stand for a thousand years to house its leaders stood crumbled into dust and ashes with only a few pillars and hallways remaining intact. But even in its devastation, Sheridan was struck by the majesty. He could visualize it as it had been with great marble pillars rising up to the sky, thousands of the devoted thronging into its forecourt to hear the fearsome speeches of its leaders, the torchlit parades down the Wilhelmstrasse stopping in front of the great Corinthian columns.

Sheridan stepped from the jeep and walked to the great front staircase that had once stretched in a marble semicircle around the exterior of the building for over a thousand meters in every direction. Sheridan reached the top of the steps and then looked back down at the city. What had he been brought here to see? he asked himself again, glancing over at Ivanov's hard-set features. The colonel was obviously a man who did things only for a reason. Why the Chancellery? Why now?

There were guards at the entrance, but they were swept away by the barest movement of the Soviet colonel's hand. To Sheridan's surprise, most of the building's long, high-ceilinged marble hall was still standing. There were a few uniformed guests being led through the vast, rubble-filled marble chambers. Sheridan could see British, American, and French generals being led somberly from one vantage point to another by their Soviet hosts. And he could hear muffled voices echoing around inside the vast interior space like voices lost in a great museum hall.

Sheridan followed Ivanov through the partially damaged but still enormously impressive rooms of the Chancellery for several minutes before the Soviet led him out to its rear gardens.

Sheridan knew that British intelligence reports said that just beyond the garden lay the entrance to the bunker. Is that where Ivanov was taking him? The underground bunker was what he most wanted to see, but then Ivanov pointed to a corner of the garden itself. Soviet soldiers stood at the perimeter of a small cordoned-off area.

Sheridan stepped off the cement walk and moved past the guards toward the spot in the corner of the garden that Ivanov had indicated. Sheridan sniffed the air. Gasoline. He looked at the ground. There was a burned-out ring of black ash. A gasoline fire set not by bombs, but by people on the ground, Sheridan guessed, but why? Sheridan felt a strong hand on his shoulder. It was Ivanov. He was pointing at a wooden shed built at the rear of the roped-off area. The shed was heavily guarded, but again, as the Russian colonel approached, the guards let them pass.

"You are the first from the West to know the truth," Ivanov said as they entered the small dark room.

Sheridan stepped forward and both men examined closely two charred shapes wrapped in Soviet blankets that were laid out along the length of a newly built wooden counter at the back of the room. The dark shapes were shrouded in darkness and impossible to see clearly, but Sheridan knew at once what they had to be and why he had been brought here to see them. He was looking at the burned corpses that the Soviets believed to have been the two highest leaders of the Reich—Joseph Goebbels and Adolf Hitler.

★   ★   ★

Camp 19 was an even greater nightmare than Debra had imagined that it or anything on earth could be.

The only way to stay sane, she told herself as she followed behind Lowry and listened to his explanation of what he and Stevenson had found, was to force herself to do her job and concentrate on every word and forget her own feelings.

"There were three basic areas," Lowry was saying. "I think we've been able to reconstruct most of what went on here. Up here"—Lowry pointed to the area adjoining the small airstrip where now there were only piles of burned rubble—"were airplane hangars for the landing field, behind which were manufacturing and storage facilities."

"What kind of capacity?" Debra asked, knowing that it was important to know, but fearing the answer.

"Enough for thousands, maybe tens of thousands of boxes," Lowry said, confirming Debra's worst fears. "There were laboratories hidden between those hills and the edge of the forest," he said, pointing across the open area that lay between the landing field and the start of the thick pine woods. "There were living quarters attached to the laboratories sufficient to house perhaps ten or fifteen men."

"I'm guessing," Stevenson interrupted, "that the Nazis brought their very best scientists in here, perhaps a year ago, as soon as they began to realize that they were going to lose the war. The scientists were given one job only. They were to come up with a superweapon, something that could reverse their seemingly inevitable defeat. And sometime in the last year they discovered Phoenix and began to manufacture and store it as rapidly as they could. But then with the Russians attacking from the east and the Americans from the west, they had to move what they'd stored out of this location and destroy their manufacturing facilities." Stevenson stopped then.

"I'm afraid the rest is worse," Lowry said. "Are you ready?"

Debra had seen a hint of what Lowry meant from the air, when they had landed at the camp's airstrip, and she knew that he was not exaggerating, but she merely nodded her head.

They continued down the hillside then, following the road that led from the airstrip to the lower camp. Suddenly a breeze moved across the low ground in front of them and the rotten odor of the Phoenix microbe stopped Debra in her tracks, and involuntarily her body began to convulse. She remembered the gas mask that Lowry had provided her and she hurriedly held it up to her nose and mouth.

"It's horrible, isn't it?" Lowry said, fitting his own mask into place. "I keep hoping that I'll get used to it, but I never do."

Debra fought to regain command of herself and her body. She was damned if she was going to show any more weakness than she already had. Finally she cleared her head and regained her composure.

Lowry kept watching her with concern. "I'm afraid it gets even worse," he said. "No place for a woman."

"I'm all right now," Debra managed through the mask's plastic mouthpiece.

"When they pulled out, they destroyed everything they could, including their own troops," Lowry said, pointing around at the nearly impenetrable perimeter formed by the combination of the natural contour of the hills and forest and the tangle of concrete bunkers and barbed wire that surrounded the base of the valley. "It would have taken an invading army God knows how long to get in here and it would have taken one hell of a lot of casualties in the process. But, in the end, the cadre here simply murdered each other and themselves. And we believe the only way they could have managed to do something that incredible was through the command structure. We're guessing there was some kind of secret elite corps within the ranks and they had instructions to murder their fellow soldiers. Then that corps' own NCOs and officers killed their enlisted personnel, and so on up the chain of command with each level believing that the killing would end just below them, but, of course, it never did. We found the bodies of the commanding officer and his exec. The C.O. appears to have committed suicide, the last link in the chain."

They continued on down into the lower camp's main street. "This area housed the barracks for the prisoners," Lowry explained. "Not very many considering all the security, but, of course, they weren't strictly prisoners," he added, and then paused.

Debra looked at him curiously. "What do you mean?" she asked, but instead of answering with words, the two men led Debra to the edge of the woods that stood just behind the row of wooden huts. Here it comes, Debra told herself, but as hard as she tried to steel herself for the shock, when she actually saw it, she was still unprepared. She looked into the woods where Stevenson was standing and all at once her legs began to buckle. She suddenly felt very weak and it was only by the force of her will that she didn't collapse entirely.

"I'm sorry," Lowry said. "But you have to see it. They weren't prisoners here, they were experimental subjects."

A few meters into the woods was a series of long open pits. The pits were filled with bodies of men, women, and children, all dressed in gray-and-white-striped uniforms, barefoot, their heads shaven. Some lime and dirt partially covered a few of the bodies. Debra forced herself to look at them. The flesh of the corpses was crisp and black, blistered as if burned by a great fire, but as Debra looked more closely she could see that the burned effect had been the result of hideous black sores that had spread along the surface of the skin, devouring the flesh. At certain points the surface damage had become so severe that some of the bodies had split open, and Debra could see that the same black blistering sores had invaded the victims' insides as well, devouring internal organs with the same voracious hunger that they had eaten away the external flesh, leaving only charred, dead blackness. Debra could barely believe her eyes. She couldn't imagine the pain, or the fear, or the horrible death that these prisoners had been subjected to. God, Debra thought. Lowry had been right: this was no place for a woman, no place for any human being.

"We don't have enough men to do all the work we need to bury them," Lowry said, turning back to Debra. "There are half a dozen pits like this scattered around the woods on the perimeter of the camp. They're all filled. We've buried some, but it's a very long job. And"—he paused—"we've purposely delayed here, because there is something more that you need to see."

Debra nodded bravely. She watched as Lowry knelt down by the edge of the pit next to Stevenson.

"There have apparently been reports of death camps at other locations inside Germany," Lowry explained as he gestured toward the bodies. "We're pretty certain these people were all Nazi enemies of one kind or another. Jews, Poles, Gypsies, Serbs, probably some political enemies too. That's been the pattern at the other camps." *Jews.* At the word, Debra felt her body tense. Don't let it show, she commanded herself. They will be looking for any sign of a reaction.

"Mass murders of Nazi enemies," Lowry continued. "But we found something extraordinary that the other camps aren't reporting." Lowry looked at Stevenson then, as if he couldn't finish.

"Twins," the elderly Scottish scientist said succinctly, once he'd realized that Lowry was unable to go on. "Even some groupings that we believe could be triplets."

Debra didn't understand at first. Her head was swimming from the impact of so much horror all at one time, but then Stevenson's meaning punched its way through to her. Twins. The Nazi bastards were using people as living experiments in their search for a superweapon. And the results were everywhere, all around her now.

Debra began to feel her knees grow weak again. If I were the kind of person who fainted, she said to herself, but then quickly told herself that she wasn't. Make your mind work, she commanded herself, but she couldn't keep it focused on the moment. For protection it drifted backward and then came to rest on her last moments in Germany before this terrible return to the country of her birth. She had stood on a deck of a ship near a gangplank so crowded with people that there barely seemed room for anyone more, not even the little redheaded girl with the trace of freckles across her nose and cheeks. Her red hair dropped in a mess of ringlets to her shoulders, and was tied with a bright yellow ribbon at the back of her head, the last time that her mother had ever been able to do that for her. And then suddenly she had realized that the boat was moving away from the shore into the open sea and that her parents were no longer with her. They had returned to the dock and she was alone with just the medallion on the gold chain that they had given her for company and her hand went to where it should be around her neck, but it wasn't there now. And she remembered when she'd taken it off and why and suddenly she felt ashamed. She was staring into the open pit, looking at faces now. But looking for what? This was not at all how she had planned the return to her homeland.

"You see," Stevenson went on explaining, and Debra forced herself to forget everything else and only to listen, "in the mass graves that we found on the other side of the camp, the bodies were in much better shape than these poor devils." He pointed at the tangle of blackened mutilated corpses that lay in front of him. "And for every body we found on the other side, there was a matching one on this side," Stevenson added, the anger and disgust thick in his voice. "They were using these prisoners as experiments to help them validate the effects of their damn superweapon. Those on the other side of the camp as controls, these as experimental subjects," he said angrily, and then added, "And as you can see, what they learned is that Phoenix is absolutely lethal, not just to plants and animals, as we already knew, but to humans as well. Even the guards we found here have evidence of the symptoms that these poor souls"—he pointed at the pit again—"were undergoing in much more advanced stages."

Debra's eyes continued roaming the pit of dead bodies. She knew what she was looking for now, but she wasn't going to find it here. These were other people's sons, daughters, mothers, fathers, sisters, brothers. But the full truth finally reached her for the first time. Germany was full of such mass graves. And her parents were probably buried in one of them, as she herself would have been if they hadn't sent her away on that day long ago. She had known the truth a few years later, when the letters had stopped coming, but she hadn't let herself see it, not until now. She felt her legs giving out from under her. But then she wouldn't let herself surrender to the moment of weakness. She held her ground, her eyes looking away from the pit, boring a hole in the back of Lowry's dark blue uniform.

"We debated whether you should see this or not, but we need Command to know as much of the truth as we possibly can communicate to them," Lowry said almost apologetically.

Debra nodded. It had to be that way, or she had no business being out here, she told herself, no business pretending to be a British intelligence officer. "You both know what Command will ask after I tell them all this," Debra forced herself to speak. "They'll want to know if we can stop it."

"There are things here that I hadn't understood before I came," Stevenson said. "Possibilities that I fear I hadn't foreseen." He hesitated before he finished. "But my answer at this moment is in all probability yes. We are working on several formulas that should be able to neutralize its effects. But we must find their entire supply of the Phoenix material quickly before . . . " He paused then.

"Before what?" Debra asked anxiously.

"Before they can find an effective way of distributing it over a large area," Stevenson answered. "If that were to happen, no one can know for certain what the result might be."

# CHAPTER
# EIGHT

Sheridan kept looking down at the charred body at his feet.

"It is unquestioningly the body of their precious Fuehr-er," Ivanov said. "There are many witnesses, much evidence."

Sheridan nodded. Then he looked at the second body lying next to it.

"That is Goebbels," Ivanov said contemptuously. "They both committed suicide, cowardly and desperate. We must let the world know the truth."

As he listened, Sheridan felt a small feeling of relief pass through him. Without Hitler there was no one left alive to lead something as mad as Phoenix. No one with the incredible mixture of power and will and absolute evil insanity that this man had once possessed. And with Goebbels and Goering and so many others captured or dead now as well, perhaps it was finally really over.

"As you can see," Ivanov continued, "the faces of both bodies, even their fingerprints, have been burned away, but our scientists have other definitive methods of identification. We've taken extensive dental imprints from both bodies. They are being looked at by our experts now. We're very much interested in having your people join with us in that investigation. I'm certain that you will agree that dental records will confirm the identifications with even greater certainty than fingerprints would have."

Sheridan nodded. Then he bent down and closely inspected both corpses. All that remained of each of their heads were two partially charred black skulls. Then he looked closely at the hands, and down the length of their bodies, but saw only more charred black remains.

When he inspected their mouths and jawlines, though, he was able to confirm that there was more than enough teeth and jaw structure remaining on both bodies to make a positive identification. And Ivanov was right: there were few better ways to identify a corpse than by dental work. To a trained examiner, no two people had dental work even remotely similar. If the dental work matched the records, this part of the investigation would be closed, and in all probability, Phoenix too would be at an end.

After several minutes Sheridan followed Ivanov out into the Chancellery garden. Ahead of them lay the entrance to the underground bunker. Sheridan hoped that would be their next stop, but Ivanov led him away from it, back toward the interior of the Chancellery.

"I'd like to see the interior of the bunker," Sheridan said.

"No," Ivanov responded bluntly. "Perhaps tomorrow. For now, it is closed."

"But isn't that where the bodies were found?" Sheridan continued, feeling his first stirrings of uncertainty.

"Come, we have much to do," Ivanov said, and signaled for his driver. And within minutes the Soviet jeep returned them down the Wilhelmstrasse to a partially bombed-out building only a few hundred meters from the Reichstag. The building had been taken over by the Russians and high-ranking officers moved up its front steps. The site had previously been used as an ancient fortress and in its cellars lay a labyrinth of dark dungeonlike cells. Ivanov led Sheridan down to the building's lowest floors. The long dark underground corridors were cold and damp, their ceilings held in place by only a series of rotting wooden beams and rusting metal supports. But the belowground structures were almost entirely undamaged, barely touched by the bombing.

Ivanov finally stopped at a heavy wooden door that lay at the end of a long stone hallway. He unlocked the door and Sheridan followed him into a windowless room with a single blackened wooden table and two long wooden benches as its only furniture. An interrogating room with a history of much worse, Sheridan thought, looking around at the cold stone walls and imagining the racks and iron maidens and other devices of torture that he was certain the room had once held.

The next several hours were filled with a succession of witnesses, most German, a few Russian. And Sheridan struggled with his abilities in both languages as he spoke to bodyguards, personal servants, clerks, generals, common soldiers, secretaries, people that had surrounded the Fuehrer during the last hellish months in the bunker below Berlin.

Almost all of the testimony fit a consistent pattern, a story that Sheridan knew the Soviets accepted as the truth and that they wanted him to concur in and to report back to Harkins and Supreme Command. The Fuehrer and most of his inner circle had returned to Berlin in January, after the German defeat in the Ardennes. The entourage had set up their operations in the underground bunker beneath the new Chancellery gardens. From January onward, the Fuehrer had not left the bunker, except for an occasional night walk around the garden. His health and his spirits had apparently begun to badly deteriorate, until on the afternoon of April 30, he and his wife of only one day had committed suicide. Their bodies had been carried to the garden, and under Goebbels' supervision they had been burned. Later, Goebbels and his wife and children had followed the Fuehrer into the next world with their own self-inflicted death. Dr. Ernst Morell, the Fuehrer's personal doctor, had seen to the burning of their bodies. And now Morell himself was missing.

The story was nearly airtight, Sheridan decided as he listened to the parade of witnesses. The dental records would tell the final story, though. They would be nearly impossible to refute. But there was still one final detail that he wanted to investigate personally. He wanted to see the bunker itself, without any interference from the Soviets. Seeing it would tell him things these witnesses couldn't.

"Forgive me," Ivanov said, looking at his watch as a uniformed guard led the last of the day's witnesses from the room. "There is something that I must attend to. We will begin again at six o'clock tomorrow morning. We have found a room for you to stay in, very near here."

Sheridan nodded a thank-you.

"You have been assigned a car and a driver. You will wait for him here," Ivanov said sharply, and then he was gone.

Alone in the dark interrogating room, Sheridan began to feel like a prisoner himself. But he was damned if he'd stay that way, he decided. He sprang to his feet and went to the room's heavy wooden door half expecting it to be locked, but he was able to swing it open. He looked down the long row of cells that lined that dark corridor. He was alone, but he knew at any moment his Soviet driver would appear.

Sheridan moved quickly down the corridor toward the stone steps that led to the upper floors and then outside. He started toward the Brandenburg Gate and within a few minutes he was standing on the Wilhelmstrasse.

It was still light. The general air of disorganization, of a country in the middle of a massive transition, was apparent. Soviet and Allied officers moved by in a slow but steady flow. No one, though, neither conqueror nor captive, seemed entirely certain of how to act in the newly captured city. Now was the time to move, Sheridan thought.

He started down the Wilhelmstrasse toward the new Chancellery. He stopped only to buy a carton of American cigarettes, using dollars to pay one of the street capitalists that filled the center of the city. As he did, he looked over his shoulder, searching for a hint of the Soviet driver that Ivanov had sent for, but there was nothing.

He continued on then to the new Chancellery and up its imposing marble steps. He crossed through the main lobby and passed into the garden, where only a few hours before the wooden shed had stood. It was gone now, as were all signs that it or the burned corpses that it had held had ever been there.

Sheridan hurried on. There was a guard at the entrance to the bunker. As Sheridan approached him, he held out two packs of the American cigarettes. The guard smiled, showing a mouthful of wire, covering over the space where his teeth should have been, but he didn't reach out for the cigarettes. Sheridan removed another pack from his briefcase and added it to the others. Finally the guard took the packages and turned aside to let Sheridan pass.

The slender American intelligence officer moved quickly down the concrete steps and into the bunker. Its cement floor was covered with several inches of sewage, and the smell choked him as he moved inside, but he pushed forward, going directly to the steps to the bunker's lower floors.

He poked his head into a few rooms along the way, hoping to find something that the Russians had missed. Although there had obviously been some looting in the upper floors, most of the lower rooms were still furnished. The Soviets had not yet had time to fully inspect all the rooms, and they hadn't placed a very high priority on what there might be to find, Sheridan realized, the deeper into the bunker that he explored. There were clothes and personal effects everywhere. Some of the rooms were still even richly decorated with expensive furniture, and large paintings and tapestries covering the cold cement walls.

Finally he was able to find his way down to the bunker's lowest floor and then along its narrow hallways to the suite of rooms that had been Hitler's.

Sheridan entered the outer room of the suite and then waded through nearly half a meter of sewage water into its living room.

Sheridan looked across the room at the red velvet settee that the couple had used during their last moments. Sheridan stood transfixed, imagining it all being acted out in front of him. Strangely the macabre actions of the participants took on a believability—almost a correctness—in the foul-smelling mausoleum of a room that it had lacked for Sheridan in the outer world. Sheridan could almost feel the madness and the despair in the ugly foul-smelling place. Almost anything was possible down here, he found himself thinking, even the bizarre double suicide that had been described to him.

He moved to the final room then—a bedroom, very military, nothing out of order. There was a metal door and behind it a narrow dark corridor. Sheridan followed the corridor to a door that opened into another suite of rooms. Sheridan remembered the testimony that he had listened to that afternoon. This was Goebbels' suite. Sheridan began searching the rooms carefully. It was opulently decorated with large pieces of furniture crowded into the small spaces. When he came to the suite's final room, a small cramped bedroom, Sheridan focused his search even more intensely. He remembered what he had been taught in London. Goebbels had a penchant for secrets and mysteries and curious trick devices. Sheridan searched the surface of the final cement wall, moving slowly down to its base. Then he saw it, a small metal lever built into the bottom edge of a chest of drawers that had been pushed up against the wall. Sheridan moved the lever toward him and the wall slowly began to open and a narrow dark corridor appeared behind it. Of course, he realized then, that was how it had to have been, a secret escape route.

Sheridan's heart began beating very fast. He could hear a sound in the hallway. Someone was coming. Just then the door to the bedroom opened. It was Ivanov and his face was contorted in rage. He looked past Sheridan to the open wall and the secret tunnels that lay behind it. Sheridan could see that Ivanov understood at once the implications of the discovery. He would have failed in the mission his Soviet superiors had given him to end the story of the Nazi High Command in the bunker. And Ivanov was not a man comfortable with failure. The Soviet colonel's hand went slowly to the flap of his holster, unbuckling it and then coming to rest on the butt of his pistol. It would be easy enough to explain the death of one American intelligence officer in all the chaos of postwar Berlin, Sheridan thought as he looked across the room into the emotionless steel-gray eyes of the Soviet officer.

★ ★ ★

Goebbels knew that he was approaching the point of maximum danger. He stood at the stern of a small motor launch. Just above the dark waves he could see the outline of the ruins of the

ancient monastery. The monastery stood at the center of the remote island that lay just off the launch's starboard bow.

The dark shapes of gunboats began appearing then, emerging out of the shadows of the North Atlantic. The launch was
surrounded by half a dozen patrol boats, their guns pointed directly at him, as they probably had been since the gunboats had
left the island. Would they fire on him? If he had miscalculated in
even the smallest detail, they certainly would, or perhaps they
would wait until they were ashore and then he and Gruening and
Lieutenant Schuman would be killed. It was an enormous gam-
ble that he was taking. But one, he reminded himself, that he had
calculated many times as well worth the risk.

It had been a long, difficult journey in the Focke-1000 from
Camp 19 across Germany to a refueling stop in southern France
and then through the lengthy, dangerous stretch of the Pyrenees
to a second nearly deserted landing strip on the Spanish side of
the great mountain range. The next step of the trip had been
made across southern Spain and over the North Atlantic and
then down the Moroccan coast to a small plot of deserted ground
that served as a final landing field for the Focke. A car had then
taken them to a small harbor where the motor launch had been
waiting to carry them the last few miles across the North Atlantic
to their destination, a lonely, abandoned island off the northwest
coast of Africa that awaited them now.

Goebbels turned his attention briefly to Schuman, standing
next to Gruening on the deck of the sea-tossed launch. The
young blond officer had seen the approaching gunboats too. His
hand had gone instinctively to the black leather holster at his hip,
but then he had remembered that all three men's side arms had
been taken from them when they had come on board the launch.
The young SS officer's face turned then not to fear, but to puzzlement. Why had they come here to this remote part of the
world? Who were these people? And why were they placing

themselves unarmed into their power? Goebbels could imagine these questions arising inside the young officer's mind. But Schuman said nothing. Seeing Goebbels watching him, he returned his expression to a blank mask and clasped his hands behind his back and turned his gaze away from the approaching boats, the picture of a good, loyal, unquestioning officer. There was no doubt that Schuman wanted to please him, Goebbels thought. But could any man, however loyal and unimaginative, as he believed Schuman to be, be trusted in the enormity of what lay ahead?

Just then the dark-bearded pilot at the helm of the launch slowed the craft. As he did, the sea's power began to churn and boil against the launch's sides, rolling it dangerously close to the shore rocks, but the pilot responded confidently, moving the tiller into the roaring wind and propelling the craft toward the narrow rock-guarded channel that led to the center of the island.

Goebbels looked out toward the open sea. This part of the North Atlantic was wild and deserted, one of the remotest spots on earth. Even the few locals there were living near this part of the Moroccan coast had long since forgotten its existence. It was only at certain times of the year that the island, surrounded as it was by enormous underwater rock formations, could be reached safely by water. And the journey could only be accomplished then by the use of precise navigational information that very few men possessed. The rest of the year the island stood remote, unreachable, making it a perfect choice for the great but secret purpose that it played within the world of the Third Reich.

Goebbels had been one of only a handful of men within the Reich that knew of the island's existence and purpose. But he had never visited the remote spot before, but now he could begin to make out the shadowy outlines of the monastery's ruined turrets and crumbling stone towers standing at the center of the island.

The monastery had been abandoned centuries earlier and only been revived when the Reich had found it and turned it to its own purpose. Millions of marks had been devoted to its refurbishment and development, but none of the improvements could be seen from the sea or even by a direct overflight by a wandering reconnaissance plane.

Goebbels could feel his body filling with expectation. For of all of the danger of coming to this place, and of all the matters that he had to accomplish in order to ensure Phoenix's ultimate success, this island and what it held filled him with the most excitement, for he knew what lay ahead of him now was something that no other man on earth, not even the Fuehrer himself, had ever experienced. No other man, of course, except one, he corrected himself. And he could see that other man now. His thin, bent figure had appeared out of the night and was standing, solitary and isolated, on the monastery's highest turret, watching the launch make its final approach to the island.

The figure simply lifted his hand and instantly the gunboats began to close in around the launch and surround it even more tightly. And Goebbels knew as he looked at the boats silently sliding up around him in the moonlight, their guns trained on his ship, that for all of his power and position in the world outside this island, he was here no better than a common prisoner, totally at the mercy of the man standing watching him from the crumbling tower of the ancient monastery.

★  ★  ★

Geli could feel Morell's penetrating stare fixed on the back of her neck. He was truly beginning to frighten her. His obsession with her had begun to show itself almost at once after they had left Camp 19. She had flown Morell and a second man, a camp prisoner, who sat throughout the flight hidden in the shadows at the rear of the interior of the aircraft, to a small military base in southern Germany where they had spent the next two days. During the journey, Geli had begun to realize that although Morell barely spoke to her, he was watching her nearly every move. They had left the air base at dawn and continued their flight across southern Germany, and still Morell's intense preoccupation with her did not lessen. She had wanted several times to turn back to him and challenge him, find out what it was that he wanted of her, but she hadn't done it. Now wasn't the time, she told herself. There was too much that was uncertain, too many things that she couldn't control. For the moment he was the master, and her fate was in his hands. A confrontation with him would have to wait, she decided, and she continued looking ahead out the window of the cockpit of the aircraft at the sharp peaks and valleys of the snow-covered Alpine mountains, and concentrated all of her own attention on the difficult job immediately ahead of her.

The sleekly built Focke-Achgelis-1000 that she had been given at the camp was the Reich's most advanced and secret helicopter. Built for speed and maneuverability, the Focke was one of only two completed prototypes that there had not been time to mass-produce. It had been hidden away solely for the use of the Nazi High Command.

At the stopover at Camp 19, Geli had been supplied with the most advanced maps and charts, and with her enormous skills and training as a pilot, she had adapted to the aircraft quickly. Gusts of icy winds were blowing furiously at the sides of the craft, though, and it was veering dangerously close to the final outcroppings of snow and rock that lined the high mountain pass that led to their destination. Great patches of thick fog blew around the craft as well, enclosing it in near darkness, making the flight even more dangerous.

Geli felt her tension and anxiety increase to an even higher
pitch as she maneuvered the Focke forward through the treacherous mountain pass. She had never been more conscious of how
well selected their destination was. She had never approached the
Berghof by air before; few people had. On her only previous visit
she had come by rail to the base of the mountain and then by car
up the heavily fortified roads that led to the top.

The Focke-1000 used the most advanced radar systems
available in the Third Reich, probably in the world, Geli
thought. Without it—and without her great skills as a pilot—the
flight across the mountain would be nearly impossible.

Geli looked ahead of the craft then, straining for a view of
their destination. Through the last of the fog she could just begin
to make out the barest outline of the massive snow-covered peak
of the Kehlstein rising formidably above the rest of the Alpine
setting. They were almost there now, Geli thought, excitement
flooding over her and temporarily replacing the fear, but then
suddenly screaming over the hill directly at them came an attack
helicopter. The attack copter was almost as advanced a design as
the Focke, but it had been built for a different purpose, not transport, but destruction. The attack chopper closed on them at a
rapid rate. After a moment, though, Geli could see that it wasn't
a threat, but a guide. The craft's lights illuminated a final opening in the mountain pass. And the opening's sides were covered
by camouflaged nets holding snow and pine branches. She would
never have seen the opening, she realized then, without the help
of the attack craft.

Geli grasped the wheel of the Focke, swinging it in a tight
arc, barely squeezing it through the small outcropping of jagged
rock that formed the opening to the snow-covered valley. And
the attack craft followed.

Geli could see the majestic Kehlstein clearly now, rising up
in front of her in all of its soaring magnificence, the great moun-

tain's snow-covered peaks resplendent in the morning sunlight. And the Berghof was coming into view now as well. It was half in ruins. Geli's eyes searched the skies above the valley. There were no enemy planes in sight, but clearly they had somehow found their way into the valley, done their work and then left. But for how long? What remained of the Berghof stood perched at the top of a high mountain peak opposite the Kehlstein, looking at the great mountain across several thousand meters of a rock- and snow-filled gorge that dropped down into a mist-filled valley.

Below the Berghof, hidden in the lowest part of the valley, lay the small town of Berchtesgaden, and Geli could see as she banked the helicopter again and began to approach the Berghof from the rear that the little town had been nearly destroyed. Did she dare land? Surely the Allies would be back to finish what they'd begun. She looked at the gas gauge. It was nearly empty. She had no other choice. She had to set the plane down now.

Geli turned her attention then to the retreat's fortifications. She was flying the craft into the teeth of the guns mounted on the hillside. They were flying so close to the giant guns that she could see the great thick outline of their muzzles, even an occasional flash of the gun crew's white winter uniforms. And she knew that dozens more lay hidden in various secret locations around the mountain fortress.

She steered the craft across the snow-covered valley. Ahead she could see a landing area at the rear of the Berghof. And skillfully she brought the aircraft down at the center of it. Within moments she could see the attack craft settling into place next to her. Uniformed men poured from the chopper and started immediately across the airfield toward the Focke.

"You will go first."

Morell had already opened the exit hatch of the Focke and two black-uniformed SS guards stood on the landing field just below the exit. Geli hesitated for a moment, but then, realizing that she had no other choice, she slid down from the craft and through the open hatch down onto the snow.

One of the guards gestured for her to cross the airfield and she was taken up the snow-covered hillside past several bombed-out buildings. The main chalet was still partially standing and Geli was taken to one of its many rear entrances and then up a series of narrow back staircases to its third floor. And then finally she was led down a long hallway to an ornately designed set of double doors.

One of the guards unlocked the tall doors and Geli stepped inside an enormous high-ceilinged bedchamber. The room was entirely untouched by the bombing. Its design was opulently Gothic, its walls painted with mythic scenes from Germany's fabled past. Beasts and naked maidens, bearded warriors fighting and making love among puffy white clouds and against a pale blue sky. Geli stepped into the enormous room. And then before she had time to turn around, she heard the door close behind her. She moved back to the high set of double doors, but they were tightly locked. There was a single window. She ran to it and threw the heavy curtains that covered it aside. Through the leaden-glass window, she could see much of the side and rear of the estate. In the distance she could see a vehicle moving on the crushed-gravel path that surrounded the chalet's grounds.

A moment later a dark sedan that had transported Morell and the prisoner from Camp 19 from the airfield slid to a stop at the rear of the estate.

Geli watched as an SS guard removed the prisoner from the front seat of the vehicle.

The prisoner was small in stature, dressed in rags, his hands shackled at the wrists in front of him in heavy irons. Morell had gone to great pains to ensure that she could never see the prisoner's face clearly, and Geli tried now to make out his features, but he was too far away.

As she watched the prisoner walk away, Morell stepped from the jeep and looked up at Geli's room. As he did, Geli felt a stab of fear slice through her. Her hands went to the ledge of the heavy leaden window, but it too was locked, and as hard as she pulled, it wouldn't open against her strength. She watched then as behind Morell, the mysterious prisoner from Camp 19 moved slowly away from the limousine and out of sight, his step slow and shuffling, his shoulders slumped, his eyes down, as if he were a man convinced that he had just arrived at the end of his final journey. She was no different from him, she realized suddenly. They had both become Morell's prisoners, their very lives totally within his power.

★   ★   ★

Had Ivanov decided to kill him? Sheridan asked himself as he looked across the bunker room at the Russian colonel.

"You are in an unauthorized area." Ivanov's words sounded as if they were a warning, preparatory to using the pistol that was at his hip.

"I had to see it for myself," Sheridan said.

Ivanov stepped past him then to the ornate wooden chest and bent down, using the lever built into the metal baseboard of the chest to close the secret opening in the wall of the bunker.

"And what did you find?" Ivanov said as he stood and turned back to Sheridan.

The American intelligence officer said nothing.

"Tomorrow," Ivanov said finally, breaking the silence. "Everything of value will be taken back to Moscow for our experts to look at more closely. And then all of this will be destroyed."

"Just like the bodies?" Sheridan asked quietly.

"Yes, just as we removed both of the bodies to Moscow a few hours ago," Ivanov agreed. "The top floors will remain for the tourists, but all of this"—his hand swept the final underground room and what Sheridan now knew to be the secret underground tunnels behind it—"will be sealed and destroyed."

"Has Supreme Command given its approval?" Sheridan asked, but the Soviet colonel refused to answer. Sheridan looked closely at Ivanov's iron-gray eyes. They were hard and unwavering.

"What do you believe happened here?" Sheridan said, turning back to the cement wall that had opened out only a few moments before into a hidden underground corridor.

Ivanov was silent for a moment, weighing his answer. "I believe that these men"—Ivanov's hands swept Goebbels' bunker room—"cannot go past this place and this time. Neither their lives nor their myths can ever be permitted to escape these walls. We must end their story here, now."

Sheridan could see that Ivanov was carrying a large manila envelope under his arm and immediately the American could guess what it contained. "The report on the bodies' dental remains," he said, and Ivanov nodded and extended the envelope toward him. "They matched exactly," he said. "My government will announce tomorrow that it is official. Hitler died in this bunker, a cowardly suicide."

"But what of Goebbels?" Sheridan said, searching the report for any mention of the Reich's second-in-command.

"He died here as well," Ivanov said, his voice flat with finality.

"But there is no mention . . . "

"Goebbels' dental records were missing from the official files," Ivanov said. "We base our decision of his death on the body we recovered, the eyewitness reports, and other direct evidence. The matter is closed—both men died here. Your government has agreed to join us in making an official announcement."

"I see," Sheridan said.

"We have arranged a place for you to stay," the Soviet continued. "I will have a driver take you there. We will begin again with the formalities of our investigation in the morning."

Sheridan followed the Soviet back through the bunker and the Chancellery garden to the Wilhelmstrasse where a Soviet car waited.

Ivanov opened the rear door of the car and moved aside for Sheridan to get into the backseat. The Soviet pointed at the long envelope in Sheridan's hand. "No matter what you believe, do nothing," he said. "Or you will be destroyed. Your government and its rules will be of no value to you here. My people fought a thousand miles. Millions of our people died, for me or someone like me to be here at this moment and to tell you the truth of Berlin. And you must know that one more death to preserve that truth is of no consequence to us." Ivanov stepped back from the window and the Soviet car started Sheridan on fogbound streets away from the center of the city.

Sheridan drew in deeply on the harsh night air. He felt safer than he had a few moments earlier, but he knew that the mere fact that Ivanov had let him leave the bunker alive meant very little. His death could be arranged almost anytime, anywhere, in the turmoil of postwar Berlin. It might even be waiting for him somewhere that very night. The car continued down a series of twisting cobblestone roads into an old commercial section in the southwest of the city.

Then it finally slowed in front of an old three-story Bavarian-style building that stood at the corner of a small commercial square.

"Second floor front," the driver pointed. "Number 3. This key opens both doors." The driver gestured toward a dark side alley.

"A car will return for you at six," the driver said, and then sped into the night, leaving Sheridan alone in the yellowish darkness.

Sheridan stared up at the outline of the building. If Ivanov had decided to have him killed in some secluded place, where no one would ever know what had really happened, he couldn't have chosen a better spot, Sheridan thought as he moved through the thick fog to the building's side alley.

Sheridan unlocked the building's back door. It was even darker inside the old building than it had been on the street, but Sheridan could make out the outline of a narrow staircase that led to the upper floors. Suddenly he heard a noise behind him in the alley. He whirled around. There was a figure standing in the fog, only a few meters away. Sheridan's hand went instinctively to his holstered pistol, but the flap of his holster was down and buttoned closed. If the figure was armed and had come to kill him, he realized in that moment, it would surely succeed, but then Sheridan could see the figure more clearly as it stepped from the shadows. It was Debra.

# CHAPTER NINE

What was there next for her? Debra felt a frightening confusion of feelings. She lay on Sheridan's bed, looking up at the ceiling of his Soviet-supplied room. The ceiling was low, water-stained, with its paint flaking off in big grimy patches, but she preferred to look up at it, rather than seeing the images that kept flashing through her head when she closed her eyes—broken, emaciated bodies lying in a pit in northern Germany. The images were beyond her understanding and yet she had experienced their reality herself only the day before. Her fingers went to the empty place around her neck and she felt embarrassment and anger, and despite the weight, and feel, and heat of Sheridan's body next to her, most of all she felt her own aloneness.

She had returned from Camp 19 and then spent the day looking for Sheridan. She had been able finally to find him through Harkins' office and she had arrived at his new Soviet-supplied room only moments before he had. Once they'd been together in his room, almost before either of them had even known what was happening, Sheridan had been taking her clothes off and gliding himself inside of her so easily and so swiftly that it had seemed the most natural thing in the world, as if they were each important missing pieces of the other that they had just rediscovered.

But their passion over, Debra could now feel Sheridan's body slowly shrinking away from her. After all they'd just had together, he still needed to be separate from her. She had gone too far in their lovemaking, hadn't she? she thought then with an old fear. Given herself too fiercely in her desire for him and in her need to stop seeing the images of Camp 19 that filled her head. She had wanted him too much, and she'd gone beyond the limit that a woman should never exceed with a man. And she wondered now if she'd lost him by showing him too much of this part of herself, as she had lost other men.

If they couldn't continue to hold each other, she wanted to talk to Sheridan, to tell him what she'd felt at Camp 19, how she still felt about the loss of her family, and why she kept their final gift to her locked away among her personal possessions, but that she didn't have the courage to wear proudly around her neck. But she believed that if she did, that might be just as quick and sure a way to lose him. No commitment, no sharing the final secret parts of themselves, not until they were more certain of the future. Those were Sheridan's rules. And if she broke them, she could truly lose him once and for all. He was already rolling away from her and lighting a cigarette. The moment for sharing secrets had passed, just as the moment of physical passion had before it. And Debra wanted to at least remind Sheridan that they were still friends and helpers and frightened that if she waited any longer, even that could slip away from her. She laughed softly.

"Look at us. The whole damn world is falling in around our heads and all we can do is jump into bed."

Sheridan smiled and inhaled deeply on his cigarette. Debra looked at him admiringly. Whatever else there was, the friendship between them was always strong. She liked him, the way he acted, spoke, the way he looked, his slim, lanky body roped with lean muscle, and his face, the long slender look of it topped with the slightly unruly light brown hair, the tough masculine chin, and the soft rounded moustache that he wore just a touch longer than army regulations permitted. But above all she was drawn to his eyes, their deep, dark blue color filled with life and warmth. And she believed in his music and his future after the war, perhaps even more than he did himself now. She believed that sooner or later he would find the success that had eluded him earlier. She knew very little about music, but it was Sheridan himself that she really believed in. She knew something about men and he was a very special man and she felt certain that his work would be special as well, when he returned to it. And she lay in his bed looking at him, hoping that there would be a chance, someday, for her to help him to see it as clearly as she could.

A long scar was forming down the left side of his body and she bent her head and kissed it gently. "Can I do something for this?" she asked, touching the long, ragged, red wound.

"I'm fine." Sheridan shook his head and stood up, moving away from the bed. God, he was a hard man to do anything for. All she wanted from him was to allow her to help him and to love him. If he didn't know how, or if he was embarrassed or too damn frightened or whatever it was right now to love her back, that was all right. She wasn't asking for that. Damn him and his stubborn American independence, she thought angrily.

Sheridan began to dress. Before he was finished he went to the window of the small room and lit another cigarette. He

115

looked out at the thick yellow cloud pressing against the window. The fog was filled with dust and ashes and debris from the destruction of the city. "I have a lot to tell you, but I think not here." Sheridan pointed to the dark corners of the room where he guessed Soviet listening devices were hidden.

"We should be used to an audience after London," she said, trying to sound casual, even though a wave of embarrassment was washing over her. She wondered if Sheridan could see the redness pass across her pale white skin. She knew that she had said and done things in their lovemaking that she couldn't bear to think of anyone else knowing about, particularly a room full of Soviet bureaucrats and audio technicians.

Debra rolled over, exposing her smooth white hip. She reached for the chair next to her where her uniform lay, removing a jeep key and a small slip of green paper that Sheridan recognized as a Soviet pass. "There's a black market café just a few blocks from here," she said, but Sheridan shook his head and pointed instead toward the roof of the building.

Debra nodded and began to dress. When she was finished, she followed Sheridan out of the room and up a dark back staircase.

It was cold on the roof and the thick yellow Berlin fog covered everything. It appeared safe to talk, though, and they exchanged information quickly and efficiently as they had been trained to do, filling each other in on what they had both been through since they'd separated in London.

Sheridan had carried a bottle of black market vodka and two glasses onto the roof with him. He poured the vodka into the tumblers and handed one to Debra. She took it and continued to listen to Sheridan's story of the burned bodies in the Chancellery bunker and the secret opening in the wall of Goebbels' room. "Hitler's dental records match the burned corpse, but there are no records for Goebbels," he said. "The official report will just gloss that part over. For political reasons everyone wants them both to be dead. They want all the top Nazi leadership to be gone, finished, the Third Reich over. Then people can feel safe and no one will be tempted to rise to their cause ever again. But what if they're wrong? What if that was a double in the bunker that the Soviets found, and somehow Goebbels himself escaped?"

"Someone flew twelve planes out of Camp 19 on the night of May first," Debra added. "Those planes could have been filled with enough poison to mount a major offensive of some kind."

Sheridan nodded his understanding. "Command's position is that without leadership Phoenix is meaningless; without a powerful figure to oversee the operation, there is very little to really threaten us. But what if Goebbels is still out there somewhere and he's running Phoenix even now? The fact that his dental records are missing must mean something. After all, it was the Nazi High Command that controlled the entire record-keeping apparatus of the country, until only a few days ago. If those records were stolen or tampered with, someone in the high command like Goebbels himself is the most likely suspect."

"You think Goebbels stole his own records or had them destroyed, so that no one could ever prove that the body in the bunker was a double?" Debra asked.

"I just need more proof," Sheridan answered. "But I don't know how to get it. The Russians have this whole damn city tied up in knots." Sheridan stopped and drank off several inches of his vodka.

Suddenly Debra knew what she had to do next. She knew that Sheridan wouldn't like it, but she had to do it anyway. She was part warrior too, and he was just going to have to learn to honor that part of her as well. She looked out at the ugly blanket of yellow fog, thinking only of the mystery of Goebbels' death that Sheridan had presented. She was certain that it wasn't the insurmountable wall of logic that Sheridan feared it to be. She couldn't quite see where it broke down yet, but she was confident that she could crack it open, with her mind, and hard work, and her relentless ability to solve problems, the tools that she always used to force the world to make sense for her. Maybe then the images in her head and the layers of guilt and doubt inside her would start to go away. She would help Sheridan and herself at the same time. "I want to work on it," she said softly. "At least until they give me something else to do. There has to be a way to break it open. I was born in Berlin. I know the city. I can find out the truth here."

★　★　★

Geli awoke feeling a strange presence in her room. As her eyes adjusted to the light, she could see that she was alone, but the powerful feeling of being watched by someone continued to haunt her. She looked over at the bedroom's high Gothic ceiling. Ugly little gargoyle faces stared down at her from the shadowy corners of the room. They seemed to be laughing at her.

She rolled over and looked at the curtained window. Shafts of sunlight were beginning to penetrate into the room through the opening in the heavy curtains.

She rose from the bed and walked directly to the window and drew the curtain aside. She tried to force the window open again, but it was still tightly locked. She knew the door to her room would still be as well. What did Morell plan to do with her? she asked herself as she looked out at the wreckage that surrounded the central core of the Berghof. A few soldiers still guarded the perimeter, camped in small tents or simply lying in sleeping bags in the open air. The enemy would return soon. And these few brave men would be no match for them. What were Morell's plans? Surely he wouldn't wait here to be captured.

There would be other skilled pilots here. And, if he decided to betray her, all he would have to do was to leave her here when he made his own escape. And if it was the Russians who captured her, she knew what her fate would be. She had heard the stories from the Eastern Front, and even if it were the Americans or the British, she doubted that it would be much different for her.

She couldn't let that happen, she told herself fervently. She had to find a way to survive.

She felt the mysterious presence in her room again. It wasn't the gargoyle faces. Someone was watching her. She could feel it. She felt a small flash of hope. Her advantage in any relationship with a man had always been her beauty and her desirability, she reminded herself. Morell would be no different. Perhaps he was watching her from some secret vantage point even now, wanting her.

She let the window curtain drop and walked to the bathroom. The room was large with floor-to-ceiling tapestries covering the walls, and the feeling that she was being watched grew even stronger as she entered it. She walked to the marble bathtub that stood at the center of the room where a bath had been prepared for her. She looked then at the wall that separated her bathroom from the next room. The wall was covered by an ancient Chinese tapestry of reds and blacks. Slowly Geli was able to make out the figures woven into the tapestry's surface. There were men and women engaged in a series of involved, obscene sexual couplings. Near the top of the tapestry were several dark designs behind which Geli knew now that someone watched her from the next room. It had to be Morell, she thought. Then she slowly removed her nightclothes, finally letting her black silken panties drop to the floor. She was naked now, her body tall and beautiful, as she slowly dipped into the bath. She lay back against the marble surface, letting the large globes of her breasts float provocatively on the top of the bathwater. She could sense then the excitement of the man that she knew was watching her from the other side of the tapestry, and slowly she spread her legs and began to rub herself softly. She could feel the elegant strawberry pink of her nipples tightening just above the surface of the water. And her fingers rubbed harder, reached deeper, and her fears began to ease with the pleasure that she was giving herself and with the power that she desperately hoped that she was gaining over Morell now.

★ ★ ★

As Goebbels' motor launch slowed to a stop, several soldiers appeared from the darkness. They were dressed in black uniforms, reminiscent of, but distinctly modified versions of, the Walther SS uniforms, their cut and style more severe, efficient, and even more menacing. They wore distinct armbands of black and scarlet. On the armbands appeared the symbol of the mythical Phoenix depicted as a sharply taloned bird of prey, its wings spread to a blood-red sky, its talons extended like blood-soaked daggers gripping the top edge of the great black swastika of the Third Reich. This same symbol flew above the masts of the gunboats that had escorted them ashore. Goebbels knew that these soldiers, like the sailors who manned the gunboats, had been trained to owe him no allegiance whatsoever. Their duty first and foremost was to the Fuehrer and then only to General Krietzer, the commandant of their order and the master of the island.

This was the way the Fuehrer had organized the very highest secret components of Phoenix. His greatest mistake, he had told Goebbels many times, was fighting the first phase of the war using an outmoded command structure. Phoenix would not be executed in that manner. In Phoenix the Fuehrer would operate at the center of a great wheel of authority with spokes of that wheel running only to him and no part of that wheel answerable to any other part of it. This would eliminate the problems of the traditional chain of command where the leader could be isolated at the top of a great pyramid, too easily betrayed by conspiracies from below. Goebbels knew the great lengths that the Fuehrer had gone to, to create this structure within Phoenix, and he knew too that the expressions of hostility on the faces of the island's elite guards as they gestured for him to disembark from the launch were very real and a testament to the planning and care that had been put into the creation of their separation from the other components of the Third Reich. And that with the Fuehrer's death they saw their only duty was to the commandant of the island, not a visitor from Berlin.

Goebbels was taken up a narrow winding stone path to where the isolated figure stood all alone in the crumbling towers of the island's ancient monastery.

As they approached to within a few yards of the figure, the guards seemed to melt away into the night, leaving Goebbels alone with their commandant.

"General Krietzer," Goebbels said, and the figure nodded slightly.

Goebbels could see the general clearly now. He was far older than Goebbels had even dared guess. His head was shaved bald, its skin badly wrinkled, and blue-veined and spotted with age. His blackish-gray eyes were small and remorseless and dead as ashes, Goebbels thought, fighting his repugnance toward the other man's grotesque appearance.

The general's body was thin and the rough wool military uniform that he wore matched those of his officers with the scarlet and black Phoenix symbol on each armband, but the uniform hung down loosely over an emaciated body, gapping at the neck and wrists. The loosely draped uniform held the insignia of the highest general in the army, but Goebbels knew that his power and authority had been in many ways even greater than that, exceeded during the war only by the Fuehrer himself.

"Why have you come?" the general hissed, letting the hatred that he felt toward his visitor show in every syllable.

He was mad, of course, Goebbels thought as he considered his reply and looked into the old man's centerless eyes. He had been warned of that by those who had known the general in Berlin before the war, in that time before he had been chosen by the Fuehrer to serve the Reich in this remote spot. He had been mentally unbalanced even as a younger man, and Goebbels could imagine what years of solitude in this godforsaken place, subjected to the duties of the island, could do to an already unbalanced man's sanity, but he had to be very careful with him, Goebbels told himself. He knew that there were half a dozen guns trained on him from the shadows and the slightest mistake now and Phoenix and his own life could both end here.

"I come as your friend." Goebbels' lie was said in a soothing, reassuring voice, but the words and their tone seemed to have very little effect on the other man.

"May we walk?" Goebbels asked quietly, gesturing toward the outer edge of the ruins, and away from the guards lingering in the nearby shadows. "What I have to say can only be heard by you."

The general nodded and the two men walked to the edge of the tower. They stood then, facing each other, the rhythmic explosions of the waves crashing against the rock-lined coastline below them.

Goebbels measured his next words carefully, for they were calculated for the power that he knew that they possessed.

"We are to continue without him," he said in a low voice, but with great intensity. "Without the Fuehrer. It was his final command, and with your help this night, we will return to even greater heights than we have ever known." Goebbels rarely used such dramatic words in private discourse, but he could see a small light come into the general's otherwise lifeless eyes and he knew that he had selected his tone well for the occasion. "Near the end, you were summoned to Berlin," Goebbels said then.

"It was impossible," the old general hissed.

"But you know what occurred there on that final night?"

"I have heard rumors," the general rasped.

"Those of us present were commanded to complete the work that he has begun."

"I can take instructions only from the Fuehrer," the general said, as if foreseeing Goebbels' next request.

Goebbels could feel the anger surge inside him. For a moment he considered taking the mad old fool and casting him backward over the ruined tower into the crashing sea below. But Goebbels knew that if he did, he would die as well. He wouldn't live to return down the stone path to the launch, much less succeed in the purpose that he'd come to this strange isolated island to accomplish. He couldn't see them, but he could sense that there were still guards standing nearby, and if he were even to raise a hand toward the general, he, not the mad old bastard, would be the one to die. No, he must control himself and play it out carefully, as he had planned it, or he would fail.

"I know your instructions," Goebbels said, forcing the soothing tone back into his speech. "But all I would see here is destruction." He smiled and looked around at the island. "That is, if you really believed what the world foolishly thinks—that it has ended. You know that I'm telling you the truth or by now the entrance to below would be locked and sealed, and all of this above"—Goebbels' hand swept the surface of the island—"given back to the sea. But there is nothing of this. Why?" Goebbels' voice was now dripping with accusation, but still the old man said nothing. "It has not ended, Herr General. It has only begun. We now have a weapon of unlimited power at our disposal that can crush our enemies and end all resistance within a few weeks, a month or two at the most."

There was a long quiet and then the general hissed, "I too know of Phoenix."

Goebbels nodded, reminding himself to be surprised by nothing in dealing with this man. Despite the Fuehrer's promise of total secrecy, the general had been told, perhaps by the Fuehrer himself, or perhaps the general had learned it somehow from his own spies.

"I know your power," Goebbels said in the soothing tone he had used earlier. "I know that except for the Fuehrer, there was no man in the Reich who can match the loyalties owed to you." As Goebbels spoke he knew what he was saying was true. The general had been there at the very beginning. It had been his great wealth and his ideas that had helped to form the party in its very early days, when there had been only the Fuehrer and the general and no one else. Soon there had been a few others. Goebbels himself hadn't come along until several years later. And many of the loyalties from those early days were still in place. And despite his location in this remote place, the general knew almost everything that happened inside the Reich: his friends and his spies were everywhere.

It was time, Goebbels decided, and slowly he unbuttoned the neck of his tunic and lifted off the ring that he wore on the ribbon around his neck and held it out toward the general. "And I also know that you are a man of absolute loyalties. The Fuehrer gave me this and commanded me to show it to you now."

The old man's aged and liver-spotted hand reached out for it. He held it closely to his eye and carefully inspected not its surface, but the letters etched into the interior of the gold band. Finally satisfied, but far from pleased, the old lifeless eyes looked up at Goebbels' face.

"You know its meaning, of course?" Goebbels said. And the old man's silence and unwavering eyes became assent, so Goebbels continued. "You know that we must obey his wishes, even in death."

Goebbels waited, letting his demand gain more power in the silence before he continued. "Your own people have confirmed all of this to you, I'm certain. So you know that what I say is the truth. And now you are compelled to do your duty. I do not have to remind you, I'm certain that you have sworn an oath to obey the bearer of this ring. I am to be treated this day as if I were the Fuehrer himself. This is as our leader demanded it to be." There was another long silence then. Goebbels looked into the old man's mad eyes and he thought of the great stakes that they struggled over now and he knew that despite everything it could be very possible that he would never leave this island alive.

"So the time has finally come," the general said, his gaze moving down to the ring that he held in his hand.

"Yes," Goebbels said, feeling the relief deep inside himself. "It is now."

"In the morning . . . " the old man began, but Goebbels angrily interrupted him.

"No, tonight," he said.

The old man waited, weighing the situation. Finally he returned the ring to Goebbels. "Follow me," the general said, and the two men moved slowly down from the lonely promontory and along a stone embankment. They passed several checkpoints as they descended into the interior of the island. Several guards, a series of locked gates, and stone walls reinforced with steel bars marked their way, until they came to a final thick metal door set deep into the island's subterranean stone base. At these depths Goebbels could no longer hear the pounding noises of the surf against the island rocks or see any traces of the moonlit night.

The final underground cavern was lit only by generator-powered overhead lamps, but in the erratic flickering light, Goebbels could see the shadows of other quiet figures moving with them through the underground labyrinth of rock and Goebbels knew that the general's protectors were still following them.

The two men proceeded down a badly lit staircase built even deeper into the earth. At the base of the stairs a final set of guards emerged from the shadows.

Behind the guards was a cement tunnel. The two men followed along it as it twisted and turned at odd angles and then finally stopped against a metal door nearly ten feet high buried deep in the rock and cement wall. Goebbels could hear the sounds of the guards and protectors moving back into the shadows. They would not be permitted to go any farther, Goebbels thought. The metal door was sealed by a series of both key-operated and combination locks. The general methodically worked his way through them, operating the complicated locking mechanisms for several minutes before he was able to move the heavy stainless-steel door open far enough to step inside.

As the heavy safelike door opened, a generator began to shift noisily into operation and lights mounted on the high stone walls of the interior chamber lit the room with an eerie amber glow.

Goebbels felt the breath go out of him as he stepped inside. What was before him now was beyond the imagination of most men, and only the general and his most trusted aides had ever seen this magnificent sight before. Even the Fuehrer, whose dreams and daring had made it possible, had never set foot inside this room. And as deeply as he had tried to prepare himself for the moment, now that it was before him, Goebbels felt the weakness in his legs and chest. No one, he realized, not even a man such as himself, could prepare completely for such a sight.

The plundered wealth of most of Europe stood in front of him in this single underground chamber. More wealth than had ever been assembled in a single place in the history of the world. Not the pharaohs, or the Romans, or Alexander or Napoleon, no one had ever dared to accomplish such a thing before, he marveled as he looked out across the vast fortune contained in the single massive underground room.

Flight after flight had landed at the remote airstrip on the northwest coast of Africa and hundreds of ships had sailed to this remote island bringing the finest and most precious objects from the territories conquered by the armies of the Third Reich.

The cavern's interior was nearly a hundred meters in length and half that again in both width and height. The walls and floors were made of the natural stone of the island, but heavily reinforced with steel bars.

There were storage areas built into every available centimeter of the chamber. And almost every ledge and shelf was filled with crates and boxes and chests made of wood or metal.

Covering one entire wall were seemingly endless stacks of gold bullion looted from public and private treasuries all over Europe. In another corner were cases stacked to the vast ceiling bulging with jewels and gold and silver coins, while other areas held artifacts and priceless antiquities from nearly every civilization known to man. Packing crates against another wall held currency from every country on earth—boxes upon boxes stacked to the ceiling containing American dollars, British sterling, French francs. Pallets stacked high with boxed paintings and tapestries and other works of art stood directly in front of him, and Goebbels walked along reading the names etched on the sides of the wooden pallets—Michelangelo, Leonardo, Rubens, Titian, and on and on.

The boxed paintings gave way to rows of statuary and antiques. And at the end of the underground room were hundreds of gold and silver altars and walls and entire ceilings and floors torn from churches and mosques and places of worship all over

Europe. One enormous golden altar inlaid with a dazzling array of jewels dominated the others. It faced out into the room, overseeing all of the chamber's great wealth. Goebbels crossed to it and climbed its golden steps toward a great altar inlaid with a dazzling array of multicolored jewels of ruby red and emerald green and sapphire blue. The tortured figure of Christ carved out of gold lay directly in front of him nailed to the great jeweled altar, but Goebbels turned from it, and from the high vantage point of the golden steps he surveyed the enormous chamber filled to overflowing with the stolen wealth of Europe.

# CHAPTER
# TEN

D ebra looked out over a vast sea of rubble and burned-out buildings. The sky was prematurely dark, the air was choking with the sickening yellow-gray fog. She was lost and she could feel panic beginning inside her, first in her chest and then spreading to her stomach. She had to keep moving. She stumbled forward a few steps and then began to run. At one time she had feared that there was someone following her, but now she just ran out of sheer panic, across the vast terrain of smoking wreckage. She fought her way to the top of a pile of charred cement, stone, and burned wooden boards and stared out at the wrecked landscape, looking for clues, landmarks, but it all seemed the same: all of Berlin, as far as she could see in every direction in the smoky yellow light, was one great junkyard. She sank to her knees, her kneeling body outlined against the great mounds of smoking rubble behind her.

Her uniform shirt was torn and her legs were cut and bleeding. She had to get ahold of herself. She was no good to anybody like this, she told herself angrily. But it was her home. Once it had been anyway. Shouldn't the school be over there? she thought, looking off toward the light fading in the west. And a row of small shops, a bakery, a tobacconist, the pharmacy, that she had walked past so many times, over there? She turned her head and looked off to the north, but again all she could see were great broken pieces of buildings and fire-blackened walls. She could still be miles away from the streets of her childhood.

That was how it had begun. She had been doing her work and she had turned a corner and seen what she thought was a familiar sight, or smelled a faint aroma of something that she had remembered from her childhood. She wasn't quite sure, but she had begun to try and walk toward her memories, confidently at first, but then with each failed landmark, each devastated block turning into another torn and destroyed vista, she had become more and more confused, until finally, lost and frightened, she had begun running from one pile of rubble to another, looking for signs that didn't appear, searching for clues that weren't there. Her childhood was gone, she told herself as she knelt at the top of yet another smoking pile of rubble. Her parents, her home, a large part of her life. She had lived in this city until she was twelve, when her parents had moved to the German countryside. Camp 19 had made any thoughts of the countryside impossible for her, but she still had longed to see the city streets of her earlier memories again, but they were gone now too, lost in this great sea of burned wreckage that had been her country. She realized now that she was crying and she wiped her eyes and began to force herself to begin to think rationally again. There were dangers everywhere, starving refugees, Nazi resisters, and, of course, there were the Soviets. She had been aware of someone following her, ever since she had begun working with Sheridan on the mystery of Goebbels' death.

She had to regain her composure and return to what was real and present. She looked directly ahead again at the light fading in the western sky. It was only midafternoon, but the light of the day was almost gone. At least she knew that ahead of her now lay the west. She would walk toward the setting sun, search carefully through the wreckage, until she could find a passageway or an alley, anything that would permit her to continue westward. She would find an open street then, and if she kept her head and was lucky, within the hour she would be back at the black market café where she had begun her search.

She started down the tower of burned-out rubble toward the ground. And then she began to walk, watching the sun, or when she couldn't actually see its faint golden rays behind the thickness of the powdery yellowish fog, remembering its position in the sky.

She walked deliberately, forcing her mind to think only about the problem of her destination. And every time that her thoughts began to stray, she insisted that her mind focus only on helping her find the way back to the café.

And soon she could see a cleared street ahead of her, where the Soviets had created a wide straight passageway in all the devastation. Debra ran to it. She could guess just about where she was now and within a few more minutes she could see her jeep parked at the side of the road near the busy black market café that she had stopped at for lunch. There wasn't enough petrol to use it to go to all the places that Debra had visited over the last two days. She'd seen over half of Berlin, and all of it had come to nothing so far. Not one lead to give her encouragement, nothing solid that would even begin to question the Soviet report on the events in the bunker. And then this afternoon she had nearly lost her head. Maybe this was the end of it, she thought as she fought herself inside the crowded café that was really no more than the converted shopfront of an enterprising young German couple. Maybe she and Sheridan were wrong after all. Maybe Goebbels' death was just like the others', a suicide of just another cowardly and frightened man. And the final end of Phoenix. Certainly she had found nothing so far that would support any other theory.

She managed to order a cup of tea from the busy shop-owner, and then she sat drinking it, her mood growing more and more hopeless as she tried to think of a new way to attack the problem, but she could think of nothing that she hadn't already tried.

She could feel the fear and confusion that she had felt when she'd first returned from Camp 19. And then the thought of telling Sheridan that she'd failed made her feel even worse. He'd angrily opposed her decision to get involved in the mystery of Goebbels' death. But he was trapped in his own round of dead-end interviews that the Soviets had set up for him and there had been nothing he could do to stop her. Her investigation had gone nowhere, though, and she felt deeply frustrated now. She couldn't quit, she told herself, but she had no idea where she was to turn next.

She finished her tea and then scraped her chair back on the café's uncarpeted floor, but before she could stand to leave, she heard a voice. Was it directed at her? Debra froze—she wasn't certain what was happening or how she should react.

"You have been looking for something," the voice said in slow precise German. Debra couldn't be certain of its origin, but she knew now that it was directed at her.

She glanced quickly around the crowded room. Then she understood. A man in a brown overcoat was bent over his table. The table was directly behind her, although she was certain that the man hadn't been there when she'd come in.

Debra sat back in her chair and waited, listening carefully.

"There is a man in the Lindenstrasse." The voice stopped then. Debra looked outside the window next to her. She couldn't be certain if the car parked across the street behind her jeep was a Soviet military vehicle or not. Or maybe there was someone in the café itself, she thought, swinging her head and looking around at the faces that surrounded her. But none of them betrayed anything. Or the man himself, she thought. Could he be one of them? Part of some kind of Soviet trap? Or was it the real break in the investigation that she'd hoped for? She continued listening, with a growing mix of fear and excitement.

"Five hundred British pounds would go far in Berlin these days," the man said in the same careful German.

Debra didn't have five hundred pounds. She didn't have anywhere near that much, but she wanted to hear more of what the careful German voice had to say. It was the first thing that she'd found since she'd begun her search that was even remotely interesting. "I have two hundred," she said, regretting her words almost as quickly as she had spoken them. There could be any number of reasons that the man was doing this. And almost all of them meant only danger and loss for her, but she waited for his reply, her breath tight in her chest.

"Place it on the table and then leave," the voice commanded.

Debra had heard, but she couldn't bring herself to act. She sat frozen in place, thinking what a wild chance she was being asked to take.

"Place the money on the table and leave," the voice commanded again.

You damn fool, Debra breathed to herself as she reached into her purse and slowly removed two hundred-pound notes, her emergency money, and placed them on the corner of the table. As she stood, she swung her head around to be certain that she wasn't being seen. But no one seemed to be taking any notice of her. Damn stupid fool, she told herself again, and let the two bank notes drop onto the edge of the table. Now standing, she felt a tug at her uniform jacket, only slight, but something, she thought as she walked toward the cashier at the door and paid her bill.

She walked outside and glanced back through the café's front window at the table that she had just vacated. Neither the money nor the man who had been seated behind her in the brown coat was there any longer.

Debra hurried to her jeep and climbed inside. For the moment she didn't give a damn how difficult petrol was to come by. She drove very fast in a straight line for several blocks and then without any warning sharply turned a corner and stopped. She looked in her rearview mirror. There was no one behind her, but she knew that meant very little. She could seldom actually see her Soviet keepers, but she knew they were there. And they would occasionally pop up at an unlikely place or time just to remind her that she was not alone.

She reached into her uniform pocket where she had felt the touch as she'd left the table at the café. Her fingers came upon a slip of paper. She removed the paper from her coat pocket and unfolded it. "33." That was all it said, just "33." It could mean anything, she thought. Debra felt her heart sink. Perhaps she'd been a fool. But she would have to find 33 Lindenstrasse nevertheless.

Debra checked the rearview mirror again. There was still nothing that she could make out, but she kept thinking that maybe the Soviets were behind the whole thing, luring her into a trap to end her investigation into Goebbels' death. She thought about Sheridan then. Maybe she should wait and go with him. But he wouldn't be free of his duties for another hour at the least. It would be well after dark then and she might have lost her chance.

Damn it, she had to risk it. She stepped down hard on the accelerator and the jeep leapt forward.

She turned down a series of dark side streets, one connected to the other by their silence and their apparent lack of living human occupants.

Debra checked her rearview mirror every few minutes as she drove. Finally she turned onto the nearly empty Lindenstrasse. The bombing had been very light along this treelined commercial street. She parked at the side of the road and removed the key from the jeep's ignition and used it to open the glove box. Inside was the .38 Webley in a small black holster that she'd been issued at the start of the war. Until now she'd always left it at headquarters, checked into the arms section. Lowry had insisted on her taking it with her from London, though, and he'd been right. She needed it now. And she was pretty good with it, she thought; at least she had been on the firing range in London against dummy targets. God knew how she would react to a real threat, and she removed her uniform coat and strapped the holstered weapon around her left shoulder and then replaced her coat over it.

She took one last look behind her as she stepped from the jeep and began to walk along the side of the narrow twisting road. Soon she could see that she had miscalculated the numbering system and she was being led off the main street and down along a winding medieval path surrounded by ancient shops and storefronts. There were only unlit gas lamps to mark her way, and the interiors of the buildings that she passed were dark, but Debra knew that there were lives being lived in those shadows as there were in many of the ruins of the bombed-out buildings that she had passed earlier. Like frightened animals, though, the people who lived on these streets didn't show themselves as night approached. Suddenly she thought that she heard footsteps behind

135

her. She stopped and listened, but she could hear nothing, only the restless evening breezes.

Why had she come here? Debra thought, beginning to regret her decision. Maybe she should go back for the jeep. But she pressed forward. The shops and storefronts were nearly intact. Almost total destruction lay on every side of this neighborhood. Why were these ancient streets spared? Debra wondered. Just one of the many mysteries of Berlin, she decided finally. The answer was, she guessed, that there was no answer—just war and its results, tangled and irrational and ultimately inexplicable.

She walked along, trying to keep her fear in check and looking for street numbers on the old buildings. Finally she came to a courtyard sealed off from the street by a high wrought-iron gate. She stopped and caught her breath. In the silence she was certain that she heard footsteps in the thick yellow fog behind her. She could feel the fear welling up inside her body, rushing from her chest to her throat and nearly choking her in panic. It had been a trap, she decided. Soviet, Nazi, someone had tricked her down onto these deserted streets. She turned to run, but her legs were weak. In front of her, there were long shadows lying across the road, barring her way. She wanted to scream, but the constriction in her throat tightened like a pair of strong hands clutching at her windpipe and she made no sound.

Then she saw it—a brass plate mounted in the wrought-iron fence. She ran to it. The plate was marked—number 33. Above the plate was a push bell. Debra's fingers went to it and pressed it hard. As she waited, her eyes searched the darkness behind the gate. There was a small cottage buried in the fog. Was there someone back there? Debra couldn't be certain, but her heart was pounding hard and her anxious finger pushed the bell over and over. She looked at the dark building, crouching behind the heavy wrought-iron gate. Its blinds were drawn, its windows closed and dark, and yet she was certain that there was someone inside watching her. Perhaps the real danger, she thought then, lay inside the walls of the house, not out here on the streets, and she suddenly removed her finger from the bell.

But then she pushed at the old iron gate and slowly it swung open. She walked inside and heard the heavy wrought-iron gate creak closed behind her. Debra hesitated for a moment, rereading the brass plate above the marking for number 33 that identified the occupant of the house as Dr. Oscar Hemel, Dental Surgeon.

★ ★ ★

Debra was frighteningly late. Sheridan kept looking at his watch. The Soviet curfew was approaching. Soon no one but Russian military personnel would be permitted on the street. Debra would never willingly have delayed this long to keep their date. Something was wrong.

She had agreed that morning to meet Sheridan for a drink in the basement bar of the Adlon Hotel at six-thirty. It was nearly eight o'clock now. Sheridan nursed his glass of strong Russian vodka and watched the door. Guests were arriving steadily, mostly Russian officers, with their British and American guests.

The hotel was far from its midwar splendor, but the Soviets needed a place to impress their foreign visitors, and the Adlon had been chosen. Most of the excitement and glamour was in its lobby and its main bar and upstairs dining room, but as the evening grew late a few of the dignitaries were filtering down to the darkly private basement bar. The cellar bar was small compared to the grand-scale rooms of the upper floors of the hotel. It was two floors below ground, cool, with thick stone walls and a large unlit stone fireplace. The Nazis had used this room for drinking right up until the final hours, Sheridan thought with a small smile. It pleased him to think of how dramatically things had changed within just a few short days.

A black man in a white dinner jacket sat at a piano in a corner of the room. He had a sweet throaty voice and Sheridan
watched his soft pink fingers on the black-and-ivory keyboard as
the entertainer softly sang "Lili Marlene." The room, he
thought, the music, it was all starting to look and feel like Germany in the thirties, and as if the war had never happened.

Sheridan drank again from his vodka, but his head jerked
up as another party of high-ranking Soviet military personnel
came into the room, but no Debra. Damn it, Sheridan thought.
Had she found something? Didn't she know it wasn't worth risking her life? He glanced again at the headlines of the London
*Times* spread out on the top of his table: "Bunker Deaths Confirmed." Every time he read it, the words struck Sheridan with
surprising power. He had known it was coming. Harkins had
brought him in for another linen-closet conference to tell him
about the announcement and to ask him if he had found anything that should delay it, and Sheridan had reluctantly said that
he hadn't. But seeing it there in print was still startling. The story
had been released worldwide. It was now official, the bastards
had both died at their own hands in the Chancellery bunker, just
as the Russians had wanted it. Hitler's burned corpse had been
identified unequivocally by matching the remains from the
bunker to official dental records. The fact of Goebbels' records
being missing was mentioned nowhere in the article. But both
deaths had become an official part of history, and with the entire
credibility of the Allied Command behind them, it would take
one hell of a lot to change any of it now, far more than he and
Debra were ever likely to come up with. So where was she?
Risking her neck for nothing, Sheridan thought angrily, and
drank again deeply from the Russian vodka, but he still couldn't
relax. Anything could have happened to her in this city, he
thought nervously. Maybe he should go out looking for her, but
where?

Then he felt a hand on his shoulder and he turned to see her face. He remembered then that there was a rear entrance to the bar that he hadn't been watching. "You all right?" he asked.

Debra nodded her head that she was, but her bright green eyes were searching the room, making certain that no one could overhear her when she whispered to Sheridan. "I think I might have something."

Sheridan set his drink down. He pointed to the headline in the London paper. Debra shook her head. "Damn it," she whispered softly, but then she added only a moment later, "Let's go. Shall we walk out together or . . . ?"

"Now, tonight?" Sheridan whispered back.

Debra nodded her head vigorously, and then she started for the rear door. Sheridan followed after her.

Within minutes they were back on the dark streets, Sheridan at the wheel of the jeep.

"Do you know where the Lindenstrasse is?" she asked, her voice still low and her eyes searching the dark fog-filled night for any sign of danger.

Sheridan nodded and moved the jeep ahead deeper into the gray-yellow Berlin fog. Once they had driven east toward the Lindenstrasse for several minutes, he turned to her.

"Where are we headed?" Sheridan pointed down the fog-bound road.

"Dr. Oscar Hemel, 33 Lindenstrasse, in the old town. Do you know it?"

"I think I can find it," Sheridan said.

"Be careful," Debra said. "I think half the time that I'm being followed; the rest of the time, I'm certain of it."

"Soviets?" Sheridan asked.

"I suppose," Debra said. "But I've never gotten a good look at them."

Sheridan turned the jeep down a backstreet that had just been reopened that morning. He knew that it would lead him within a few blocks of his destination, but might not yet have attracted Soviet patrols.

"What will we find at the Lindenstrasse?" Sheridan asked as he pressed his face forward toward the windscreen, straining to see down the unlit Berlin backstreet.

"I found a man named Hemel, Dr. Oscar Hemel, or at least I found his son, Dr. Hemel Junior," Debra said, gathering her thoughts. "But he's almost as good, in some ways even better. He's willing to talk. His father might not have been. You see, his father was a dental surgeon who served Hitler and most of the rest of the Nazi High Command including Goebbels, until sometime in mid-1943. Then for no reason whatsoever, he was replaced, at least for no reason that Dr. Hemel could understand, but I'm wondering if it might have had something to do with Goebbels' missing official records."

"What?"

"I'm not certain yet. I'm hoping Dr. Hemel Junior might be able to tell us." Debra pointed ahead through the fog toward the Lindenstrasse.

"His father," Debra continued, "was ordered to return his files, notes, X rays, everything that he had concerning his illustrious patients back over to the Nazi officials."

"But he didn't," Sheridan said, the first stirrings of understanding beginning inside of him.

"He didn't keep everything," Debra continued. "But he did keep a few things as souvenirs. He wanted to prove to his grandchildren someday that he'd actually been the personal dentist to the great men. You see, Hemel was a good Nazi, but his son isn't, far from it. He has his reasons, though, and they're damn good ones." Debra paused for a moment and then continued in a slightly calmer voice. "You see, in August of 1943, within weeks after he was dismissed from his job as the personal dentist to the Nazi High Command, Dr. Hemel Senior was severely beaten up in his office by someone or some group and his records ransacked and destroyed and Dr. Hemel was left to die. Sound like the work of the SS to you?" Debra asked, and Sheridan nodded his head. "Well, it does to his son as well. And he hates the Nazis. He said that he would do anything to help us. He remembered that his father had removed his souvenirs of the work that he'd done for Goebbels and some of the others, probably Hitler's too, from his regular files. Dr. Hemel thought he could find them. I've been talking to him for hours. He wanted some time to look through his father's things. So I drove back to the Adlon. But he should be ready by now," Debra said, glancing at her watch.

"It should be enough to reopen the investigation," Sheridan said. "It'll take some doing, though. London's credibility is behind the Soviet report. And the entire world is convinced the bastards are dead now."

"Well, maybe the world's wrong," Debra said. "And if it is, we may just have found a way to prove it."

# CHAPTER
# ELEVEN

Geli awoke from a nightmare. In the dark dream she had gripped the Chinese tapestry in her bathroom aside and found not Morell, but the hideous laughing gargoyle faces from the ceiling of her bedroom. And the gargoyles were alive, laughing and snapping bloodstained teeth at her face and neck. She awoke in fear, sweating, strangling a scream. She sat up then, finally remembering where she was. Her room was dark and she knew that the horrible, ugly faces hid in the shadows above her. She sat on the edge of the bed, her eyes staring down at the thickly carpeted floor of her room. The earlier feelings of hope that she could somehow use her sexuality to win her battle with Morell had only given way to more anxiety and fear. How much longer could she live like this? She was used to a life of action and movement. Trapped in this hideous locked room, living in fear of Morell and what he might do to her, she was slowly going to go mad.

Once or twice she had seen his grossly overweight figure walking back and forth in the garden behind her room. They had not spoken to each other or formally seen each other since their arrival at the Berghof, but Geli was certain now that it was his eyes on her as she slept or bathed or dressed. And when she was permitted to walk in the garden herself, she could see him standing on the balcony of his room, staring down at her.

It was almost time for her morning walk and Geli went to her dressing table. She dressed quickly, admiring herself in the mirror as she finished. The enforced discipline of her life at the Berghof, the walks, the rest, the simple meals, had one consolation. The khaki slacks that she wore for her walks clung skintight to her high round hips and they were very becoming. She looked even better than she had when she'd left Berlin, in fact more beautiful than she'd ever been, she thought, smoothing the smallest of wrinkles from the rear of the slacks, then fixing the last of her hair and makeup.

There was a knock on the door and she went to it. It was the guard who accompanied her each morning on her walks. She followed him out of her room and down the hall, but rather than being led to the main staircase, the guard took her down the corridor, to a door set in the middle of the long hallway, next to her room. The guard knocked on the door and at a command from inside, he opened it and Geli stepped past him into a large bedroom. It was even grander than her own room, she thought as she moved inside, larger and nearly untouched by the bombing. Morell sat in an armchair near the center of the room. And as she entered, the large man rose with great difficulty and began his way toward her.

Geli looked closely at the man's grossly overweight face. It was even more encased in excess flesh than she had remembered it. But Geli knew that she had to be very careful to contain both the disgust and the fear that she felt at his presence. She was more certain than ever now that Morell held the key to her survival.

"Has everything been done for your comfort?" Morell asked.

"I am quite comfortable," Geli said, and then watched as Morell turned and walked toward the balcony of the luxurious room, stopping to pour himself a large brandy in a cut-crystal tumbler. He stepped onto the balcony then and looked out past the wreckage on the grounds of the Berghof at the snowcapped Kehlstein.

Geli followed him to the balcony and stood behind him. Morell turned back to her. His eyes, behind the gold-framed glasses, were damp from the brandy and there were small, dark brown stains on his shirtfront. He had been drinking for some time, Geli realized. Probably working up his courage for what she could guess lay ahead now. But how monstrous he was, she thought as she looked at him closely. In Berlin he would not even have been asked to most of the parties and receptions that she had been so highly sought after to attend. And yet, here in this place, at this moment, he was ruler of everything, including her very life. How grotesque he looks, though, despite his momentary power, Geli thought, the mixture of hatred and fear that she felt for him growing even more intense. Like some strange fat animal that you might see at the zoo, but up close there was nothing tame about his face and eyes. He was shrewd and brutal and full of unresolved ambitions, Geli decided, but she was very careful to continue smiling at him, revealing nothing of her feelings in her own expression.

Finally he focused his attention directly at her. "You know that I will be leaving here soon," he said.

Geli nodded calmly, although inside she could feel her nerves growing taut. Would she be taken with him or left behind for their enemies? She had to be enormously careful now, she told herself. The next few moments could well determine her future.

There was a long silence then. Geli fingered the buttons on her blouse nervously, aware that Morell was staring at her body with alcoholic intensity through his gold-rimmed spectacles.

He set his brandy glass down and, still staring at her, spoke slowly in what Geli guessed that he imagined to be a seductive voice. "You look quite beautiful today," he said.

She was careful in her reply, not yet certain of what she should do. "Thank you," she said.

Morell nodded his head several times, sloppily. Then he turned away from her and looked again at the great snowcapped peak of the Kehlstein. "We are in the midst of matters of great importance here," he said in a grave alcoholic voice.

Geli held her breath, hoping that he would go on, not daring to say anything for fear of it being the wrong reply.

"Without fear of being overly dramatic," he continued, "one might almost say momentous, historic events."

Geli could see that her silence was impossible this time. She had to speak. "I wish with all my heart to continue to be a part of them," she whispered.

Morell whirled around. "Do you?" he said. "Do you really?"

Geli remained silent, puzzled by his strange reaction. She must be very careful. One slip with this half-drunken madman and she could be in grave danger.

"I don't think you fully understand," Morell said. "You see, to be part of what is about to happen, it is not safe. In fact, it is highly dangerous. No one would ever question what happens here. At this moment I am the ruler of the Berghof."

"I know," Geli answered softly.

Morell set his fat black cigar on the rail of the balcony. He took a step toward her. She could see from the obscene way that he held his body thrust forward toward her that he was sexually aroused. He looked at her and laughed. "There is, however, a way to ensure your safety," he said in a throaty excited voice, stepping even closer.

Geli felt a moment of confusion. She hadn't expected anything this crude, even from a man like Morell. But she had to decide what to do very quickly. Morell was no fool, despite his half-drunken state. However disgusting he was to her, for this moment he held her fate. There was no one else at the Berghof who could help her. He could save her from the future of being left behind for the Americans, or a swifter, surer ending at the hands of one of the SS. She saw herself on her knees before him, or lying in bed next to his fat body. The pictures disgusted her, but she had done far worse and with much less to be gained. It was her very life that was at stake now. She looked up into his passion-filled face. He was sweating heavily with excitement.

"No," she said. The word seemed to just burst from her, although she was far from certain that she was doing the right thing. "No," she said again, this time with even greater conviction. "Never," she said, looking deep into his watery gray eyes, and knowing the great risk that she was taking by denying him now.

There was a long silence then, intense and punishing, and Geli felt the fear deepening inside of her. Morell stared at her through his steel-rimmed spectacles. In that moment she thought that she could see his true full ruthlessness and ambition. But still she didn't break his gaze. Had she made a terrible miscalculation? Was he going to kill her now without even giving her another chance?

"Of course," he said finally, reaching for his drink and taking a long swallow of it. "Yes, of course," he added regaining at least a veneer of composure and civility. Geli began to back toward the door, but he brushed by her suddenly and called out for the guard. Geli watched him walk away. As she did, she could feel the fear pour over her. She had overplayed her hand, she thought, miscalculated badly. She would have been better off giving in to his demands. Sharing his bed, as repulsive as it might have seemed at the moment, might have been the better alternative to what very likely lay ahead for her now. She had gambled and lost, she thought. And she was growing more certain by the moment that the stakes that she had just played with this disgusting but powerful man had been her own life.

★   ★   ★

"Oh my God." Debra saw it before Sheridan did, a bright red-and-orange light in the sky and a pall of black woodsmoke rising straight up into the yellow-gray fog.

Sheridan slid the jeep to the side of the road, parking it deep in the protection of the darkness of an overhanging storefront.

He hopped from the jeep and started toward the blaze. Two figures appeared in front of him. They were running from the fire. Sheridan stopped by the small storefront and strained against the fog and darkness to recognize the figures, but it was useless.

Suddenly a ragged hole burst in the rotten canvas awning just above Sheridan's head. Then a bullet cracked into the edge of the brick storefront, sending a shower of brick dust into his face and eyes. He reached out, momentarily blinded and took Debra by the shoulders, pushing her to the ground and then covering her with his body. He looked up just in time to see another muzzle flash of the attacker's weapon. The bullet whistled past him, striking the cobblestone street and sending up flashing sparks of orange-yellow. Sheridan removed his own .45 and aimed it at the spot where he'd seen the muzzle flash and fired. It was quiet then. Debra managed to climb out from around the corner, crawling toward the edge of the shopfront. Sheridan moved ahead of her. He could make out a vehicle now. It was moving, its lights off, through the fog toward them. Sheridan fired his weapon at the vehicle, but just as he did, its headlights flashed on, blinding him. Sheridan could hear a motor running loudly and the light raced closer, glowing inside the layer of fog. He was blinded, but he could hear a pistol firing and bullets cutting through the air around him. He returned the fire without seeing his target. The vehicle sped by him in the darkness.

Debra had already begun her way toward the sheet of flames that roared into the night sky. Sheridan followed after her. They moved down narrow winding cobblestone streets toward the source of the flames, until they came to a heavy wrought-iron fence that separated the road from a small courtyard. Inside the courtyard a building was in flames. Debra threw the gate open and dashed inside. She was running toward something. But what? Then Sheridan saw it. A man's legs and hips protruded from the front entrance of the burning cottage. The man's body was facedown with flames leaping around him. Sheridan ran through the courtyard toward the body. The fire had spread to the overhead trees and Sheridan was surrounded by flames as he leapt onto the cottage's front porch and dragged the body by its legs, until it tore free of the jammed door. As it did, fiery debris tumbled down around the entrance.

Sheridan pulled the body safely onto the grassy area at the center of the courtyard before he bent down and rolled it over.

Sheridan looked over at Debra then and he could tell from her expression that the body was that of the man they'd come for. Sheridan could hear the sounds of the building collapsing behind him, burying their hopes for a breakthrough in their investigation under hundreds of pounds of fiery wreckage. Someone had gotten to Dr. Hemel and his evidence before they had.

# CHAPTER
# TWELVE

Sheridan could hear the sounds of the Soviet fire brigade approaching. The Russians had taken over the Berlin fire department, and judging from the wailing sound in the air, the first of their fire trucks would be arriving momentarily, to put out the blaze that in all likelihood their own people had started, Sheridan thought angrily. He stood up and reached out for Debra's hand. "They're almost here," he whispered.

She began to run alongside him and they were back at the jeep within seconds. Sheridan waited for the first of the Soviet trucks to speed past the shadowy storefront where he was parked before he started the jeep's engine and headed it back across town.

He and Debra drove in silence for several minutes, both lost in their own thoughts. "Did you see who it was that shot at us?" Sheridan asked finally.

"No, nothing," Debra said, and then added sadly, "but it had to be the Soviets. They must have followed me this afternoon."

Sheridan nodded his agreement. He couldn't be certain that it had been the Russians, but it made sense. They controlled the city. They had no desire for anything to question their official version of events in the bunker and they could have easily known about Debra and followed her.

Sheridan turned the corner into the small commercial square that held his billet. He could tell immediately that something more was wrong. Lights blazed in the window of his room.

He'd been a fool coming back here, he realized. The Soviets weren't going to stop at destroying the evidence, they were going to destroy the investigators as well.

Suddenly a vehicle pulled out of nowhere and blocked his jeep from moving into the square. Headlights flooded into his eyes, reminding him of the blinding lights on the Lindenstrasse. Sheridan reached for his .45, but he knew that he and Debra weren't much better than sitting ducks in the open jeep. Then, instead of a spill of gunfire from the other vehicle, a voice called out, "Major Sheridan."

Sheridan recognized the voice and slowly his hand let the .45 drop back into the holster. He squinted into the headlights. A slender figure emerged from the bright glare. It walked slowly toward him. It was Dwyer, General Harkins' aide.

"Where the hell have you been?" Dwyer asked, and then didn't wait for an answer. "New orders," he continued. "We have only a few minutes to get you to Tempelhoff. We're seeing to your gear now." The lieutenant pointed toward Sheridan's room, where the lights were still blazing.

Tempelhoff, a flight, but where? Sheridan couldn't guess and he was too disciplined an intelligence officer to ask. Like everything else on an assignment, he would be told only what he needed to know, when he needed to know it.

He looked over at Debra. She was pretending to be the good soldier too, but he could see in her darkening green eyes that events were happening too quickly for her.

Sheridan turned back to Dwyer. "Do you have someone that can escort Lieutenant Marks to her billet? We've been through some trouble tonight." Dwyer nodded and then headed toward his parked vehicle.

Sheridan slid out of the jeep's driver's seat. "You'll get a full report to Command about tonight," he said, although he knew it wasn't necessary. Debra always did her job and did it well. There was nothing that had happened that night that would change that. Sheridan took one last look at her face and then he quickly looked away. Seeing her in danger at the Lindenstrasse had affected him deeply. She had performed well, but it had filled Sheridan with fear. The fear was turning to anger now as he thought about it—anger at her for risking herself the way she had.

"For God's sake," he said, leaning close to her so that the others couldn't hear. "While I'm gone, stop all of this. Your part in this thing with Goebbels is over."

Debra looked away from him, saying nothing for a moment. "I can't," she said finally. "It's my fight too, you have to see that."

Sheridan looked deeply into her eyes for a moment. Then he merely nodded and turned away from her, following after Dwyer.

"Good luck," Debra called out as he walked away, but he didn't turn back. Sheridan could hear the engine of her jeep starting up, but he forced himself to just walk to Dwyer's staff car and get in. From the backseat of the car, he could see only the red of the jeep's taillight and then it turned the corner of the square and was gone.

Sheridan sank back into the staff car's rear seat and lit a cigarette. What the hell was it that she was trying to prove? She was going to get herself killed. It wasn't worth it—nothing was worth losing her. He'd already had too damn much death and loss. They both had and losing her would just be too much. How could he make her see that? But he had no answers for his angry questions and the drive to Tempelhoff passed in silence.

At the airport Sheridan's driver took him through the security checks and stopped the staff car less than fifty meters from an American Air Force transport that was warming up near the edge of the airstrip.

"You open this once you're airborne," Dwyer said, and handed Sheridan a manila envelope containing his orders.

Sheridan quickly crossed the dark airfield and showed the envelope to the air force captain waiting at the base of the steps that led up into the belly of the cargo plane. The officer waved Sheridan on board.

There were three rows of metal benches bolted into the rear of the aircraft. Sheridan eased his long body into one of them and buckled a restraining belt around his waist. The transport held only two other passengers, both officers, neither of whom Sheridan recognized. Where the hell were they headed? Sheridan wondered again, balancing the manila envelope on his lap.

The plane began its taxi to the head of the runway and within minutes they were in the air. There was a porthole near where Sheridan sat. He unbuckled his seat belt and slid over to it and looked out at the lights of Berlin shrouded in the darkness and the clinging yellow-gray fog. It still held many of the mysteries of Phoenix, he thought, but perhaps his new destination would lead him to at least some of its solutions.

He reached down and cracked the manila envelope open and read his orders. When he was finished, he folded the typed instructions and placed them in his inside breast pocket. They contained General Harkins' own signature. They were highly extraordinary orders, and Sheridan could feel his excitement and anticipation mounting. His destination was not London, but a small town in southern Germany named Berchtesgaden.

★   ★   ★

Dr. Stevenson watched the ugly, highly dangerous organism move under his microscope. The elderly Scottish scientist still couldn't believe what he was seeing. Over fifty years of scientific inquiry and he had thought that he had seen, read, or at least heard of every type of bacterial and viral conduct that there was, but the Phoenix organism broke all the rules.

Stevenson bent back over his microscope. The activity that he had noted on the glass slides was continuing before his very eyes, but still didn't seem possible.

Stevenson's entire body filled with fear. This monstrous thing was truly a phenomenon beyond all belief and current scientific understanding, at least within the Allied scientific community, but obviously not beyond the understanding of the scientists of the Third Reich. Unless, of course, he was just tired and wrong.

In his frustration his hand shot out and swept a tray of clean glass slides to the floor. The equipment shattered on the cold ground. What a foolish thing to do, he realized immediately. Foolish and careless, but he was too old to be expected to deal with something like this alone, he thought as he very carefully began picking up the broken remnants of glass and returning them to his worktable.

When he had finished, he looked around at the interior of the tent that stood near the site of what had been the commandant's office at Camp 19. He had been at work here for several days under these crude conditions and he was tired and it was very possible that he could simply be mistaken about what he was seeing, he told himself.

He could hear the plane from Berlin beginning its descent toward the airstrip located above the camp, and he went to the door and walked outside. It was almost sunset in Camp 19 and a cold wind blew the stink of the pits at the rear of the camp in his face. And the rotten smell drew him even deeper into despair and confusion.

Lowry was already crossing the main camp street to a waiting jeep, and Stevenson hurried after him and took his place in the vehicle's passenger seat. It was the first flight to arrive from Berlin in nearly two days and both men were anxious to meet it.

As the jeep moved down the desolate camp street and up the hill toward the airstrip, Stevenson was tempted to tell Lowry of his findings, but he decided against it. The consequences of what he had found were too alarming to say anything without being absolutely certain. But he knew that he couldn't wait much longer. Lowry was under considerable pressure from London to report something of his work as soon as possible.

The trouble was, Stevenson decided, he'd been out of touch with his colleagues back in England for several days now. That was a very bad mistake. He had sent them samples from each of the sites he'd found at the camp, and undoubtedly they were running many of the same tests and analyses at Hillborn that he was here, but their equipment was so much superior to his. And, he admitted grudgingly, maybe at this point their brainpower was better than his as well.

With any luck, there would be a report from his colleagues on this plane, Stevenson thought as the jeep reached the crest of the hill and he watched the plane from Berlin settle down onto the airstrip and then taxi across its paved surface to stop only a few meters in front of him.

Lowry was the first of the two men out of the jeep and across the field to greet the arriving aircraft. Stevenson moved after him several meters to the rear.

A general officer disembarked from the aircraft. Oh Jesus, Stevenson thought as he watched Lowry start his way toward the arriving general. The scientist knew what the new general's presence meant. Command had grown impatient with his delays and sent someone out to see the situation firsthand. He would have to make a report on his findings very soon now.

Stevenson continued on toward the plane, taking a wide berth around the newly arrived dignitaries.

"Dr. Stevenson." The elderly scientist turned toward the runway. One of the new junior officers from Command was crossing the field toward him. He had a long brown envelope in one hand. Apprehension gripped Stevenson—the long-awaited information from his colleagues back at Hillborn. He suddenly wished that it had never come, because somehow he knew from the envelope's shape and size alone that it was not good news.

The senior officer extended the envelope to Stevenson, who took it and turned away saying nothing.

There was an overturned oil drum at the edge of the field. Stevenson went to it, his fear becoming even more intense. With anxious fingers he tore the envelope open. A thick sheaf of papers fell out of it into his nervous hand. And after a few minutes of reading through the material, his worst fears were confirmed. When he looked up, he saw Lowry standing above him. Behind Lowry, he could see the newly arrived officers being led off to their billets.

"I got rid of them for now," Lowry said. Stevenson nodded, saying nothing. The two men looked deep into each other's eyes. "I told them," Lowry said, pointing over his shoulders toward the newly arrived officers, "that there would be a briefing at 1700."

"Yes," Stevenson said slowly and haltingly. "But it won't be good news," the old scientist added, pointing at the papers in his hands. "Hillborn's reporting just what I've been finding here."

"I thought you were working on countermeasures that could destroy the damn thing," Lowry said, incredulous.

"Yes, and I think over time, we'll find something that will neutralize its effects."

"Time is something that we may not have very much of," Lowry said.

"I know," Stevenson said. "But there's an even greater problem." He stopped then. What he had to say now made no good scientific sense to him, but now Hillborn had confirmed it and he had to report it.

"Yes," Lowry urged.

"The real problem is its extraordinarily high level of effectiveness and concentration. We have determined that each of the Phoenix sites that we've seen so far, including the crash site here"—Stevenson pointed out toward where the Nazi transport had gone down—"has been caused by only a very small amount of the material."

"But an entire transport crashed," Lowry said. "Wasn't it filled with Phoenix materials?"

"No, we don't think so," Stevenson said. "Our tests indicate that there was only a gram or two of the substance on board at the very most."

Lowry shook his head, deeply puzzled. "A gram or two. I just don't understand," he said finally.

"All we know for certain," Stevenson continued, "and my findings match Hillborn's precisely on this point, is that, if the aircraft had been filled with the material when it crashed, the destruction here would still be going on. And frankly, I can't even imagine where it would have stopped—hundreds of kilometers from here at least, I would suspect, perhaps into the thousands.

The extent of the damage that the microbe does is directly related to the amount of the material released at any given site. We're certain of that much now."

"So perhaps the other transport planes that left here that night held only a small amount of the material as well," Lowry said hopefully.

"Perhaps, but I don't think so," Stevenson said. "We've discovered something else about the crash. It wasn't an accident."

"Not an accident?"

"No," Stevenson said. "There was a small explosive device in the aircraft's engine. We've found remnants of it. The crash wasn't an accident. It was done on purpose, probably as a warning. It was a way to draw us quickly to the site and to show us just how deadly and how extraordinarily efficient the material is. We couldn't know that from the earlier sites, because we had no way of guessing when the process started, and by the time we reached those sites, the material had completed its work and was no longer active. This is the first time that we've been able to know precisely when and where the material was released and to measure its effects. I think the crash of that plane with only a gram or two of the poison on board was planned as a final warning to us. They want us to know the full potential horror of Phoenix. They want us to truly fear the possible consequences, if we don't capitulate to their demands, when the time comes for them to deliver their final ultimatum."

"So what the hell do I tell them?" Lowry pointed toward the visitors from Command.

"The truth," Stevenson said. "We have to continue to look for ways to stop it, but if they've been able to manufacture it in any significant quantity—say, if the other eleven cargo planes that left here were actually filled with the material—they will be at a tremendous advantage, because of its enormous concentrated power. And if they do launch a successful attack with it somewhere, they could easily destroy an entire country's vegetation, perhaps even that of an entire continent. And along with the vegetation, it could destroy the entire ecological chain, set off a reaction that could end all life in the area, threaten the entire world, for all we know." Stevenson paused for a moment before telling Lowry his worst fears. "We have to tell them that Phoenix is an even greater threat than we'd ever imagined. Phoenix may be the most efficient killing machine that science has ever produced."

★   ★   ★

The knock on the door came in the middle of the night, loud and unremitting. There was no way to ignore it. Geli bolted awake in fear, feeling the horror and hopelessness that so many others all over the world had felt for the last several years.

She had made a vital mistake with Morell. What a fool she'd been. Geli's thoughts were a frightened jumble as the door opened without her going to it and a Nazi SS officer, wearing a full-dress uniform, stood in the center of it.

She could not see the officer's face, hidden as it was in the shadows of the doorway, only his body and uniform, an anonymous assassin, she thought. She would have preferred to see his face, she thought strangely, and then quickly realized that, of course, it didn't really matter.

"You are to dress," the officer said, and Geli nodded. She went to her dressing room and opened the wardrobe that stood against one wall. Dress for what? she thought, staring blankly at the line of clothes that she had arrived in, khaki slacks, blouse, and knee-high, black leather boots.

She turned away from the wardrobe and looked at the Chinese tapestry, begging for a reprieve, but she could feel no presence watching her from behind it that night.

She took a quick look around the large room, but there was no exit. There were a few small windows high on the wall, but they were far too small for her to attempt to use them to escape.

She went to the mirror and began to fix her hair and makeup, working without emotion, as if in a trance.

As she put her long blond hair up into a roll at the nape of her neck, she could hear the guard growing restless in the next room. She looked at the marble ledge beneath her. Fresh toilet articles had been laid out by the maid: soap, small cosmetic items, a razor and fresh silver blades. Geli studied the edge of the blades carefully. Was this why she had been permitted these moments alone? She considered one of the blades' sharp metal edges for a long moment and then rejected it. There was still a chance, she told herself. There was really no telling what the next few moments held. There was always a chance. But as she turned back for the door and saw the tall, powerfully built SS officer waiting for her in the center of the bedroom, the dull ache of fear inside her grew more powerful. Would she soon regret not having taken the opportunity with the sharp silver-edged blade, just as she now deeply regretted having made the wrong decision with Dr. Morell the night before?

# CHAPTER THIRTEEN

G oebbels watched as the vast shape rose out of the sea, dispersing great quantities of water off its metal back as it came to the surface.

The *Leviathan*, as its crew had nicknamed her, was the latest in a series of German U-boats that at one time had ruled the Atlantic, and, Goebbels thought as he watched this powerful new model emerge from the sea, they soon would again. They would rule both the Atlantic and the Pacific and all the other great oceans of the world.

Goebbels turned back and took a final long look at the ruined towers of the ancient monastery that he was leaving now. There was no sign of General Krietzer, but Goebbels knew that the old man watched him from some hidden vantage point. Goebbels felt dissatisfied and anxious at all the vast treasure that he was leaving behind, but he knew that he must, at least for now, and he turned away from the island and returned to watching the great U-boat that was to take him on the next leg of his journey as it cut across the surface of the ocean toward him.

The *Leviathan* was a greatly modified design to its predecessors, with a wider and deeper hull permitting greatly expanded cargo space with no loss of underwater maneuverability. The speed of the new boat would have surprised her enemies too. Even with the increased storage capacity, the newly designed craft would be able to cross the Atlantic in much less time than they would be able to anticipate.

As he watched the powerful metal beast emerge from the sea and come to a rest on its storm-tossed surface, the hatch opened and a single uniformed naval officer climbed up onto the ship's topside bridge. The man was dressed in the bluish-gray uniform of a German U-boat captain. He stood waiting stoically as Goebbels' launch crossed the last few meters of open sea and came alongside the great metal ship bobbing on the surface of the North Atlantic.

Lieutenant Schuman was standing in the bow of the launch alongside Goebbels. The young SS officer had taken this trip dozens of times over the last few days, moving between the island and the U-boat. And he went first now, taking the short jump from the launch to the U-boat's flat metal deck and then across to the rail of its conning tower. A moment later Goebbels followed and climbed down the metal ladder into the interior of the craft. Immediately the heat and smell of burning oil and the sounds of machinery in the small interior space rushed at him. A long journey on this cramped vessel would be extraordinarily uncomfortable, and he considered for a moment leaving it to others, but when he thought of all that awaited him at the end of the passage, his reservations were removed. The discomfort was nothing compared to all that he would soon achieve.

As he had requested, the crew remained at a distance as he passed through the ship, and he was able to move easily through the U-boat's narrow passageways and down its interior ladders to the cargo hold. There was no reason for anyone except the captain to know that he was on board, and even the captain did not know the full purpose of his journey.

Just before they reached the final set of double cargo doors, the captain stopped and unlocked the entrance to a small room that held two beds and a pair of wall lockers and little more. Gruening sat on the edge of the bed nearest the door. He looked up at the captain as the door opened, but neither man said anything. Lieutenant Schuman's gear was already piled on the cabin's other narrow metal-framed bed. Goebbels watched as the young SS officer disappeared into the room and then, as he had been instructed, locked the door after him.

Goebbels lifted a hand to dismiss the captain, and the gray-haired officer returned up the ladder to the ship's upper levels, leaving Goebbels all alone in the shadows of the final belowdecks companionway that led to the cargo hold.

Goebbels waited a moment to be certain that he couldn't be seen. Then he moved to the compartment's metal door and unlocked it.

He stepped inside and turned on the overhead light. All was as he had ordered it. The compartment itself had been heavily modified during construction. The cargo space was far larger than the standard designs in many particulars, lengthened and widened considerably and with much more vertical space than a standard submarine design. But for all of its size, the compartment was nearly filled. There were hundreds of neatly packed metal and wooden boxes lining the walls, each box marked in a code that only Goebbels understood.

Goebbels had carefully selected from the island's underground treasure chamber some of the most easily disposed of its assets: gold, silver, currencies, cut and uncut jewels. Then Lieutenant Schuman had overseen the transfer of the boxes to the cargo compartment of the modified U-boat.

Goebbels walked to a box at random. He removed a sharp-bladed bayonet from a scabbard at his belt and pried the metal box open. A great splash of cut diamonds sparkled out at him.

Goebbels could feel the great U-boat's engines readying themselves for the journey. He moved to the compartment's only porthole, another modification he had demanded be made to the underwater craft's normal construction. He pushed back the metal shade that had covered the opening. The launch was moving past the island. Goebbels took a final look at the ruins of the monastery outlined by the final rays of the sun against the rough gray water of the North Atlantic. It hurt him to leave this place, he realized. He could feel a pull in his chest for the vast fortune that he had left behind in the storage vaults beneath the ruins of the old abbey. He looked back at the cargo compartment filled to overflowing. Certainly there was enough wealth in this room to accomplish any human undertaking, but in removing it from the island's storage chamber, he had barely made a small dent in the island's vaults. It was the incomparable fortune that he was leaving behind that he thought of now, rather than the enormity of what he was taking with him.

Dark seawater bubbled over the porthole and Goebbels turned back to it, but he could no longer see the sky or the sunset or the island. In his mind's eye, though, he could still imagine almost every detail of the underground treasure room. He vowed to himself that someday he would return to it.

Slowly he slid the protective cover over the opening and turned back into the room. At his request, a cot had been made up just beneath the window, and what few personal things that he had managed to bring with him were packed into a single footlocker that lay beneath the bed. He would eat and sleep in this room throughout the entire journey, he thought, walking over and seating himself on the edge of the cot.

He looked at the shapes of the boxes and crates that filled the compartment. From this angle by the side of the room, he could see the compartment's other cargo. Stowed away at the very rear of the *Leviathan*'s cargo hold were several hundred gray-colored, coffinlike metal boxes.

So far, he had done his job well, Goebbels thought, feeling the great metal beast under him pull away from the coast of northern Africa and head toward the open sea. He looked back and forth between the gray metal boxes and the wooden crates filled with treasure. He had before him now, contained within this very room, not only enough wealth but enough raw destructive power to rule the world.

★ ★ ★

He was very close to his prey now, Sheridan thought, rereading his orders as he had several times during the long flight from Berlin. He knew that Berchtesgaden contained above it the Fuehrer's personal retreat—the Berghof. And the orders stated that Command had a recent report of the arrival at the estate of a strange group of people, two men and a woman. Could Goebbels himself be one of them? Elements of the 101st Airborne were already cracking their way into the mountain stronghold. They were anticipated to break through at dawn. Sheridan was to join up with them as quickly as he could and to intercept and ascertain the identity of the chalet's mysterious visitors.

His flight reached Berchtesgaden slightly before dawn. The next few hours were not going to be easy, he decided as he saw the lights of the tiny Alpine village below him. The Berghof was well fortified and manned by the infamous SS Death's Head squads, the best and the most ruthless of the Nazi soldiers.

The aircraft circled the small airport once. And as the plane began its descent, Sheridan could hear the sound of artillery. Whether any of it was directed at his plane he couldn't be certain, but he noticed that the pilot used all of the precautions required of landing in a combat zone, a quick steep approach with all lights remaining off until the last moment and then switched off again immediately after touchdown.

Sheridan hopped off the plane with his gear in his hand. The airstrip was filled with smoke and chaos. American planes were landing, bringing in troops and supplies, and the strip was under sporadic sniper and artillery fire. A tough-looking army sergeant in full battle gear, steel pot, web belt, his bayoneted rifle strung over his shoulder, greeted Sheridan as he jumped down from the aircraft. "Sheridan?" The crusty sergeant managed a halfhearted salute.

"Yes." Sheridan returned the salute with only a little more formality.

"We got a radio message on you. I'm supposed to get you up the hill." The sergeant, whose name tag read "Landa," gestured up toward the outline of the high Alpine mountains that rose above the airfield. "Only trouble is, nobody's broken through yet. There's about five miles of winding mountain road, most of it straight up. The road's narrow, the woods flank it on both sides, and they're filled with snipers and deserters. There's a lot of fighting on the road and I don't know how close we can get right now." The sergeant looked up at the sky. The first traces of light were just beginning to crack into the horizon. "They'll be making their final push at dawn. We could wait and see how it goes." Landa stayed silent then, leaving the decision whether to proceed to Sheridan.

"Let's go up and take a look," Sheridan said, and started toward the sergeant's waiting jeep, parked at the edge of the runway.

As he crossed the airstrip, Sheridan could hear incoming artillery rounds whistling nearby. His instinct was to throw himself on the deck, but he could see Landa sprinting past him and then hurling himself behind the protection of the jeep. Sheridan did the same. Shrapnel rained on the landing field where they had just been.

Landa lifted himself onto one knee and looked directly at Sheridan. Are you sure? his expression said. Sheridan's answer was to swing his long legs up over the passenger side of the jeep. This veteran sergeant followed after him and within minutes they were speeding down the road that ran along the outskirts of what remained of the devastated Bavarian town. They could hear the sounds of the fighting coming from the mountain range that rose up from the edge of the highway intensifying as they approached the army checkpoint established at the base of the Berghof road.

The sergeant stopped the jeep and Sheridan surveyed the situation. There was a short convoy of jeeps and trucks passing through the checkpoint on their way up toward the fighting at the top of the mountain. Sheridan nodded toward the convoy and the sergeant edged the jeep into the caravan and moved through the checkpoint without being challenged and started up the narrow mountain road with the rest of the convoy.

Sheridan looked ahead of him. Dawn was breaking and the details of the pine-covered forest were coming into focus. He could hear sniper fire farther up the road and then automatic-weapons fire. Sheridan withdrew his .45 and placed it on his lap.

The mountain road was just as steep as Sheridan had been warned. It was narrow and winding with thick pine woods flanking it on both sides. The convoy began to string out and a few of the heavier vehicles pulled to the side of the road to let the others pass. Soon Sheridan's jeep was near the lead.

Sheridan stayed low and studied the darkness of the pine woods. He could hear the sounds of gunfire growing louder as the minutes passed and the top of the mountain neared.

Suddenly, from somewhere behind him, a burst of automatic-weapons fire cut loose. Bullets smacked against the metal side of the jeep. And then its front windshield shattered with the impact of the incoming rounds.

"You okay?" Sheridan called out as he crouched below the jeep's front seat and moved into position to face the danger.

"Uh-huh," Landa managed as Sheridan's eyes scanned the woods, looking for the spot where the rounds were coming from, but he could see only thick forest and occasional traces of orange flame cutting through the air.

Sheridan fired his weapon into the woods in the direction he guessed the shots had come from, not waiting for a precise target. There was a return of more angry automatic-weapons fire. Bullets exploded against the tailpipe, but then the jeep was past the next switchback curve in the road and moving up the mountain again. Sheridan looked behind him. The truck next in the convoy was being engaged by fire now. One of the soldiers stood in the rear bed of the vehicle and hurled a grenade into the woods. Its explosion rocked Sheridan thirty meters from where it went off. The automatic-weapons fire stopped and there was only the sporadic rifle fire from the other side of the road. The soldiers in the truck turned their attention to it as Sheridan's jeep continued up the mountainside. He could hear more gunfire ahead of him as well, but the jeep advanced to a clearing near the top of the mountain without taking any further direct fire.

The sergeant stopped the jeep in front of the remnants of an iron gate embedded in blocks of concrete. The gate was blown open and it hung in bent and twisted wreckage from its concrete base. Bodies of a dozen German soldiers were draped over the edge of the concrete structure. Landa stopped the jeep only for a moment and then wove his way through the twisted remnants of the protective barrier and proceeded down a long entrance road, overhung with arching tree branches. Sheridan could hear intense gunfire directly ahead of him. The jeep continued on down the long tunnel of trees, until their overhanging branches opened out into a wide courtyard. Sheridan could see the front of the Berghof directly ahead of him now. Much of the Berghof's main structure and its outbuildings were in charred ruins, but the central core of the house remained intact.

Smoke blew in great clouds, obscuring the chalet's entrance, but Sheridan could tell at a glance the state of the battle. A squad of American troops was advancing across the estate's formal courtyard toward its high, double entrance doors while the fortresslike chalet was being defended from its front steps by black-helmeted German soldiers.

Sheridan slammed a fresh clip into the butt of his .45 and then leapt from the jeep. As he did, automatic-weapons fire sprayed the interior of the vehicle. Landa was already lying on the crushed stone of the entry, returning fire at the new source of danger.

Sheridan hit the ground and rolled to safety behind a low garden wall. He crept forward along the edge of the wall, until he could see the front of the Berghof. The lead squad was at the entrance now, engaged in hand-to-hand fighting with the last of the German guard.

There was another flurry of gunfire and Sheridan flattened himself in the dirt behind the stone wall. When the firing ended, he stole another quick look at the front of the chalet. A shower of grenades had just shattered the Berghof's thick oak front door, splintering it into shreds, and a rush of American troops started through it. Sheridan followed at a sprint. He could hear more gunfire, even see the stone steps beneath his feet splintering with the impact of the rounds. But he made it up the steps and into the chalet's front entrance.

Several bodies, both American and German, lay across the entry hall, splattering the expanse of white marble with the crimson of their blood. Servants were lined up against the walls, their arms in the air, begging for mercy, terrible looks of fear on their faces, as the invading American soldiers began the process of searching them and taking them prisoner. Sheridan continued on into the first of several magnificent reception rooms and then he followed two other American soldiers up the winding, ornate front staircase. From the top of the stairs, Sheridan looked below him. More American soldiers were spilling into the lower rooms, their olive-drab uniforms looking strikingly out of place against the formal white marble entrance and the grandness of the richly decorated room.

Sheridan turned back to the upper floor, searching his memory for the details of the house's design that he had been shown in London.

There was a burst of gunfire and the soldier in front of Sheridan fell. Sheridan lifted his .45 and fired in the direction of the shot. A black-helmeted SS officer tumbled forward over the second-floor landing and fell onto the marble entry.

Sheridan and the other soldiers continued up the staircase to the third floor, where more servants stood with their hands in the air. Suddenly more gunfire erupted behind him. A servant dressed in gray livery was firing a handgun at the advancing American soldier just ahead of Sheridan. The soldier returned fire on the single servant, who fell to the hallway carpet, still firing his weapon. The servant waved the gun wildly and the advancing soldier continued firing at him until the servant dropped to the floor, the pistol spilling from his hands.

Sheridan continued down the hallway. He was leaving the other Americans behind, but he had a sense of where he was going. He held his .45 out in front of him as he charged past a last few startled servants. When he reached the final door in the long hallway, he fired his pistol into its heavy lock, splintering it open, and then he rushed into a large, elegantly appointed sitting room. A meal was laid out on a wooden table at the center of the room. There was a double door open at the room's far side. Sheridan ran to it. The canopied bed in the adjoining room was wrinkled and used. He was so close to him now, Sheridan thought. He could almost smell the sour fear of his prey.

Sheridan looked quickly around the large bedroom. He could remember the discussions in London about the possibility of a final set of secret rooms. The speculation was that it might be accessed off one of the bedrooms on the third floor, perhaps from the master bedroom itself. Sheridan's eyes searched the walls of the grandly decorated room. There was a trail of smoke escaping from a narrow opening in the far wall from between a large ornate mirror and one of the room's vertical supporting beams. This was too convenient, Sheridan thought. He'd felt one too many times since he'd been pursuing this man that things were not as they appeared, that he was being helped along by more than mere chance, and he approached the opening carefully. There was a fireplace in the room and Sheridan went to it and withdrew an iron poker from its hearth. He thrust the poker into the opening, forcing its jaws apart far enough that he could move his entire body through it. There was a narrow staircase in front of him and Sheridan started slowly up its steps. He drew his breath in tensely. Was it a trap? At the top of the staircase was a small hidden room.

The smell in the closed-up room was intolerable. Sheridan recognized the smell at once. It was the same mixture of gasoline and burned flesh that he had smelled for the first time in the Chancellery garden. Smoke hung thick in the air as Sheridan crossed the room to the bed that stood in the far corner. There was a man's body lying on it. What remained of the corpse was still giving off the sickening smell of gasoline and burning flesh. The bed's linens and mattress were still smoldering as well and filling the room with a heavy pall of smoke. Sheridan could almost hear the body's blackened grinning face laughing at him. They had beaten him again, the laughter said.

Sheridan could hear soldiers at the foot of the secret staircase that led up to the final room. He went to the head of the stairs. It was Landa. Sheridan made the calculation very swiftly, the same one that he knew Command would soon make on a worldwide scale. No one else could see the contents of this room. If word got out of what it held, Allied credibility would be smashed.

"Sergeant, seal off this room," Sheridan commanded. "Be certain that no one else comes up here."

"Yes, Major," Landa replied quickly.

Sheridan returned to the partially burned corpse and knelt down over it. Part of the man's face and almost all of his hands and most of his body were burned away, leaving only remnants of a gray uniform tunic and matching uniform pants and black leather boots. But from what remained of the face, Sheridan realized that this body, just as the one in Berlin, looked in every possible way to be the final remains of Reichminister Joseph Goebbels.

# PART
# THREE

# CHAPTER
# FOURTEEN

Which of the two bodies was really Goebbels? The one in the Berlin bunker? Or the one here in Berchtesgaden? Sheridan had been working without rest to find the answer to that question and the other mysteries of the Berghof for nearly the last twenty-four hours.

The key was knowing what was real and what wasn't, Sheridan told himself as he crossed the burnt-out shell of Hitler's study on the chalet's first floor. He had been using one of the headquarters' tents that the 101st had set up at the rear of the Berghof to interview its servants and guards all morning, and now he wanted to see what remained of the chalet's interior. It was like playing chess with a great grand master, who was unseen and unknown. There were always traps within traps, boxes within boxes, another mask to remove and find another mask beneath it, all designed to hide the master's real strategy. It was the only way a truly skillful operation worked. And Phoenix was the most skillful operation that he had ever seen.

There were things on the upper floors of the chalet that he needed to examine for himself now, he decided, and he started up the remains of the massive white marble central staircase.

He stopped for a moment when he reached the landing between the grand staircase's first and second floors. He looked below at the mixture of charred ruins and desolation of what remained of the Berghof's grand interior design. The exterior of the chalet and most of its surrounding buildings had been destroyed by fires set by the SS guards before the dawn attack, and only parts of the central core of the house were still intact. What the hell had really gone on here? he asked himself again, and then angrily continued up the staircase toward the chalet's upper floors, where several of the core rooms had been untouched by the fires.

When he reached the second floor, there were guards from General Harkins' staff posted at the entrance, but they recognized Sheridan and let him pass. The general and some of his people had arrived only a few hours after Sheridan had found the second Goebbels body in the secret upstairs room. Debra and some of the rest of the Phoenix team had arrived with him. And they had been undertaking the official inspection and formal interviewing of the captured prisoners. Sheridan felt better knowing that Debra was out of Berlin. And maybe she could learn something more than he had here, he thought hopefully as he moved inside the first door at the head of the long upper hallway. His investigation had so far revealed only an overview of recent events at the Berghof, and nothing of its real meaning.

A small party had apparently arrived at the estate shortly after the Soviets had taken Berlin and overrun the bunker. It was clear to Sheridan that Dr. Ernst Morell, the personal physician to only the most elite members of the Nazi High Command, had been one of the men. And the man whose burned body lay now in the secret upstairs room that may or may not be Joseph Goebbels had been the other. But there had also been one other member of the group, a beautiful young blonde woman, and Sheridan had learned that she had stayed in this second-floor room. None of the servants could identify her, but they were all consistent in their testimony that she had arrived with the others. And then just before the 101st began its attack, a chopper had been seen leaving a pad at the rear of the estate just before dawn. Sheridan was guessing that Morell had been on it. Had the mystery woman as well? And who could she be? And what role did she play in Phoenix? Sheridan asked himself as he looked around at the bedroom's bizarre gothic design.

The blonde woman's presence made no sense to Sheridan and that was why he was so interested. He was trained to look for the extraordinary elements in the otherwise understandable set of circumstances. He'd found they were usually the keys to his enemy's weakness.

Sheridan approached the room's large four-poster bed. The corners of the bed were thrown back and the sheets rumpled. The bedclothes smelled slightly of perfumes and scented powders. The smell was delicately seductive, intensely female. He remembered the servants' description of the woman's stunning beauty and he felt himself being drawn toward the mystery woman. Careful, he reminded himself as he forced himself to turn away from the bed and search the rest of the room. He wanted this woman to become his enemy's vulnerability, not his own.

"Who was she?"

Sheridan turned back to the bedroom door. It was Debra. She carried a large crystal decanter filled with dark brown liquid and two cut-crystal glasses.

179

"I was hoping that you could tell me," Sheridan said, trying to remain cool and distant.

"I don't know yet," Debra said, shaking her head and stepping inside the bizarre gothic bedroom and then kicking the heavy door closed behind her with the heel of her uniform shoe.

"I thought we'd put what we have through London," Sheridan said. "Maybe they can identify her." He quit his search of the mystery woman's room then and walked over to a dramatically curved gold and scarlet silk couch that wrapped around the room's pink marble fireplace and sat down. His eyes moved to the ceiling of the room where women with long golden hair and mighty mythic warriors on horseback appeared against a pale blue-and-white backdrop of painted clouds and sky.

"Brandy," Debra said as she crossed the room and set the crystal decanter and glasses on a small black enamel table that stood in front of the fireplace. "The bastard's private stock," she said, pointing at the bottle. "Harkins got nearly half a case, but I managed to steal us some."

Sheridan finally smiled at her, feeling the anger and distance between them melt away as it always seemed to sooner or later, and then he lifted the decanter and poured the rich brown liquid until it was nearly overflowing the two crystal glasses, and handed a glass to Debra, who took it gratefully. "Why two bodies? Wasn't one Joseph Goebbels one too many?" Sheridan said, and drank from the brandy.

Debra said nothing for a moment, using her free hand to remove her hard, black uniform shoes and then the dark blue wool socks. Then she lifted her bare feet up onto Sheridan's lap.

"And, if Goebbels is dead, who the hell is running Phoenix?" Sheridan continued as he began rubbing the soles of her feet, an old ritual between them. "I'm not ready to give up on the investigation just because of this, are you?" He pointed up toward the hidden room where he'd found the second Goebbels body.

"No," Debra said, and then added, "What if it is still Goebbels that's behind everything, always has been?"

"What do you mean?"

"Well, this is what I've been thinking. Did any of the servants absolutely identify Goebbels? Could any of them positively place him here over the last few days?"

"Nothing that couldn't be explained away," Sheridan said thoughtfully. "Some of the staff that I spoke with thought that they saw him, but always from a distance, or at night, something."

"That's what I got too," Debra said, warming to the idea. "The body here could have been a double just as easily as the one in Berlin. What if neither one was really Goebbels?"

Sheridan stopped rubbing Debra's feet for a moment and reached for his glass. "Twins," Sheridan said, understanding now. "Camp 19. They could have brought one of them to Berlin and one of them here."

Debra nodded her agreement. "They used them like animals, collected them from all over Europe. They could have easily found a set that looked like Goebbels, perhaps done some cosmetic surgery to enhance the resemblance, dressed them in his clothes."

Sheridan nodded. "Both bodies could be only a cover or a diversion of some kind. A complex double trap to convince us that Goebbels is dead and the threat has ended, just another device to keep us busy trying to solve a mystery of which body is really his, when in reality neither one is. He could still be very much alive and is somewhere even now, moving Phoenix into its final stages."

★   ★   ★

Goebbels watched from the U-boat's conning tower through a thin curtain of rain as the gunboats pulled alongside and then began to surround his craft.

181

There were half a dozen ships in all, each armed with mounted automatic weapons at their bows and stern. They flew no flags, nor did these fast deadly ships bear the markings of any country. And the sailors that manned the sleek deadly launches wore no uniforms. Goebbels knew their allegiance, though. It was blindly and unquestionable to Phoenix and to the "New Reich."

Goebbels could smell land even through the curtain of warm rain that surrounded him. The South American coast lay less than a thousand meters away. The gunships had intercepted the *Leviathan* minutes after it had surfaced off the Argentine coast. They had quickly surrounded it and were leading it now toward a narrow bottleneck that connected the open Atlantic to a narrow river channel that led into the interior of the continent.

At the narrowest point of the bottleneck guarding the entrance to the channel stood a wooden dock and boathouse. Stone steps wound up a high rocky promontory behind the dock to the sprawling, reddish-brown Spanish-style hacienda, built at the top of the tall cliff.

A lone figure stood on the dock, watching as the *Leviathan* was escorted toward shore. The figure was dressed in black military-style hunting clothes, with a long black cape blowing around him, that protected him from the rain. Count Heinreich, Goebbels thought with contempt, a minor figure in Berlin before the war. But now the master of this desolate but vital outpost.

As the U-boat passed slowly through the entrance to the inland channel, Goebbels stepped to the edge of the ship's conning tower and extended his arm out toward Heinreich in a Nazi salute. "Heil Hitler," he called out against the blowing gray air, and the figure on the dock returned the stiff-armed salute with great energy.

Despite the storm, Goebbels could see the man a little more clearly now. He was of slightly above average height with short-cut, almost bone-white hair. And from the brief time that he had met with him in Berlin, Goebbels remembered the man's bright blue eyes and chiseled Aryan features. The prefect Aryan type, the Fuehrer had called him when he had chosen him for this important assignment, Count Albert Heinreich, a German nobleman, with an aristocratic family that could be traced back for centuries. Goebbels had never liked or respected the man, but he hadn't tried to stop the Fuehrer when Hitler had insisted that Heinreich be given this lonely and difficult assignment. He could only hope now that the Fuehrer had been right and that he would find everything as it should be.

The U-boat slid by the dock and began its way inland, down the narrow river channel, turning and twisting through the semidarkness caused by the storm and the layers of jungle foliage that grew above the passageway, until finally the craft turned at a hard angle toward its starboard side.

Goebbels looked over anxiously at the U-boat's captain, who stood in the topside conning tower with him. Was he mad? The U-boat was within seconds of crashing into what appeared to be a solid wall of branches and overhanging vines and yet the captain's gray-bearded face showed no emotion.

Goebbels braced for a crash, but the center of the seemingly impenetrable wall gave way and the U-boat slipped through what proved to be only a thin curtain of vines and undergrowth and entered into a long dark tunnel of thick foliage that opened out after nearly fifty meters into a small harbor, built into a natural crescent-shaped bay. The harbor was surrounded by a scattering of barracks and warehouse buildings. And at the far side of the bay was a series of wooden docks built into the shoreline with a few intermediate-size ships tied into them. And floating at the center of the harbor was a small fleet of pontoon aircraft.

Even though he had been the one to select the site and approve the designs, it was Goebbels' first look at the reality of the secret coastal base and he was pleased with the results. It would serve its purpose as a transfer point for Phoenix quite efficiently, he decided.

Satisfied with all that he saw, Goebbels took a final deep breath of the warm, storm-laden air and then went below, returning to the subterranean cargo hold at the third and lowest level of the great underwater ship that had been his headquarters for the long voyage.

Ten days below the Atlantic, he thought, unlocking the massive metal door of the hold and stepping inside its dark cavernous interior. Ten days and almost every moment spent in these cramped makeshift quarters. Ten days of tension and danger as the U-boat had evaded the enemy's screens and blockades. There had been one long chase off the coast of West Africa with a British destroyer and several desperately tense moments as the U-boat eluded enemy ships or drifted, its engines off, hundreds of meters deep underwater, while Allied sounding gear searched for their location. But they had come through untouched, as had every ounce of their precious cargo, Goebbels thought, looking across the hold to the rows and rows of neatly stacked, gray metal boxes and next to them the more unruly piles of wooden and iron treasure boxes that had shared the entire tension-filled trip across the Atlantic with him.

He turned away from the rows of boxes when he heard a knock on the bulkhead door. He walked across the hold then and slid its heavy metal bolt back.

Schuman stood in the entrance. The events of the last few weeks had changed him, Goebbels decided as he looked briefly into the officer's face and eyes. He was no longer simply the naive, unquestioning young man that he had selected from the ranks in Berlin. But that was to be expected, Goebbels told himself. Schuman had seen and experienced too much since then to be the same, but the question of trust hung anxiously in the air between the two men for a long moment.

"Is all in readiness?" Goebbels asked, finally breaking the silence and using his forefinger to punctuate his words by tapping it hard against the young officer's chest. Goebbels had meant for the action to be intimidating and he took pleasure in the small flicker of fear that he saw sweep across Schuman's eyes.

"Yes, sir," the young man answered.

Goebbels pushed past him and swept out of the hold and down the narrow dark corridor to the stairs that led to the bridge. He moved up the twisting metal staircase, without even a backward glance at the room that had held him for ten long days and nights across the Atlantic.

He hated leaving it all behind now to men like Schuman and Heinreich, but he knew that he must. He had other work to attend to, even more important work. He could be pleased, though, he told himself. He had completed another part of the task successfully. He had brought enough sheer destructive power to change the course of history to the very doorstep of his enemy.

★   ★   ★

To her surprise, Geli had survived at least for the moment, but she had to stay strong and watchful, she kept reminding herself. She couldn't let the fear that fluttered around the edges of her thoughts gain a grip on her. There were still dangers on every side and they could destroy her at any moment.

To keep her mind alert and strong, she traced back over every mile of the long journey that had begun in Berchtesgaden several days before.

After she had been awakened in the middle of the night at the Berghof, the SS guard had led her down the chalet's back stairs. She had been led past the estate's gardens and across the crushed-gravel path that ringed its grounds. And then she had been taken down the hill to the landing field at the rear of the estate.

The Focke had been warming up in the cleared area near the edge of the valley, its powerful rotor blades cutting great circles across the dark, nearly cloudless sky. Dr. Morell and a pilot were the aircraft's only other passengers. And almost as soon as she was on board, the aircraft had lifted off its pad.

A moment later she had heard the first of a series of explosions that rocked the helicopter from side to side and nearly hurled it back to the ground, as it fought to climb above the valley. She had looked behind at the Berghof. The entire estate was lit by great waves of orange and yellow flames. There were more explosions then, followed by the sound of gunfire coming from the road that led up the mountain to the chalet. And she had watched flames shooting from the roof of the great structure as the Focke made its ascent, escaping the jaws of the valley and the blasts of the explosions, and then disappearing over the snow-capped crest of the Kehlstein into Austria.

They had flown south and west then. After a brief stop for refueling, the Focke had continued on. She had tried to gauge its direction, but soon it became very difficult. When the aircraft set down at a small farmhouse hidden deep in miles of barren hill country, Geli could no longer be certain of exactly where they were, but she guessed it to be somewhere in southern Spain.

The Focke had been met by several men carrying rifles. The men had been dressed as farmers, but they had the speech and bearing of highly trained German soldiers. These men had taken her and Morell to a small stone farmhouse, where she and the others had stayed until the morning of the ninth day, when they had been driven to an abandoned military air base and loaded onto a large military transport. The aircraft bore no markings, but Geli recognized it as a reconfigured pre-War German transport.

At dawn, the powerful aircraft had taken off again, flying south by southwest, away from the rising sun. It had been refueled somewhere on the western tip of Africa late that night and then continued on at the same southwesterly course.

Geli had slept and woken several times since Africa and she had lost track of both time and the precise direction of the aircraft, but she could feel the plane beginning its final rocking descent now and she knew that the great landmass of South America lay somewhere very close ahead.

Then through the blowing sheets of rain that surrounded the aircraft, Geli could see a long sweep of coastline. There was a break in the coast, a small bottleneck that led from the sea inland down a narrow river channel. To one side of the channel lay a small bay and harbor filled with ships. In addition to the ships, there were at least a half dozen pontoon aircraft bobbing on the surface of the water. Geli's plane continued on past the bay, until a small airstrip was visible at the end of the narrow river channel.

She looked over at Morell as the aircraft began its rocking descent toward the small airstrip. He sat across the aisle from her, his thick fingers drumming nervously on the arms of his chair. After a prolonged skidding on a rain-slick runway, the plane came to a stop.

Morell was the first to exit the aircraft. Geli followed, the rain swirling around her, but she was struck at once by the warmth and delicacy of the South American air despite the freakish summer storm.

As she descended the aircraft's exterior stairs, she could see that the staircase was surrounded by a squad of waiting men. They were dressed as the squads in Spain had been, as farmers and ranch hands, but as Geli approached them, she noticed that they were carrying German infantry weapons, and despite their informal clothing, they had precisely the same bearing and manner as the most elite Nazi Death's Head squads that she had known in Berlin.

There was a long black Mercedes limousine, its doors closed against the rain, its window glass tinted a dark gray, waiting on the edge of the runway. When the vehicle's door opened, Geli could see a single uniformed figure seated in the limousine's rear seat. It was Goebbels. And in the shadows next to him sat Gruening.

Morell hurried across the landing field to the open limousine door. Geli could see him leaning into the limousine and talking to Goebbels. She knew that they were deciding her fate. Suddenly Goebbels raised his hand and gestured to one of the guards standing at the edge of the airfield. Geli felt her stomach tighten in fear as the guard crossed to her and pointed at a waiting jeep parked on the far side of the runway. Geli started her way toward it, and as she did, two more soldiers, their rifles unstrapped and carried at the ready across their chests, fell into place on either side of her. What had Goebbels' decision been? Geli's thoughts were filled with fear. Had she survived the Berghof only to lose her life halfway across the world on the rain-washed coast of South America?

★　★　★

Goebbels watched the beautiful young blonde woman carefully as she entered the rear of the jeep. He felt a struggle inside himself. She was very desirable and he wanted deeply to make love to her, but he knew that would not be wise. She could easily become a risk to the entire operation. Morell should have seen to her elimination in Berchtesgaden and a new backup pilot chosen from the ranks available to him there. But perhaps Morell was even more taken with her beauty than he was himself, Goebbels thought as he looked over at the doctor's wide fleshy face.

"Why did you bring her?" Goebbels asked as the limousine sped off, away from the airfield.

Morell shook his head, openly troubled by the question. "Her skills as a pilot, nothing more," he said. "We learned in Berlin that we must always be prepared for any emergency."

Goebbels nodded his head, seeming to accept the explanation, but his doubts remained. "I see," he said.

The sedan continued on away from the airfield, moving slowly along a narrow road built between the jungle and the river that ran back into the interior. "As soon as we arrive at the final staging area tomorrow," Goebbels said, turning to Gruening, "I want her eliminated. We will have no more possible use for her then."

Gruening nodded, saying nothing. They drove on in silence until the small secret bay and harbor came into view ahead of them. Goebbels turned back to Morell. "You will be in charge here," Goebbels said. "Lieutenant Schuman has already begun the transfer of the materials, but he must be watched carefully. Count Heinreich"—Goebbels pointed up at the red stone hacienda at the top of the cliff—"has been in command here until our arrival, but he is a man of no real consequence. He will not challenge your authority." Suddenly Goebbels stopped. He could see down to the harbor. There was a flurry of frenzied activity, most of it centered around the anchorage that held the *Leviathan*.

The jeep pulled down the harbor road and stopped within a few meters of the docked U-boat. The boat's captain, a large burly man in a dark navy sea coat, was striding angrily toward him.

Suddenly Goebbels understood what must have happened. "Schuman," he called out as the commandant approached the side of the limousine.

"Yes, sir," the captain answered, "and two of my own men."

Goebbels stepped from the rear of the vehicle, limping on his damaged leg as he moved across the dock. He made a small clumsy step to the topside of the *Leviathan* and crossed its metal deck to the conning tower.

Within minutes he stood before the heavy outer door to the cargo hold. The door was ajar. He pushed it open and went inside. The hold was a mass of confusion, boxes smashed open and left lying on the floor, currency, jewels, and gold coins scattered everywhere in the contained space.

Goebbels hobbled to the rear of the hold. He knew at a glance that a dozen, perhaps more, of the treasure boxes were missing. What fools, he thought. A single box would have been far more than three men could have spent in a lifetime. The extra boxes would only serve to weigh down their craft and slow their escape.

But what he saw next was even more foolhardy and far more dangerous. The theft hadn't ended with the treasure. They had also taken with them one of the gray metal boxes of Phoenix.

# CHAPTER
# FIFTEEN

Goebbels stood in the U-boat's cargo hold for only a brief moment. Suddenly he knew Schuman's destination. Goebbels had studied the charts of the coastline for months. Once Schuman was out of the bottleneck and into the open sea, only a fool would head north up the coast back toward Buenos Aires or try to take a small boat into the open Atlantic to the east. Schuman would head south. Less than fifty kilometers down the coast, the shoreline broke into a network of inland passageways that led deep into the interior, most of them overgrown with dense forest. They would make finding a single launch almost impossible. And if Schuman succeeded in escaping, it could be disastrous. He could go to the Allies or stupidly somehow fall into their hands. That could endanger Phoenix itself.

"Two ships have been dispatched," the captain said as he entered the hold. "One is to search the coast to the north. Count

Heinreich is personally piloting the other south. We will find them."

"Prepare another ship. The fastest one that you have available," Goebbels said, and then added, "But with sufficient firepower."

Goebbels returned to the dock and waited anxiously until his order had been obeyed.

When the long sleek gunboat finally arrived and sped to a stop in front of him, Goebbels immediately went aboard. And within seconds the launch was under way, cutting across the vacant harbor and down the tunnel of dense foliage and then out into the narrow, rock-lined river channel that led through the bottleneck to the open sea.

The sleek craft began its way south down the coast at a speed that Goebbels knew could not be matched by Schuman's heavily loaded craft.

After a few minutes Goebbels went below and spread out the charts of the coastline. They must catch the stolen launch before it reached the entrance to the inland passageways at Puerto Nueve or not at all, he decided, placing his finger on the map at the spot of the break in the coastline, just past the first small fishing village on the coast. And Schuman's own greed would determine the outcome. The enormously heavy extra boxes of treasure that he had loaded onto his small craft could just be enough to make the difference, Goebbels thought as he made a series of quick calculations in his head. It would weigh the stolen launch down and permit his own craft to reach it and then to sink it.

Goebbels went back on deck then, carrying with him a pair of field glasses from the captain's cabin. He stood in the prow of the ship and searched the horizon line, looking for any sign of the renegade launch. But there was nothing.

An hour went by and then another, still nothing. The rain built to a driving frenzy, but Goebbels stayed in the prow, searching the ocean for any sign. He was cold and his body ached with dampness, but still he stayed above, sweeping the turbulent sea with his field glasses. Outwardly he remained calm, but inside he was fighting a feeling of disaster. This was the first major mistake in the entire operation, but it could be enough to ruin everything.

A small fishing village passed by on the craft's starboard side. Goebbels knew that it had to be Puerto Nueve and that they were now only a few kilometers from the first of the inland passageways that undoubtedly Schuman would take, and then within a few minutes he would disappear into the interior.

Suddenly there was a hint of something on the rain-swept horizon line ahead of him. He'd been right. Schuman's launch was headed for the coastline at precisely the spot that he had predicted. And he'd almost made it. Goebbels called out to his ship's captain and pointed ahead to where he had seen the blurred shape against the panorama of windswept rain.

The captain lifted his field glasses and searched the horizon. A moment later he nodded his head, confirming what Goebbels had seen.

The captain cut the wheel of the chase craft, heading it for a point to starboard where the coastline broke off into the first of several small bays and inlets.

The chase craft cut through the water at high speeds, leaving a sharp vee of white water in its wake. With each passing moment, the slowly moving launch ahead of it got closer, but so did the mouth of the bay.

After several minutes it became apparent to Goebbels that he was going to lose the race. The launch was going to gain the entrance to the inlet before he could reach it.

Goebbels looked up at the heavy guns mounted on the upper deck of his ship. If they opened fire now, even from this distance, there was a chance they could bring the launch down. But did he dare? There was Phoenix to consider. Schuman's craft held a box full of the deadly microbes. If he fired on the launch and sank it, the poison would be spilled into the bay and the entire area would be contaminated. The destruction would bring local officials and in all probability his enemies. But by then he and the rest of Phoenix would be hundreds of kilometers away, halfway across the South American continent, ready to launch the final strike. But if Schuman escaped and fell into the Allies' hands? He knew so much. He knew the location of Phoenix' final staging area in the interior. He knew Phoenix' real target. He knew almost everything. It had to be done, Goebbels decided. He couldn't risk letting Schuman escape. "Fire," Goebbels commanded. And he watched as Schuman's slower, heavily weighted craft made its way ponderously the last hundred meters toward the safety of the bay. And then just at the final moment before the launch disappeared into the inland waterway, the first of the heavy rounds fell into the sea a few meters from the bow of Schuman's launch. Then another exploded near the stern, but the launch was untouched.

"No!" Goebbels screamed into the storm. He could just see the last of Schuman's launch as it moved safely into the inland passageway. But then out of the gray air came another ship. It was the chase ship manned by Count Heinreich and his crew. It cut across the stern of Schuman's small craft and opened fire with its own heavy guns.

Schuman's launch burst into flames. Heinreich's ship came alongside and continued firing and Schuman's craft began sinking fast. Goebbels could see figures jumping from its deck into the water.

194

By the time Goebbels' ship arrived at the side of the launch, there was nothing left to do but watch the launch sink below the waves and let Heinreich's gunboat methodically chase down the struggling figures in the water while Heinreich himself shot each of them as they attempted to swim to shore. Schuman was the last of the three and Goebbels watched through the storm with considerable pleasure as Heinreich stood on the bridge of his ship and opened fire on the young lieutenant, who, mortally wounded, sank beneath the waves.

Heinreich saluted Goebbels across the stretch of storm-laden air that separated the two men's ships. And Goebbels returned the Nazi salute and then motioned for his captain to turn the craft back up the coast.

Quite impressive, Goebbels thought, feeling grateful and more than a little surprised by Heinreich's actions. The time out here at this lonely outpost had changed the man. The Count Heinreich he had known in Berlin would never have been capable of such actions. And for a moment Goebbels even considered if it would be possible for Heinreich himself to have a fate different from the one planned for him, but Goebbels knew that was impossible. Soon the wreckage of the launch would bring the enemy and that would make it even more important than ever that there be no more deviations from the original plan. Phoenix must go forward precisely as scheduled.

★   ★   ★

Sheridan stood at the entrance to the main headquarters' tent established by the 101st at the rear of the Berghof. It was almost sunset and the final rays of sunlight were reflecting off the surface of the snowcapped mountains that bordered the great estate. The dying light was giving off a prism of colors, phosphorescent blues and sparkling emerald greens, with momentary flashes of sherbet pinks and rose-tinted reds.

For a moment Sheridan felt a hint of the intoxication of what it must have been like for Hitler and Goebbels and the others to stand in this room and look out at all this magnificence. But all they had seen was a world to conquer or destroy, he thought. How was that possible? Sheridan shook his head angrily. It was impossible for him to ever really understand the evil of his enemies, he realized then, as the last of the sun slipped away in the western sky. He only knew that he had to beat the bastards.

Sheridan turned when he heard a sound behind him and General Harkins entered the tent through a side opening, Debra only a few paces behind him.

Harkins went directly to a large metal field desk at the center of the large tent and sat down behind it.

Harkins lit one of his large black cigars and pointed it at Debra as he spoke. "Lieutenant Marks says that you have something that you want to show me."

"Yes, General," Sheridan said, and crossed to the field desk and placed a copy of a report from the British embassy in Buenos Aires in front of Harkins. "It came in late last night to London. They sent it right on to us."

Harkins picked up the report and began reading.

"A shipwreck on the Argentine coast and deadly poisonous material spreading back into the interior. It could be Phoenix," Sheridan said as Harkins finished.

"It could be," the general said thoughtfully. "But it could be a lot of other things too."

"We looked into it last night," Debra said, sliding a map of the South American continent onto the desk in front of Harkins. "Argentina has over fifteen hundred miles of coastline between Buenos Aires and Punta Norte in the north and Cabo San Diego in the south. The Nazis have been running a U-boat in and out of there practically unchallenged throughout the war. Lately the traffic has even increased, bringing wealthy German refugees into the area. They could have easily found a way to put a secret base somewhere along that coastline. The locals are sympathetic to them, and the farther south you go the more the terrain becomes wild, rough, desolate, much of it overlain with thick foliage. It would be nearly impossible for us to search all of it effectively. But maybe this spill or wreck—or whatever it is—has given us the break we need."

"If it is Phoenix out there, sir," Sheridan said, "they're within striking distance of the United States. And destroying America or bringing it to its knees is the only way for them to have a true final victory. It's far better than just setting Phoenix loose on Europe. America holds all the cards now, our strength has barely been tapped. If they're going to win that's the place to strike."

"And if you're wrong, and whatever remains of Phoenix is still in Europe, you've lost four, five days, a week, that we don't have," Harkins said.

"Captain Lowry's finished at Camp 19," Sheridan countered. "And God knows we've run out our leads here and in Berlin. This thing's all we've got right now," he added, pointing again at the report on Harkins' desk.

As Sheridan finished, Harkins looked down at the map of the South American coast and studied it for a long moment. "Well, I will say this. If I were going to use this damn stuff to attack the United States, that's sure as hell one of the spots I'd choose to launch the strike from," he said, pointing his cigar at the long stretch of Argentine coastline. "But if I send you out there, Command's going to tell me I'm crazy. They know how potentially dangerous Phoenix is, but Hitler's dead, and despite what the two of you believe, Goebbels probably is as well. That leaves no one to run an operation of the magnitude and complexity required to strike the United States. Command's going to tell me to concentrate my efforts in Europe." He paused before turning to Debra. "What do you think, Lieutenant?" he asked.

"It's the way the Nazis work, General," Debra answered thoughtfully. "We've seen it now for years. They confuse their enemies, divide us, lull us into a false sense of security, then they strike. But what they don't do is they don't quit. They don't stop themselves. In the end, we've always had to beat them. It's my belief that Phoenix is no different. We have to end it. And the only way to do that is to push at them, keep after them. We can't stop now and we can't underestimate them ever. Or we would be making a very bad mistake."

As Debra finished, Harkins remained silent, thinking. He drew in deeply on his cigar and then slowly let out an enormous cloud of smoke.

"General?" Sheridan prompted, uneasy with his silence.

"I think," Harkins said slowly, reaching his decision even as he spoke, "that Lieutenant Marks here probably knows as much about how these bastards really think and operate as anyone does. So I guess we'd better listen to her." He turned to Sheridan. "I wish you both good luck out there, but I hope to God that you're wrong."

★   ★   ★

Geli awoke slowly. For a moment she lay in the darkness not knowing where she was. Then finally she remembered. After she had arrived on the South American coast, at Goebbels' command she had been taken to a small, one-room cabin near the secret harbor that she had seen from the air. There had been a cot in the room and she had gone to it, meaning only to lie down for a moment, but she must have fallen asleep.

She looked at her watch and then went to the cabin's only window and looked outside. The first streaks of light were just appearing in the east, against a dark rainy sky.

There was food and water on a table in a corner of the room. She went to it and began ravenously eating hard bread and cheese and drinking stale, cold coffee.

Suddenly there was a knock on the door and two armed guards entered. She was led outside past a series of wooden docks. A great metal U-boat was anchored at the center of the harbor. And next to it, several small amphibious aircraft, equipped with twin pontoons locked into their undercarriages, bounced in the shore swell of the bay. The interior of one of the aircraft was lit against the gray morning. And Geli was taken across the harbor in a small launch to the brightly lit aircraft and escorted inside.

Goebbels was seated at the back of the craft, and as always now Gruening sat next to him. Goebbels nodded at Geli as she entered, but he said nothing. A young dark-haired pilot was at the controls. The young man had a small black leather bag on the floor next to him. Geli noticed the bag at once. It was in all probability a basic survival kit that all pilots were taught to carry, particularly when they flew over unpopulated or dangerous territory. Inside would be maps and a flight plan, a compass, probably local currency, a flashlight, a little food, and with any luck a loaded pistol and ammunition. Everything, she realized in a flash, that she would need to make a successful escape.

A few minutes later the aircraft lifted off the surface of the bay and headed west into the interior of the continent.

Geli watched the dark-haired pilot carefully. She soon was certain that she would have no trouble flying the aircraft, if she needed to. She also had very little doubt that if she was given even the slightest opportunity, she would act. She was going to have to be very careful, though, and wait for her chance. If she was patient, she knew it would come.

Within only a few minutes of takeoff, the storm blew away into clear, bright skies. And as the aircraft continued westward into the South American interior, Geli could see through the window next to her a seemingly endless stretch of dry brownish-gold scrubland, but then after several hours it gave way to a range of high grayish-colored mountains. And then on the other side of the mountain range a thick green carpet of tropical forest began. Geli guessed that they had now passed from western Argentina into the forests of eastern Chile. And as the aircraft began its descent she could see the thick forest open up and a large body of silver-gray water appear below the plane. A few moments later the aircraft's pontoon undercarriage settled down onto the surface of a large dark water lake hidden deep in the South American interior.

The pilot moved the aircraft skillfully across the surface of the lake, finally stopping it at a long metal pier that extended out from the forest, nearly a hundred meters into the water.

Geli looked out the window of the aircraft. She could see now that the lake was fed by a high silver waterfall to the east and emptied out into a series of rivers and streams to the west. It was late afternoon and the overhanging foliage blocked out much of the remaining light from the dark orange ball of the setting sun, but she could still make out the shapes of several ships tied into the pier and along a series of docks built at the water's edge.

There were a few barracks and warehouse buildings behind the pier and a small two-story headquarters building nearly buried in the tropical forest, about halfway up a short hillside behind it.

Goebbels walked by her, and without even pausing to speak, exited from the aircraft, with Gruening following closely behind him.

Geli stood carefully. There were guards with rifles standing on the pier, watching her every move, but as Gruening exited the aircraft, his broad shoulders brushed the aircraft's door and pushed it partially closed. For a moment Geli was blocked from the guards' view. This was her chance, she decided.

She sprang forward and removed the flight bag from the copilot's seat. The dark-haired young man was so busy with the controls that he didn't notice at first and Geli was able to unzip the bag and plunge her hand into it. The pilot turned to her then. Geli's hand moved through the papers and odd shapes until it came across the cold steel handgrip of a Luger. She removed the pistol from the flight bag and pointed it at the pilot. Would it be loaded? Geli could see instantly from the man's face that it was. She leapt to the cabin door and locked it. The pilot started to call out and Geli whirled and with the full force of her powerful body swung the side of the pistol in an wide arc and dashed it against the side of his head. The pilot sank to the floor. Geli pushed his body aside and took the controls. The engine was still humming. She pushed forward on the wheel. The aircraft rose slightly into the air, but then rammed hard against the edge of the pier. She twisted the wheel, pulling the restraining ropes free of their ties, and started the aircraft at full speed across the surface of the lake. Behind her the sound of automatic-weapons fire began and bullets ripped through the metal exterior of the plane's cabin.

Geli jerked the aircraft's stick back and drove the nose of the plane up at a vicious angle. Bullets tore into the side of the airplane and the plane began to swing violently from side to side. She knew that any more direct thrust upward with the unsteady fuselage could tear the fragile craft to pieces, but the end of the lake couldn't be very far ahead, and if she didn't get sufficient altitude soon, she would crash into the thick wall of forest that lay just outside its perimeter. She brought the stick back as far as it would go. The aircraft responded at first, climbing up even higher into the fierceness of the wind. But then more gunfire ripped into its tail section. Geli rammed the stick all the way forward then, but the craft failed to respond. She pulled back on the wheel with all of her strength, but the aircraft dove out of the sky and crashed into the surface of the water and she was jolted forward against the plane's front panel. For a moment she was dazed, but then she quickly unsnapped her restraining belt and started for the door to the cabin, stepping over the body of the pilot. She stopped only to pick up the black leather flight bag and to strap it over her shoulder.

She could smell smoke as she moved through the darkness to the compartment's exit door and crashed through it with her shoulder, falling onto the wing and rolling through the windswept air to its edge. She could see flames above her and big pieces of the fuselage breaking apart and sinking into the dark waters of the lake.

The aircraft rocked violently and tossed her to the very tip of the wing. She could hear gunboats cutting across the lake toward her. She slipped down into the dark water and began to swim. And once she was clear of the flaming wreckage, she spotted the shore. She swam for several minutes toward the dark wall of forest at the water's edge. Soon her feet could touch the silty bottom of the lake and she walked ashore. She unslung the flight bag from around her neck and sank to her knees, exhausted. She looked back at the spot only a few hundred meters away where the pontoon plane had gone down. There was very little to see now, except the lights of the arriving launches. The last of the burning aircraft was just sinking below the waves.

It would take her pursuers some time to determine that she was no longer on board. That was just the time she needed to make her escape, she thought, and she unzipped the flight bag. Just as she'd guessed, maps, a compass, food, a thick stack of currency, an entire survival package, and there was even a flight plan, which pinpointed her precise location. She would make it, she thought, looking back at the dark tropical forest that rose up behind her.

She rested for another moment and then lifted the flight bag and swung it over her shoulder. A few moments later she disappeared into the dense forest.

★   ★   ★

Debra hurried across the runway, her short, nicely turned legs moving smartly beneath the dark wave of her uniform skirt. She was aware of the stares of the nearby men. But she was too filled with expectation and excitement to think very much about it.

She looked over at Jill, who was moving with her through the light early morning mist on the runway and managed to smile. They were used to it, two attractive women in a world of men. Jill smiled back at her, but there wasn't time to slow their pace or even to exchange words. The others were already on board and the airliner's propellers were at full throttle.

The two women had traveled from Berlin and their plane had arrived in Lisbon several hours late. They knew that the Pan Am Clipper would not wait for them. There were long lists of people trying to get a place on this flight, or any flight out of Europe, and if they missed the departure, there was no telling when they would get another chance.

But their goal was in sight now and they hurried toward the long silver fuselage with the Pan American logo emblazoned on its side and then up the exterior ladder and down the aisle of the aircraft, just before the doors were closed and the exterior metal staircase wheeled away.

Debra buckled her seat belt around her narrow waist just as she felt the big airliner begin its powerful movement down the runway. She patted some of the morning mist off her dark red hair and looked over at Lowry, who was seated across the aisle from her, watching her with the same detached amusement that she remembered only too well from London. You would have thought that after more than a fortnight at Camp 19 there would be something new in the young officer's face and eyes, but Debra could see nothing there but the same smug complacency.

She turned her gaze to Stevenson. The elderly Scottish scientist was seated on the aisle next to Lowry. There were marks of change in Stevenson, though, Debra thought. His once supremely confident face looked hurt and confused.

Debra glanced out the window as the Clipper reached full runway speed and then burst into the air, heading immediately and directly west, toward a part of the world that she had never dreamed of visiting before, the Americas, the New World. How strange that her last thoughts on the old soil of Europe had been of Camp 19. She breathed in deeply then, committing herself once again to the job of keeping anything like it or Phoenix from ever spreading to the other side of the Atlantic.

Debra turned to Stevenson. He looked over at her with sad, weary eyes, but he wasn't so changed that he could forget greeting her with a few sharp words. "You were smart to get out of Camp 19 when you did," he said gloomily.

The words stung as they always did. Damn him, she thought. She had heard the same implications many times, so many different ways. She was a woman, a Jew, a German, and therefore she never had and never really would put herself on the line the way the rest of them would.

She wanted to tell him to go to hell, and she thought of her parents' Star of David that she had packed away among her personal things. She should take it out and wear it, wave it in Stevenson's face, she thought angrily, but she contained herself. There was Phoenix to consider. It was more important than her personal feelings and they all had to work together toward its defeat. "I would have been even smarter never to have gone out there in the first place," she said, forcing herself to smile and doing her best to deflect the blow.

Stevenson didn't return the smile and Debra unsnapped her restraining belt and stood up. She glanced around at the cabin, looking for Sheridan. She knew that it was unlikely, but she had still hoped that he might be on the flight.

"Tom will follow us in a day or so," Lowry said, standing up with her and guessing what was on her mind. "He got held up in London. Harkins asked him to make his case directly to Command before coming out."

Debra nodded her understanding, slightly amused at the discomfort that Sheridan would feel at making a report directly to all that brass. He would handle it well, though, she thought. He was always impressive in circumstances like that, as much as he disliked them.

"I see," she said, steadying herself against the seat back as the Clipper hit a pocket of unsteady air. "Stevenson looks like hell," she whispered, motioning briefly back toward the elderly scientist. "I don't think he's delighted with my presence here either."

Lowry nodded. "He thinks this whole trip is a waste of time."

They both turned toward the tail section of the aircraft, letting their bodies and the noise of the engines cut off any possible chance that anyone on the commercial flight could overhear their conversation.

"It didn't get any better at Camp 19 after you left," Lowry said then. "All we know for certain is that the stuff is one hell of a lot more lethal than we'd ever guessed."

Debra nodded. She'd been briefed about Stevenson's findings on the effects of Phoenix. "We finally just had to pack up and get out," Lowry continued. "They're still working hard at Hillborn, but they're not making any real progress there yet either. If the Nazis do manage to deliver Phoenix somewhere, we're practically defenseless against it. There's no telling the damage it could do."

They were both silent for a moment.

"It doesn't look like it's going to be the scientists that save us this time," Lowry added finally.

"Then maybe it will be us," Debra said, looking out the window of the Clipper. She had a strong sense that those questions that Stevenson and the others had about her—and that sometimes she even had about herself—of how she would perform when the stakes were high and a great deal was really on the line would be answered very soon.

# CHAPTER
# SIXTEEN

T he tide of death," the locals called it, and Debra could easily see why now, as the police launch approached the beach. It was Camp 19 all over again.

The last hundred meters of ocean between the outer reef that protected the shoreline of the bay was black with decaying sea life. Dead fish floated in the low tide, and the black water was spilling up over the narrow sand beach and had already begun to spread its death and devastation inland into the coastal jungle.

Immediately after their arrival in Buenos Aires, Jill and some of the others had begun to set up a temporary headquarters at the British embassy, while Debra, Lowry, and Stevenson had driven south to the small fishing village of Puerto Nueve on the Argentine coast.

The local constable, a big, dark-skinned man, had offered to take them out to the site of the shipwreck in the morning, but

Stevenson had insisted on seeing it at once. Reluctantly the constable had agreed, swearing angrily in Spanish at the freakishness of the summer storm that swirled around them as they traveled down the coast to the small blackened bay.

It was raining even more heavily now as the small police launch approached the shore and the blowing gray air filled with rain obscured Debra's ability to see the mainland clearly, but she had smelled the damp decay-filled stench coming from the coast for the last several kilometers. "The tide of death" was Phoenix. She had no doubt of it. And when she looked over at Stevenson's lined and deeply worried face, she knew that he had become convinced of it now as well.

The constable drove the launch to within a few dozen meters of shore and then cut the engine off and anchored the boat in the low tide. He started to swing his heavy body over the side into the water, but Stevenson reached out a hand and stopped him. "No," the elderly scientist said. "Captain Lowry and I will go. It's dangerous."

Lowry turned to Debra. "I'd like you to take a look at the wreck." He pointed out toward the reef. "And if this storm doesn't get too bad, search the coastline north of here. If you find anyone, make inquiries. Someone must have seen something."

Debra nodded her understanding. Then she waited while the two men pulled on their protective gear and stepped over the side of the launch into the shallow, blackish water.

"Give us a few hours here," Lowry called back to her. "We'll stay in touch," he added, patting the radio strapped to his pack.

Debra watched for a few moments as the two men waded through the black tide toward shore. She turned back to the constable and he slowly swung the police launch out to sea, cutting a sharp wake through the poisonous black tide.

Ahead of her through the thin curtain of rain, Debra could see objects floating on the surface of the water, trapped against the reef that ran roughly parallel to the shore, three or four hundred meters out to sea along the entrance to the bay. And as the constable brought the launch closer, Debra could make out what some of the objects were. There were splintered pieces of the hull of a ship, with them, debris that Debra knew at once were fragments of one of the gray metal boxes that she had seen at Camp 19.

The constable began to sweep the bow of the launch into what appeared to be the source of the debris bubbling up to the surface of the water.

"No," Debra called out over the intensifying sounds of the wind and rain. "No, don't. *Muerte,* death," she said, and then noted the spot along the reef where the surface of the water was the darkest and where the most wreckage had piled up along the outcropping of rock. She knew that the sunken ship lay somewhere beneath the water near that spot. But they would need equipment and trained personnel to deal with it properly. "Where could this ship have come from?" she asked in Spanish, pointing at some of the worst of the wreckage. "Is there some kind of a harbor, a port near here?"

"There is nothing, only a few fishing boats in Puerto Nueve!"

Debra looked from the debris-strewn reef up the coast. She knew from her study of maps of the area that nearly three hundred miles of coastline stretched in front of her, between here and Buenos Aires. And to the south was over a thousand miles of wild, rough, only sparsely populated Argentine coastal terrain. Finding anything in those miles of coast would be very difficult, but now they knew that at least some of the poisonous Phoenix materials had crossed the Atlantic and there could be a great deal more of it out there somewhere. She had to try.

209

"Let's take a look." Debra pointed north into the growing curtain of rain. And the constable swung the craft free of the reef and began his way up the coast.

Debra stood under the tarp that stretched across the bridge of the small police launch and watched the jagged cliffs on the shoreline. An hour went by and Debra had found nothing. Occasionally she would see a light or a shadow or a structure high up on one of the great walls of rock that rose up along the coast, or she would see a small cluster of fishermen's huts built into the protection of a small bay, but mostly there were only the great lonely rock cliffs washed with rain, and rolls of surf pounding over a seemingly endless coastline of narrow sand beaches. She knew that she should be turning back, but she hesitated to give the order.

The wrecked launch that had held the Phoenix microbes had to have come from somewhere, Debra thought. But where? She traced and retraced the coastline on the maps of the area that she'd obtained in Buenos Aires, but there was nothing, no clues of any kind to help her in her search.

The day was growing late. The rain was beginning to come down even harder than it had and the wind was blowing the gray-green surface of the sea in rising, turbulent waves, and she knew that she would have to turn back soon, but directly ahead the map showed a small bottleneck on the coast that led into the interior. It was a possibility, Debra thought. Just a few more kilometers, she decided.

Suddenly the radio mounted beneath the wheel of the ship began to crackle and Debra went to it and lifted the receiver to her ear.

"Lieutenant Marks." It was Lowry's voice crackling through the speaker.

Debra acknowledged Lowry's call and then waited.

"Return immediately to our location. Something important has come in."

Debra could hear the urgency in Lowry's voice. What could have happened? She didn't delay for an instant in her acknowledgment of the order. She would have to search the bottleneck later. Then she turned to the police constable and instructed him to return to Puerto Nueve.

As the launch began to make its turn in the rain-washed sea, Debra noticed high on the rock cliff above her a large red stone hacienda. "Who could live in such a place?" she called out to the constable.

"Europeans," the man answered with a hint of contempt. "A man named Heinreich and an old woman, his mother. They have been here for many years. Haters of the Nazis as you," the constable said, and then completed the turn of the launch, heading it back up the coast.

"I see," Debra said, storing the information away for further reference. A son and his mother who hated the Nazis could be a useful ally when she returned to complete her search of the area.

★  ★  ★

The Eastern DC-3 broke the clouds and Sheridan got his first look at the coastline of Argentina. It looked deceptively smooth and unbroken along this stretch of the northern coast, but Sheridan knew that as the coastline moved south it became ragged with inlets and coves, much of it spilling over with dense tropical foliage. Innumerable places for the Nazis to secretly land U-boats filled with boxes of Phoenix and then to resupply, refuel, and do whatever repairs were required to launch an attack against the east coast of the United States.

The stopover in London had been difficult. He had reported to a room full of one- and two-star generals. He had managed to convince them that the mission to South America was not entirely foolish, and to send a trained combat team into the area for his use if they did find something that deserved a closer look. But he could feel his own confidence shrinking now as he stared down at the start of the long desolate coastline. They were going to need one hell of a lot of luck to find anything down there.

It would take a fleet of ships and dozens of aircraft to search the area properly and they had only a limited amount of support available to them. How the hell would they ever find one small harbor in all that coastline? Sheridan asked himself as he continued looking out the window of the commercial flight that had taken him from Miami. Berlin to London, London to New York, and then hopping down the coast from New York to Miami in just over twenty-four hours, and now the final leg of quick-hops ending in Buenos Aires. And soon the great Argentine city appeared in the distance, up the Río de la Plata, a wide, sparkling blue waterway that stretched from the Atlantic westward into the continent, before it curved northwest past the city.

Sheridan could make out a cluster of central high-rises, visible through a faint shimmer of heat at the horizon line. Then Buenos Aires' large central harbor and the straight intersecting grid lines of its wide palm-lined boulevards came into focus as the plane grew closer. And Sheridan could see the great network of rail and internal roads and waterways that fanned out from the center of the city. Only Rio de Janeiro, to the north, near the center of Brazil, rivaled it for dominance of the continent's Atlantic seaboard.

It was a beautiful city from above, much of it newly minted and clean, barely touched by the horror and devastation of the European cities that he had just left. A new start, a new hope to get it better, Sheridan thought as the plane settled softly down onto one of the runways of the newly built airline terminal south of the city.

Sheridan was on his own in the Buenos Aires airport. He had requested no special treatment that might call attention to him. His cover story was thin as it was, he thought as he moved through the crowded terminal. Thomas Sheridan, a mining engineer from Colorado, in Argentina to explore business opportunities. And in order to look the part, he'd exchanged his field uniform for a lightweight khaki-colored suit, white shirt, and wide maroon print tie. It was the first time in nearly three years that he'd worn civilian clothes.

Buenos Aires was full of spies and counterspies, traitors and patriots. And Sheridan knew how much he stood out from the rest of the crowd despite his civilian clothes, a lone American male, and he could feel the eyes of a dozen officials and probably a dozen other freelance information peddlers and intelligence agents, both friendly and enemy, on him, as he proceeded through the busy terminal.

He waited for his bags at Customs. And when they arrived, he knew they had been thoroughly searched, but there would have been nothing to find. He had left anything even remotely suspicious in London, including his U.S. Army issue .45. He had given that up reluctantly, but he knew that if someone found it, it would only heighten suspicions about him. It made him feel even more vulnerable than he already did, though, plunging into the strange and dangerous new country without it.

Sheridan crossed the crowded terminal with his bags and entered into a warm, breezeless South American morning.

He took the first taxi in line and gave the driver the name of his hotel.

Sheridan sat in the back of the cab, his eyes carefully searching the traffic on the wide boulevard behind him. Once or twice he felt a hint of something wrong, something that shouldn't be there, maybe the gray sedan with darkly tinted windows that seemed to be following him at a distance, but it was impossible to know for certain in the crush of the big-city traffic.

The taxi passed by several low thatch-roofed resorts, sprawling across the beachfront, finally stopping at the El Mirador, a modern metal and glass high-rise located right at the water's edge.

Sheridan carried his own bags into the crowded, colorful lobby. Tourists and white-suited businessmen mixed in noisy animation inside the air-conditioned room. The large lobby was tropically decorated with bright colors of reds and golds. Palm trees, tropical plants, and potted palms stood everywhere, reflected against shiny metallic and mirrored surfaces. At the far end of the room, high glass windows displayed an enclosed tropical garden and a large blue-green swimming pool, surrounded by women in revealing bathing suits and darkly suntanned men. Sheridan stood for a moment in the center of the lobby taking it all in.

He went to the desk and checked in and then started toward the elevators. Suddenly he saw her across all the color and activity of the busy room.

Debra was seated at one of the small tables in the garden bar just outside the lobby's plate-glass windows. She wore a light tropical dress of pinks and deep emerald greens, cut low, but with a matching top covering her shoulders.

Sheridan crossed the crowded lobby, his eyes only on her, and walked outside to her table. It was warmer on the terrace, but a cool breeze from the sea lightened the air.

"You look awfully damn good as a civilian," Sheridan said, smiling at her as he approached the glass-topped table.

"You'd think that you'd never seen me without my uniform," Debra said, and smiled back slightly.

"That's not quite right," Sheridan said, and settled into a wicker high-backed chair across from her.

A dark-skinned waitress came and Sheridan ordered a rum and Coke. It came quickly, cool in a tall frosted glass.

"How was London?" Debra asked softly.

"It seems a million miles from this," Sheridan said, waving a hand at the sparkling blue-green swimming pool.

"I wish that were true," Debra said, and Sheridan could sense her deep seriousness.

"What is it?" he asked.

"Were you followed from the airport?"

"Probably. I couldn't pick them out for certain, but I think they were there."

Debra nodded her understanding. "It is Phoenix," she whispered. "Not six hours' drive from here." She pointed down the coast.

"God, how bad is it?" Sheridan breathed out, remembering the devastation he'd seen in the German river valley.

"Pretty bad."

"So the target is the U.S., then," Sheridan said tensely. "A total and final victory in one strike."

"It looks that way. And probably pretty damn soon."

"I suppose it could be another trick of some kind," Sheridan said. "Plant some of the poison out here so that we chase it, while they finalize their plans to strike somewhere else."

"I suppose it could be," Debra said thoughtfully. "But if it is a diversion, it's a very subtle and skillful one. What we found seems to truly be an accident of some kind. Wait until you see the site."

"I'd like to."

"There's something else first," Debra said, and removed an envelope from a leather case that lay by her chair and slid it across to Sheridan. "Something very important has come up. It may be just the break we need. You requested this from London."

Sheridan lifted the envelope off the table and opened it. Inside was a photograph of a beautiful young blonde woman. She was drinking champagne and was surrounded by high-ranking Nazi officers. "The woman from the Berghof," he said, guessing the truth at once.

"She is beautiful," Debra said, watching Sheridan's face carefully as he studied the photograph, but Sheridan didn't respond. He just continued looking at the photo and then began sorting through the remainder of the envelope's contents.

"It seems Command has quite a file on our mystery woman," Debra continued. "Her name is Angelique or Geli Von Stahl, a German aristocrat, an intimate of most of the Reich's High Command."

"Including Goebbels?"

"Including Reichminister Joseph Goebbels. And apparently at one time, even Adolf Hitler himself. It's all in there." Debra pointed at the long brown envelope.

Sheridan's eye turned again to the black-and-white image on the photograph. The woman could easily be the most beautiful woman that he'd ever seen, he thought—tall, slender, with long blond hair, a striking figure in a close-fitting white satin evening gown.

"She's here in South America," Debra said, breaking Sheridan's thoughts. "She's been in contact with one of our agents in the interior. She's in hiding, but she wants to arrange a meeting with a high-ranking Allied intelligence officer, preferably British or American. Harkins says that's you. She says that she's willing to exchange what she calls secret information for her personal safety."

"Safety from what?"

"From the Nazi network here in South America, I guess. I don't see how we can ignore it, do you?"

"No," Sheridan said. "I don't."

She handed a second, smaller envelope across the table to
Sheridan. Sheridan opened it. Inside it were two train tickets.

"It's been arranged," Debra said. "We're to leave for the interior tonight. A meeting, but entirely on her terms. We're to
check into the Hotel Central in a town called Neuguén. That's
nearly at the Chilean border. She will contact us there."

Sheridan looked up at Debra. He hesitated only for a moment
as his hands scooped up one of the two train tickets and placed it in
his inside coat pocket. But she knew what that hesitation meant.
Sheridan wouldn't question their orders, but the last damn thing
that he wanted was to be assigned a truly dangerous field operation
with her as his partner. She was going to have to prove herself now
even to Sheridan.

★   ★   ★

Goebbels stood on the dock of the secret base deep in the
Chilean jungle and watched the last of the pontoon aircraft settle
onto the surface of the dark lake.

Six aircraft, flying around the clock for two days and three
nights, stopping only for refueling and repairs. It had been very
difficult, but this was the last of them. And all had gone safely
and well.

Hundreds of long gray metal boxes of the poisonous material had been brought in from the transfer point on the Argentine
coast. Now all that remained to be done was to load the boxes
onto the assault ships and prepare the ships for departure. And if
all continued to go well, the ships would depart in less than two
days' time, and once they were under way, nothing would stop
them. They would each take separate routes through the maze of
Chilean rivers and waterways to the Pacific and then up the coast
to their targets on the unprepared southwest coast of the United
States. Before the enemy could mount a defense, San Diego, per-

haps even Los Angeles, would be devastated by tons of the poisonous microbes. Final victory was only days away now.

The last of the pontoon aircraft slid to a stop near the edge of the dock in front of him. And sailors working the docks tied it into the anchorage. A moment later the aircraft's hatch opened and Morell clumsily exited from it.

Goebbels greeted him with a sharp Nazi salute as the big overweight man crossed the dock toward him. Morell returned the salute. "All was done precisely as you ordered it," Morell said then. "There is nothing left in Puerto Nueve. The base has been destroyed. All aircraft and equipment dispersed or on their way here."

Goebbels nodded his acceptance of the report. "And Count Heinreich?"

"The hacienda, the count and his mother, the servants, all destroyed by fire, lost in the flames. Nothing remains of the base or the house," Morell said, and then looked around at the jungle enclave. "Is all well here?" he asked. "What of Miss Von Stahl? I understand there were problems."

"Nothing," Goebbels replied angrily, waving a black-gloved hand dismissively at Morell. "She escaped temporarily. But we will find her. And when we do, she will be killed, as she should have been long ago."

Morell nodded his understanding.

"And very soon now Phoenix will commence," Goebbels said. "And once it begins, nothing else will matter."

# CHAPTER
# SEVENTEEN

It had been hot and bright on the balcony of Sheridan's room at El Mirador, but the day's heat was fading now. He stood, his shirt off, feeling the last of the sun's warming rays on his chest, a cool rum and Coke in his hand. Across the busy street in front of the hotel, Sheridan could see the blue-green surface of the harbor.

In the distance the lights of the high-rises and the red and green neon of the city's nightclubs and cafés were just starting to glow against the evening sky. Sheridan stood and watched, drawing in deeply on his cigarette and letting the smoke pour from his nose and mouth.

Debra was up and moving across the room from the unmade bed and past the table stacked with discarded room-service plates and a half-finished bottle of wine.

She came to him and stood next to him, joining him in looking out over the slowly emerging South American night.

Sheridan turned back to her and held her long and hard, swinging her around in a powerful embrace, kissing her with all the passion of the lovemaking that they'd just enjoyed. The kiss meant something different, though, than the lovemaking had, letting her know that he felt more than one kind of passion for her, and when they broke, Debra buried her face in his chest for a long moment.

Sheridan could have stood on the balcony above the city and the river in the cooling night holding Debra next to him for days, but his eye caught a flicker of something over her shoulder and he broke the embrace.

"What is it?" she asked.

He pointed down to the boulevard in front of the hotel. A gray sedan had parked at the curb and two men in dark business suits had emerged. One walked into the front of the hotel. The other disappeared down a side alley.

"I think that's the car that followed me from the airport," Sheridan said, but Debra had already understood and she had returned to the interior of the hotel room and was quickly completing her dressing.

Sheridan came back into the room. Debra had tossed a small package wrapped in brown paper onto the unmade bed.

"That's for you," Debra said, and Sheridan bent down and picked up the parcel and unwrapped it. Inside was an American Army officer's standard-issue .45 and a package of shells.

"Harkins said to be sure you had one of these."

"What about you?" he asked, and Debra removed the Webley and its holster from her suitcase and strapped it on over her shoulder before she covered it with a short navy blue jacket.

Sheridan picked the pistol up, loaded it, and went back to the balcony. The mysterious gray car was just making another slow circle in front of the hotel.

"They're probably only trying to keep an eye on us," Sheridan said. "But it could be more than that."

Debra nodded. "Let's get out of here, I've got a car in the alley," she said, and Sheridan went to the door of the room and opened it slowly. The hallway was clear, and he motioned for Debra to follow him down the corridor past the elevators to the back stairs. They moved down several flights, but then Sheridan could hear the sound of heavy footsteps climbing up the uncarpeted staircase toward them. He motioned for Debra to follow him back into a hotel hallway and then to the entrance to the fire escape at the end of the corridor.

They clambered down the metal staircase and leapt the final few feet to the narrow dirty alley that ran behind the hotel.

As Sheridan hit the ground, he looked up at the entrance to the alley. There was a big man in a dark suit leaning against a back wall, waiting in the shadows. The man stepped out into the center of the alley, blocking their way.

Sheridan heard noises above him. He glanced back at the fire escape. Shadow figures holding guns danced downward in the fading light.

Debra was already running toward a beat-up convertible parked at the side of the alley. Sheridan began to follow, but suddenly the big gray embassy car slammed around the corner of the alley and began speeding at them. Sheridan raised his .45 and laid down a fast line of fire across the width of the alley.

The sedan's front window blew out, but there was a barrage of return gunfire from inside the car and then streaks of dangerous crossfire from the running man behind them.

Debra was the first to jump to the side of the alley as the speeding car roared toward her. The sedan sliced along the plaster wall, sending out bright metal sparks within only a few meters of where she lay.

The sedan continued on toward Sheridan, but the American agent dove headlong into the doorway just as a barrage of bullets slapped against the dirt of the alley where his diving body had been.

Sheridan lifted his head from the dirt floor of the alley just in time to see the running man stop and extend his revolver, locked in two hands in front of him, the barrel of the big pistol pointed at Sheridan's head.

There were several loud explosions. Bullets clipped against the plaster wall above Sheridan's shoulder and he returned the fire. The big man fell to the ground, the front of his dark suit a mass of spreading blackish crimson. Sheridan looked up to see the gray sedan trying to brake to a sliding stop, but its brakes weren't holding in the soft dirt and it slammed into the back wall of the alley and its impact swung it nearly in a circle. In another moment it would be headed back toward them. Sheridan stumbled to his feet and he and Debra sprinted down the alley and into the waiting convertible. Debra took the convertible's wheel and it sped out of the alley and onto the palm-lined street that ran in front of the hotel.

Sheridan watched the streets behind them as Debra skillfully turned the car down side roads and back alleys, until they arrived at the crush of traffic at the very center of the city and then they melted into the great jumble of downtown traffic and found the main rail station.

Debra parked the convertible on a dark side street. "I'll go first," Sheridan said, and stepped out onto the curb. He stood for a moment then, wanting to say something more to her, but he couldn't. They'd made their plans in the room and he would just have to trust her to do her job, he told himself again. He didn't like it at all, but that's the way it was and there was nothing he could do about it. So, without turning back to her, he moved inside the crowded early evening station. He glanced at his watch.

It was hours before he could board his train. He found a coffee stand where he could sit and watch the boarding passengers and ordered a beer and tried not to think about Debra.

The station was of soaring modernistic design, with great square rows of windows cut in its high domed center, and as it grew late, moonlight began filtering into the station through the cut-glass windows, bathing the cavernous interior in shadows. Sheridan drank the beer and smoked a cigarette and watched the shadowed activity swirl around him. He held his breath when he saw Debra moving with a small group of passengers down the platform.

Sheridan's eyes searched the crowd around her. Everything looked normal enough, but he knew that he couldn't be certain.

After she was safely on board, he continued nursing his beer and waited, still watching the crowd. When the hands on the station clock rose to nine, he left the table and crossed to the platform, where the train for the interior was making its final preparations for departure.

He mounted the steps to the first-class car and handed his ticked to the uniformed conductor.

The conductor led him to a small, private compartment and Sheridan locked the door after him. The intelligence agent removed his coat and threw it on the bed, but he left the .45 tucked into his waistband.

He went to the window of his compartment. He could feel the train beginning to gather strength beneath him and hear the steam hissing from its undercarriage. In another moment the platform would be left behind as the train pulled out of the station. But then suddenly he saw a flicker of movement, and two men, one in a light brown trench coat, dashed quickly from the shadows of the station and into the train, a single car ahead of his own.

Was it the men from the car in the alley behind the hotel? Sheridan didn't know. The train gathered force then and began to pull away into the night.

Sheridan's first instinct was to find Debra and to warn her, but he knew he couldn't. They had made very precise arrangements. They had a night and a half day of travel ahead, moving first south to the coastal town of Bahia Blanca and then west into the interior and their destination of the Argentine city of Neuguén. They had agreed not to speak or to acknowledge each other in any way until their arrival in Neuguén. He wouldn't change things if it were another agent, and he knew that as difficult as it was for him, he had to work the same way with Debra or he would only wind up putting them both into even greater danger.

So Sheridan arranged the compartment's only chair so that it was pointed at the window and sat down, his legs up, resting on the sill.

He was tired, but he didn't want to sleep. Instead, he lit another cigarette and smoked it as the train headed south through the outskirts of the city.

He remained at the window, smoking his cigarette and watching the city of Buenos Aires slip from the shiny new architecture of its downtown into the poorer, crowded suburbs, and then the train plunged through a long, dark tunnel. And as the train emerged on the other side, Sheridan watched the small shabby houses give way to scrubland and tropical forest along the edge of the tracks. And soon the darkness and the hard, steady rhythms of the train, and the deep fatigue inside his own body, rocked Sheridan into a deep sleep.

Nearly three hours later, he awoke with a start. It was still dark outside, but there were bright lights coming in the window of his compartment and someone knocking loudly on the glass.

Sheridan tried to shake the sleep out of his head and fumble for his pistol. He looked out the window. An old woman with a smooth dark-skinned face stood just outside. Sheridan started toward her, but as he did, the old woman dropped an envelope through the narrow opening at the top of the window and then she was gone.

Sheridan could see now that the train had stopped at a station platform. A clock above the station read a few minutes before midnight. Sheridan remembered then that the train had a brief final stop at Bahia Blanca, a small riverside resort town on the coast before it headed west into the interior.

Sheridan knelt and retrieved the envelope. Inside was a single slip of paper. It was a ticket for a steamship, the *Marianne,* leaving at midnight for Buenos Aires.

There was a blast of the train's horn. It was preparing to continue its journey. Sheridan looked out the window of his compartment. The passengers who had been on the platform were beginning to return to the train, but there was something more. On the far side of the small rail station was a short line of green-topped taxis. And there was a woman standing behind one of the cabs, watching him. She was a tall woman, with a slender, shapely figure. She was dressed in a tailored white linen suit and wearing a matching wide-brimmed hat that held her face in shadows, but Sheridan knew immediately that it had to be Angelique Von Stahl, the Geli of the Berlin photographs, an intimate of both Goebbels and Hitler. Very clever, he thought, both in anger and admiration, as he watched her duck into the taxi and the green-topped cab pull off down the crowded main street of the riverside town. Keep your opponent off guard. Surprise was a basic law of survival in this business and the German woman seemed to have learned how to do it well. She had never intended to keep the appointment in Neuguén. She would meet him only on her own terms. He looked again at the steamship

225

ticket in his hand. She was forcing him to make some very quick decisions. He scrawled a few words on a slip of paper outlining the change in plans and cupped the paper in his left hand. He went to the door of his compartment and started down the narrow corridor. He had to find Debra, but he could feel the train already beginning to move from the station.

He flew between cars, not knowing where he might find her. Suddenly he caught a hint of a man, maybe two, following behind him. One wore a brown trench coat and Sheridan remembered the blurred brownish shape that he had seen crossing the platform and entering the train in Buenos Aires.

Then in front of him he could see Debra moving with a clump of passengers, returning from the station platform to their compartments. He tightened his hand around the crumbled note as he pushed against the incoming passengers, until only Debra stood barring his way to the exit. He brushed by her, saying nothing, but he pushed the slip of paper into her hand as they passed. He could hear the sound of a scuffle behind him then, and Sheridan knew that Debra had understood at once that he was in trouble and was doing her best to block the narrow corridor. She was gambling that the men following him didn't recognize her. That could be a mistake, Sheridan thought, and he wanted desperately to turn back and help her, but he knew that he couldn't. Their mission was too important. It had to be completed, whatever the personal cost to either of them. And Debra was part of it now. It wasn't just his own life on the line anymore, but hers as well. It was one of the hardest things that he'd ever done, but instead of turning back he leapt from the train down onto the station platform.

Then he wove his way through the crowded station at high speed. He didn't look back until he reached the small terminal's central lobby. The man in the brown trench coat had just exited from the train. He was followed by another man. They stopped and looked around at the interior of the station. When they saw Sheridan, they started across the platform toward him.

Thank God, Debra had been right, Sheridan thought as he continued on through the terminal building and out onto the street that ran in front of it. The men hadn't recognized her. They were only interested in him. He slowed his walk then to blend into the street traffic.

It was Saturday night in a busy riverside resort town. Couples strolled along the promenade built along the town's river embankment just a few hundred meters away across a busy commercial street.

Sheridan crossed the street and melted even deeper into the crowd and then shot a quick glance behind him again just in time to see the two men from the train emerge on the sidewalk in front of the station.

Sheridan mounted the steps to the riverfront promenade. The raised boardwalk ran along the water's edge, its inland side lined with bars and cafés, shooting galleries, puppet shows, and all the noisy, glossy diversions of a busy resort town at full season.

At the end of a long promenade, Sheridan could see pleasure boats tied up to a wooden dock, and farther along past the smaller pleasure boats a large double-decked steamship was anchored. The steamship's gangplank was down and it was taking on passengers. As Sheridan looked, its whistle blew, indicating that it was ready for departure.

Sheridan could guess that it was the *Marianne* and that if he hurried, he might just be able to catch it. But behind him the two men from the train had mounted the steps to the promenade and stood less than fifty meters away, carefully searching the crowd.

Sheridan ducked into the first open doorway. Inside was a small dimly lit café. Through the smoky air, he could see a mirrored bar and above the bar, the crossed flags of Argentina and the Third Reich. More Nazi memorabilia littered the walls.

Sheridan could feel the eyes of nearly every person in the room on him as he moved through the smoke-filled interior and ordered a beer, using his best German accent. While he waited for his drink, he watched the door nervously and searched the rear of the café for a back exit in case the two men from the train had seen him duck into the café. He jumped when a sailor and his girl pushed their way into the dimly lit room. And as soon as the beer came, Sheridan placed an Argentine bill on the bar and then turned back to a table by the door.

Did he dare return to the boardwalk? The men from the train could still be searching the promenade for him. And there could be others. But Sheridan knew that he had to risk it. He couldn't afford to miss the steamship and be left with nothing.

He set his beer down on the table and walked as nonchalantly as he could out onto the boardwalk.

As he emerged back on the promenade, he heard a final departing blast of the steamship's horn. He looked down the raised walkway. The last of the passengers had boarded and the big ship was making its final preparations for departure. The two men from the train were nowhere in sight. Sheridan hurried his pace.

The gangplank was up when he arrived at the side of the ship, but he waved his ticket at the officer, who was standing in the bow, and then leapt from the dock up onto the deck of the big steamship. The officer took his ticket just as Sheridan could feel the ship beginning to pull out into the dark waters of the harbor.

Sheridan walked to the rail and lit a cigarette. He looked back at the lights of the riverfront town. He could see no sign of the men from the train, but Sheridan knew that he couldn't let down his guard. The Nazis apparently still had a formidable network of operatives in this part of the world and they were intent that he learn nothing about Phoenix, and perhaps they even knew about his meeting with the German woman and were trying to prevent it. There could be agents on board this ship, he realized, looking carefully around at the ship's passengers.

The ship sailed slowly past the train station. The tracks were empty. The train had long since disappeared down the dark railroad tracks to the west of the town toward its destination in the interior. Was Debra still on it? Was she safe? There was no way for Sheridan to know. And he felt a wave of fear pass through him, but he knew that he had to continue to concentrate on his own situation. For the moment it was the only part of the puzzle that he could really do anything about.

And he began to carefully study the details of the steamship that was returning him back up the coast of Argentina. It was a gambling ship, the outline of its smokestack, rails, and superstructure strung with bright gaudy Christmas tree lights of red and gold. Fashionably dressed men and women strolled its decks. The men dressed mostly in dinner jackets, the women in elegant formal dresses in springtime colors of white and pastel pinks, light greens and soft yellows. The purpose of the ship was obviously strictly pleasure. It would arrive in Buenos Aires in the morning after a slow trip up the coast.

There was an orchestra playing softly and light strands of rhythmic South American music floated up onto the deck, and Sheridan moved from the rail in the direction of the sound.

He looked for Angelique Von Stahl among the elegantly dressed passengers, but he didn't really expect to find her. She was in control now and in all likelihood she would find her own way to contact him.

Sheridan passed down a glittering mirrored corridor and into a beautiful interior salon. There were linen-draped tables surrounding a dance floor, and mounted on a stage above the floor was a large formally dressed orchestra, and at the far end of the room a long chrome and glass bar and bright green felt gambling tables.

Sheridan moved through the crowded room to the gleam-
ing chrome bar and ordered a rum and Coke. He hadn't been
drinking it long when a steward appeared behind him.

"Señor Sheridan?" the steward asked cautiously.

Sheridan nodded and the steward extended an envelope.
The American took it and then returned with it to the deck before he opened it. Inside was a key with the number 18 printed
on it.

Sheridan moved down the steps to the lower deck and then
down the ship's gleamingly bright corridor to the cabin marked
18. He stopped for a moment outside the door and removed his
.45 from the waistband of his pants. Then with his left hand he
inserted the key into the lock and opened the door.

The room was dark, but Sheridan could make out the figure of a woman standing by the cabin's only porthole.

"Come in," the woman said in German.

Sheridan moved into the room as the woman stepped from
the shadows into what little light there was in the small cabin.

Now Sheridan could see how incredibly beautiful she was.
She was tall and her long blond hair fell down her back beneath
her shoulders and he could see the taut shape of her powerful
body under the tight-fitting white linen suit that she wore. It
was definitely the woman from the photograph and she was
even more beautiful in person, and far more deadly as well,
Sheridan thought as he noticed that she held her right hand just
out of sight behind the curve of her hip. Sheridan was certain
that the hand held a small pistol and he could guess from the
confident way that she held it that she knew precisely how to
use it.

"You wanted to see us," Sheridan called into the dark room.

The slender woman said nothing for a long moment. Sheridan could feel the rocking of the ship beneath his feet, hear the

rhythmically sensual South American music from the salon and the sounds of gambling from the ship's casino.

"Are you alone?" the blonde woman asked finally, speaking again in German. She stepped forward then. And Sheridan's hand tensed on his .45 as the woman's right hand swung out away from her body, but then she dropped the small-caliber pistol that she had been holding onto the table in front of him.

"His people are everywhere," she said, and Sheridan heard what he believed to be real fear in her voice. "They are here on this ship. They may even try to kill us before the night is over, or surely when we try to go ashore tomorrow in Buenos Aires. They will do anything to stop our meeting."

"Why would anyone want to do that?" Sheridan said, locking the cabin door behind him and moving carefully into the woman's cabin.

Slowly he began relaxing his hold on his pistol, but even as he did, he continued watching the woman's movements very carefully. He'd be damned if he'd let her beat him again, he told himself angrily.

"They fear for their precious operation and I know everything," she said. "I know their plans. I know their weaknesses. I even know how they can be stopped."

"Tell me," Sheridan said.

The blonde woman lit a cigarette. "I will need protection and long-term safety. I need to have your government promise me that."

"No, I can't make any promises," Sheridan said. "All I can do is try to get you safely back to our embassy in Buenos Aires. And then I can get you to someone who can make a decision about the future. But that's all I can do, and I can only do that if I think your story is really worth as much as you say it is."

"It is," she said softly.

Sheridan nodded. "Then tell me."

The blonde woman sat silently for a moment, considering Sheridan's terms and slowly smoking her cigarette. "All right," she said finally, and then began. "Have you ever heard of something called 'Phoenix'?"

# CHAPTER
# EIGHTEEN

Sheridan stood at the railing of the steamship looking back at the curl of churned-up white water that the powerful ship was leaving in its wake.

It was less than an hour to dawn and the ship's arrival in Buenos Aires. Would there be people waiting there to kill both him and the German woman? Or were there assassins already on board somewhere ready to attack at any moment?

He was moving ahead into danger and he could have no assurance of what the outcome would be. The thought made him tense and made his stomach move uneasily, but he was confident that he would perform well once the action began. It was just the damn waiting.

He flipped his cigarette overboard and watched it wash away in the dark water. He turned back and looked at the ship itself. Its decks were empty, the bright lights turned off, the music of the night before silent and the revelers gone to bed.

Sheridan was left alone to consider the enormity of the woman's story. Could it be believed? If it was true, it changed so damn much and Command had to know about it as soon as possible. Goebbels alive, just as he and Debra had suspected, and mounting his final attack, not from the Argentine coast, but from a secret staging area deep inside Chile. Sheridan thought again of the details of the map and flight plan that the woman had given him to help prove her story. Goebbels' staging area in the Chilean interior had direct access down a series of rivers to the Pacific Ocean. From there the lower west coast of the United States lay open and vulnerable to his attack. Whatever defensive assets that Command had at its disposal had to be moved from the east coast to the west and they had to be moved quickly. That is, if the German woman was telling the truth. And her story was full of so many small true pieces, things that he'd confirmed for himself at Berlin and Berchtesgaden. But still he couldn't be certain. There was only one way to know absolutely. If he survived the next few hours, he was going to have to mobilize the combat team that Command had placed at his disposal and go into Chile and take a look for himself. For the moment, though, none of that mattered, he thought, and threw his cigarette over the railing. First, he had to get both the woman and himself safely back to Buenos Aires. And that was going to be damned hard enough to do all by himself.

He walked back belowdecks to cabin 18.

The lights were off inside the room. And Sheridan could see the scattering of woman's clothing thrown over the chair next to the window.

Angelique Von Stahl lay naked across the bed, beautiful and inviting in the cabin's half-light. Her long blond hair was thrown back and draped across the pillow, her rose-tipped breasts tilted up seductively toward him, her long, white silky legs parted, leaving just enough room for Sheridan to slip between them. "I'm frightened," the exquisitely beautiful woman breathed as she slowly raised her tantalizing body up, offering it to Sheridan. "Protect me, Major," she whispered. "Take care of me."

Sheridan crossed the room to her and sat on the edge of the bed, barely thinking of what he was doing.

He reached out and held her in his arms, her naked breasts pressed up against his shirtfront. He could feel her body trembling in his embrace. He could smell the intense smell of powder and perfume and beautiful women that he had sensed only a hint of at the Berghof. "You do believe me, don't you?" she whispered. "Everything that I've told you?"

He could feel his hands running over the sides of her naked body to her tight bare hips. He bent to kiss her and he looked down into her sapphire-blue eyes, beautiful but cold as ice. And then he stopped. An image passed across his consciousness, an image of Goebbels, perhaps even Hitler himself, making love to the woman who lay naked beneath him now. And Sheridan froze, his hand becoming like stone on the warmth of the woman's body. He turned away from her then and stood. He went to the cabin door. "An hour to dawn," he said through a thickly filled throat. "I'll be back then."

He returned to the ship's steps and stood again on the windswept deck. He went to the rail and used his lighter to light another cigarette. He only then noticed that his hands were shaking. He was a damn fool, he thought. Men were supposed to take whatever they were offered. And he remembered again the naked beauty of the woman's body, but then her words returned to him as well. "You do believe me?" she'd asked. And the doubt that he'd felt about her earlier intensified. She was trying too hard, Sheridan thought. Or maybe she just seduced every man that she met. Sheridan took a long draw on his cigarette and let the smoke out slowly into the cool air of the morning. Or maybe he was just that damn irresistible? He laughed at himself then. He'd been around women long enough, he thought, to at least eliminate that possibility.

★ ★ ★

Sheridan waited, watching the departing passengers move by the corridor outside cabin 18. He had hoped that Debra might have found some way to dispatch help to him, but there was nothing. And he was running out of time. He was going to have to move now, before the last of the passengers departed and he and the German woman were left alone and vulnerable.

"All right," Sheridan said, and he could see the fear in Geli's eyes as she moved toward the door. She knew the stakes they were playing for as well as he did. Over the next few minutes their lives would be directly on the line.

"My pistol," she said, anger and fear coming through in the hard edge of her voice.

Sheridan thought for a moment, wavering in his decision. Two guns would be far better than one in what lay ahead, he thought, but she was his prisoner, not his partner, and he would play it out that way, remembering his suspicions of the night before. "No," he said as he reached down and picked up the pistol from the table and dropped it into his own coat pocket. "Just stay close to me."

He stepped out into the ship's corridor then. He could feel Geli moving behind him. And despite the wall of anger between them, she seemed to know instinctively how to survive and she did precisely as he had instructed her and stayed at his side as they moved down the ship's corridor. Sheridan's stomach and chest were knotted with expectation. The enemy could be anywhere. The next few minutes, the short trip up the stairs, across the crowded deck, and down the gangplank would be some of the most dangerous moments of his life.

He pulled Geli even closer. He could feel her soft full breasts pushed against him as they started up the steps to the main deck. Sheridan's other hand was deep in his coat pocket, his fingers wrapped around his .45.

He saw something that he didn't like almost immediately when they came up into the early morning sunlight of the upper deck. There were two European men in dark business suits standing slightly apart from the rest of the passengers, watching the crowd carefully. The men from the train, Sheridan realized in a flash.

He didn't hesitate. He moved his prisoner, guiding her back down the staircase. As he did, he glanced at the men who stood by the railing. One of them had moved into the crowd and was pressing forward toward him.

"Come on," Sheridan called out, and the German woman ran with him across the long, belowdeck corridor into the deserted ballroom. The salon was empty, the gambling tables covered, and empty champagne bottles and used glasses stood on soiled linen-draped tables and along the shiny chrome bar.

They threaded their way through chairs and tables and across the confetti-littered dance floor toward the salon's rear exit.

Near the door, Sheridan heard a noise behind him. He turned to see one of the dark-suited men from the main deck.

The man had a raised gun pointed at Geli. Sheridan turned and dove at the legs of the blonde woman, knocking her to the floor, just as a bullet splintered a champagne bottle on the table next to her and a rush of golden liquid poured out across the white linen-draped table.

Sheridan removed his .45 from his waistband, moved up on one knee, and fired at the gunman. The man ducked behind a row of tables, turning one of them over, spilling glasses and bottles onto the floor.

Sheridan began moving quickly in a half-crouch around the perimeter of the room, staying below the line of empty tables. Hearing an explosion and a bullet impact against the chair next to him, Sheridan turned to the sound and fired his own pistol. The dark-suited man tumbled forward, overturning tables and glassware.

Geli was already running at full speed toward the ballroom's rear exit. Sheridan followed after her. They sprinted down the lower-deck corridor and then up the back staircase.

When they reached the main deck, Sheridan pushed his way ahead of her. There was a panic caused by the gunshots. Passengers were fighting to exit down the ship's gangplank.

Sheridan took the woman by the hand and plunged into the crowd. He could hear screams and shouts of confusion. Then ahead of him he saw a small group of people making their way up the gangplank toward him. One of the oncoming figures Sheridan recognized as Lowry. He felt a stab of relief. Debra had managed to get him some help. But then he felt his prisoner tug on his shoulder and he turned to see the dark-suited companion of the gunman pushing his way through the rear of the crowd. The man was coming fast, scattering the frightened passengers as he moved toward Sheridan. There were screams as the man cut his way through the confusion. Sheridan pulled Geli after him. They were nearly at the gangplank, but there were still several people ahead of them, blocking their way.

Sheridan raised his weapon and spun back to the gunman. The man was just emerging from the crowd. Did he dare risk a shot in the middle of all these people? Sheridan hesitated and in that moment the gunman freed himself from the other passengers and raised his own weapon and pointed it at Geli.

Sheridan felt one body brush by him and then a second. A figure leapt into the space between the gunman and the German woman, blocking the assassin's line of fire. It was Debra.

Sheridan had only enough time to briefly feel the horror and loss of what he was witnessing, and in that moment he saw the flash of the gunman's pistol.

Sheridan dove forward, knocking the dark-suited man onto the deck. The man's pistol fired again, but Sheridan smashed his fist into the man's wrist and the pistol fell to the edge of the gangplank.

Someone grabbed Sheridan by the shoulder and lifted him back off the gunman's fallen body. "Get out of here. We've got this bastard." Sheridan turned and saw Lowry. He was pointing down at a waiting car parked on the Buenos Aires dock.

Sheridan pushed his way through the crowd of bodies. As the crowd cleared away, he could see Debra hurrying Geli down the gangplank toward a waiting staff car. Behind Debra, the railing of the ship was splintered and broken where the gunman's bullet had smashed into it, missing both women by only inches.

# CHAPTER NINETEEN

Sheridan followed the two women down the gangplank. There was a second waiting dark sedan parked behind the car that Debra and Geli entered. The driver of the second car motioned to Sheridan and he slid into its front seat.

The two cars made a fast-paced caravan from the harbor across town to a quiet tree-lined residential street at the south of the city.

A three-story, colonial-style building buried in tall trees stood behind an iron gate. A small bronze plaque at the front of the gate identified the building as the British embassy.

There was a uniformed guard at the outer gate and another at the embassy's front door. Two more guards met Debra's car as it pulled up at the center of the wide circular drive built at the front of the embassy building. The guards escorted the German woman inside. Debra turned and approached Sheridan as he exited from the trail car.

"You all right?" Sheridan asked, and Debra nodded.

Sheridan stood for a moment looking at her, saying nothing. He could feel the anger inside of himself, but he could feel something else now as well. He felt strangely proud of her. Something had happened to him in that moment on the ship's gangplank when he had seen Debra place herself directly in the line of fire. She had performed with courage and effectiveness. It wasn't a game with her either, he realized then. She was as deadly serious about defeating Phoenix as he was. And no one had earned the right to be in the fight any more than she had. He could only imagine the dangers that she'd had to overcome even to arrive back in Buenos Aires in time to help him.

"Rough night?" he asked finally, using the same respectful toughness and understatement he would have used with Harkins or with a small handful of fellow soldiers that he had fought side by side with over the last few years.

Debra smiled, understanding. "There were some bad patches," she said, answering with the same understated code of the fellow soldier, but then Sheridan stepped toward her and they held each other close for a long moment, breaking the soldier's protocol with the power of their even deeper feelings toward each other.

Finally they broke the embrace and Debra turned from him and led Sheridan inside the embassy building to a large room dominated by a long dark wood conference table.

"What did she tell you?" Debra motioned back toward the embassy steps where they had last seen the German woman.

"One hell of a lot. It could be the break we've been looking for. I'll show you," Sheridan said, spreading out the map and flight plan that Geli had given him across the long oak conference table.

"Her story," Sheridan began, "is that Goebbels is still alive; both the body in the bunker and the one at the Berghof were only doubles, just as we suspected. And he's running Phoenix even now. She says that she's seen the staging area that he's using to launch the attack, but it's not on the Atlantic Coast at all. It's here." Sheridan put his finger down on the map near the west coast of the South American continent, deep in the tropical forests of Chile. "She says that she was flown from Europe to a location on the central coast of Argentina below the Gulf of San Matias, nearly a thousand miles south of Buenos Aires, but it was only a transfer point. From there, she and Goebbels were taken inland to the final launching or staging area in Chile. And look." Sheridan pointed at the map again. "If she's telling the truth, from there a squadron of intermediate-size ships could move west through Chile on this network of rivers and waterways"— Sheridan traced the area with his fingers—"and be in the Pacific within a day or two. The lower west coast of the U.S. would be wide open to attack. The United States is the target, but we were dead wrong about the rest. It's the Pacific coast, not the Atlantic, that's in danger."

"What about Puerto Nueve and the shipwreck?" Debra asked.

"If she's telling the truth," Sheridan said, "it's meaningless, probably just another diversion. The shipment of Phoenix materials from Camp 19 was landed at a transfer spot somewhere on the central coast below the Gulf of San Matias, over five hundred miles from the shipwreck and then immediately shipped into Chile. If we believe her, what we saw at Puerto Nueve was just a decoy. But God knows how much of this is true. I don't know yet whether to trust any of what she's said or not."

Debra shook her head in desperation. "We'll begin her interrogation at once," she said. "But it could take days to find out the truth."

"I know," Sheridan said. "And I can't wait for you to find it. Phoenix could be launched at any moment. I've got to go in there now."

★ ★ ★

Sheridan listened to the low steady drone of the C-147. He could feel his heart beating fast. They were almost at the drop zone now and Sheridan wasn't surprised by the tense feeling in his chest. There was always tension before a jump.

His men, as good as they were, would be feeling it too. There was only one cure for it. Make the jump and do it as skillfully as it could be done.

He stood then and walked over to the metal racks built into the rear bulkhead of the plane and pulled out his chute and hoisted it up onto his back and then buckled its straps tightly into place around his chest and waist.

No one had said anything about him jumping first, but it was the way it should be done, he thought. These men knew each other well, but they had no idea about their new leader. And he went to the lead line and belted his chute onto the very front of it—a small gesture, he thought, but a necessary one.

He didn't look back at the other seven members of the squad, nor did he issue an order to them to begin their final preparations, but he knew that he didn't have to: he could hear them moving into position behind him. The rest of the squad had all been together in Europe for the last two years. They had seen plenty of action and they would perform well when the time came, Sheridan thought. He didn't have to worry about them. The operation was sound as well. They'd had plenty of time to go over it and work out the details during the long flight. But what worried Sheridan the most was the limited intelligence available to them. What they had was based entirely on the German woman's story. He hated going into something as dangerous as this operation without some kind of secondary confirmation, but given the circumstances, he knew that was impossible. They would just have to take their chances. They'd know the truth soon enough, he thought, and slid the buckle of his chute along the safety line to the edge of the exit door.

A few seconds later the copilot came out from the cockpit and crossed toward him. Sheridan knew what that meant. They were over the jump zone. "Okay?" the copilot called out, and Sheridan nodded and then waited while the copilot pulled the exit door open.

Cold air rushed into the interior of the aircraft and Sheridan braced himself against its force as he fought his way forward and took a powerful jump up and out.

The chute opened and he dropped through a layer of cloud cover. He could see the ground below him, a large cleared field surrounded by thick forest with a narrow dark thread of winding river valley beneath it. He looked above him then, to where a half dozen dark figures were dropping through the clouds, just as it had been planned.

A moment later he felt the impact on the ground and tumbled to his side, the chute billowing out around him, until he could catch it in his arms and unstrap it.

The assembly went like clockwork as well and within minutes the eight men started into the thick forest toward the winding river valley.

Suddenly Sheridan dropped to one knee on the forest trail. He could sense danger ahead. He raised his hand in the air and then lowered it sharply, signaling for his squad to seek cover.

He raised his automatic weapon and rested it for a moment at an angle across the front of his chest at the ready.

There was a strange presence out there in the darkness. Sheridan quickly reviewed the plan. There should be nothing here, nothing or no one for several more miles.

Sheridan called out the sign, pronouncing it carefully in Spanish. Then he waited a long tense moment until the counter-sign floated back across the night air.

Sheridan stood then and carefully advanced into the thick forest. A figure approached him from out of the shadows.

It was a young man not more than eighteen, slightly built but with a very big automatic weapon slung over his shoulder.

"My name is Ramón," the young man said, and looked at Sheridan with great dignity, as if he expected the American to say something about his youth. Sheridan was surprised, but he said nothing. They would be lost in this country without a local, even one as young as this boy, Sheridan thought, looking around at the dense forest.

"I brought the boat upriver," Ramón said. "There were patrols at the location near the bend where we were to meet."

"Patrols?"

"Yes," the young man said. "From the camp."

Sheridan removed the map from his pack and pointed to the place that the German woman had told him was the secret Nazi staging area for Phoenix.

"Yes," Ramón said, nodding at Sheridan. "There are men there. I have never seen the camp. No one has, but we know there are Germans there."

Sheridan felt a surge of hope. There was his confirmation. And he felt then that he was finally moving toward the very heart of Phoenix.

★   ★   ★

Debra looked across the table of a small upstairs room at the British embassy in Buenos Aires into what were at once the most beautiful eyes that she had ever seen and also, perhaps, the most chilling. She had risked her own life to help save this woman and yet she had received not even the smallest flicker of gratitude from her, only the unrelenting, coldly beautiful stare.

The small upstairs room had been converted into an interrogating room, and experts and high-ranking officers from all over the area had been brought in to listen to and question Angelique Von Stahl.

And Sheridan had been right: if they believed her, it changed everything. Changed Command's entire strategy for defending against Phoenix from an east coast to a west coast defense and either saved or put at even greater risk tens, maybe hundreds, of thousands of lives, to say nothing of the longer-term potential for an even greater disaster. And Debra could tell from the faces of the men in the room that they did believe her, believed her words, believed in her beauty, her vulnerability. But Debra didn't. It had been something in her story, some small piece among all the convincing details that the woman had supplied, that had tripped her up. Debra couldn't quite bring the mistake into focus yet, but it had been there. She was certain of it. Debra knew, though, that she had to be careful. She couldn't let her feelings of loathing for this woman color her judgment as to whether she was telling the truth or not. The stakes were far too high for that.

General Nelson was breaking the session now. The big white-haired general was the senior man not only in the room but in the entire South American area.

Debra let the others wander out into the hallway, until she was left alone in the small room with just Angelique Von Stahl and a single uniformed guard.

"You don't believe me, do you?" the blonde woman said very quietly as she lit a cigarette and slowly wreathed the first breath of smoke out around her face and shoulders.

"It will be looked into," Debra said, returning the other woman's coldness. "But if something goes wrong . . ." Debra started, but then didn't finish her threat.

The German woman didn't break her cold, expressionless stare, and Debra could see that she didn't believe her warning. Debra searched inside herself and knew that the German woman was wrong, for Debra truly had the anger and the power to keep her threat.

"I think you're lying," Debra said into the other woman's hard cold eyes. "I don't know why yet, or precisely where the lies are in your story, but I know that you're lying."

"You know nothing," the German woman said. She had totally dropped now the mask of seduction and vulnerability that she had used with the room full of men, and Debra knew that she was looking at the real Angelique Von Stahl now, not a frightened, vulnerable woman fighting for her survival that she had portrayed to the others, but a cunning, manipulative woman, very much in control of what was happening to her.

"I think you lied to us and I think very soon that I will know why."

"I think not," Geli said, and began to laugh.

Debra stood for a moment, looking across the room at her, saying nothing. Then she turned and started into the hallway, but Geli's voice stopped her.

"Lieutenant Marks," the German woman said. "It is already too late for you and for Major Sheridan."

Debra refused to turn back. Instead she moved into the hallway and closed and then locked the heavy oak door after her. But she could hear Geli's laughter of scorn echoing in the hallway through the thick wooden door. "It is already too late," the German woman called out again.

★　★　★

Sheridan nodded, approving the change in plans that Ramón had requested, and the young man led him down an embankment and uncovered from the shadows of a narrow riverbed a small light boat about twenty meters in length with an outboard engine attached to it in the stern. A perfect craft, given the conditions, Sheridan thought, looking downstream. It would be fast and highly maneuverable, although it would take great skill to operate in the shallow, fast-moving, rock-filled channel.

Ramón took the tiller, and the single engine mounted at the craft's stern started easily. Soon the entire squad was on board and the strangely built seacraft was headed downstream at high speeds, just barely avoiding the river's treacherous rocks and bends.

After a few kilometers the channel opened out into a wide turbulent river. And finally there was a break in the dense forest. In the distance Sheridan could see a set of lights of a small town and above him he could make out the shape of a pale, nearly full moon. He removed the map from inside his uniform shirt and spread it out below him.

"We are not far," Ramón whispered, and pointed ahead to where the jungle closed in again on both sides of the river.

The launch wound its way downstream for several more minutes, until Sheridan could feel the powerful pull of the current beneath the craft increase to a furious pace. It was all Ramón could do to pull the craft into the shallow water at the edge of the river. Ahead lay a tumbling wall of white water, a great roaring waterfall that fell hundreds of meters into the forest. And the squad moved from the craft across the forest to the edge of the falls.

Sheridan dropped to his belly at the rocky edge of the great tumbling sheet of silver-white water. All he could hear was the roar of the cascading falls, its ice-cold water splashing across his face and shoulders.

He removed his night binoculars from his pack and looked through them. He could see below him the enormity of the high, sharp rock cliff and beneath the cliff, a short sand beach rimming a great dark water lake. And then there it was, a temporary encampment built near the far perimeter of the lake with ships and pontoon aircraft bobbing at a series of wooden docks built along the water's edge.

The ships were of intermediate size. Small enough, Sheridan guessed, to navigate the river passageways that led from the lake through the South American continent to the Pacific Ocean, but large enough to then move up the Pacific coast and deliver Phoenix directly onto the U.S. mainland. He brought the focus of his glasses down across the surface of the water toward the lake's far side, until he saw a long steel pier, protruding out for several hundred meters into the water. There were lights illuminating the pier and the temporary warehouse buildings standing behind it. And as he watched, men in black uniforms carried gray coffinlike boxes onto one of the ships.

He'd found it and it was precisely as the German woman had described it. It was the final staging area for Phoenix, and from the look of it, he'd been right: the enemy was only hours away from launching its final attack.

But there was only a moment to consider what he'd seen, because as the brightly lit pier came into focus, there was a sound nearby, very close. The sound of men approaching and barking dogs moving rapidly through the underbrush toward where he and his squad lay in the open at the top of the cliff.

★ ★ ★

Debra awoke suddenly in the middle of the night. There were sounds in the embassy's upstairs corridor. She sprang to her feet and removed the Webley from its holster on the chair next to her. A rush of adrenaline brought her even more alert as she felt the heft of cold steel in her hand, and she ran to the door of her room.

There was gunfire in the hallway. She swung the door open and looked down the darkened corridor. There was more gunfire and figures running at the end of the hall. She sprinted toward the sounds, the Webley in her hand. She stopped when she saw a figure lying on the floor below her. It was one of the embassy guards, the one assigned to the German woman's room. Debra ducked her head into the bedroom where the prisoner had been held. It was empty. She could hear more gunfire in the downstairs landing. Debra ran back to the corridor and then down the staircase. A second guard lay dead at the center of the first-floor entrance.

She sprinted down the front stairs and outside. Just past the reach of the embassy's floodlights, figures were running through the darkened grounds. Debra saw a flash of long blond hair. One of the running figures was the German woman. There was a man next to her, and he appeared to be moving her along at gunpoint.

Then on the street in front of the embassy, Debra could see a dark sedan speeding toward the embassy's front gates.

An embassy guard knelt by the gate firing at the oncoming sedan. A return of gunfire came from inside the speeding car. The guard toppled to the ground, and then the sedan burst through the double iron gates, leaving behind a tangle of twisted metal. In another instant the running figures reached the vehicle and disappeared into its rear seat.

By the time that Debra was able to cross the embassy grounds to the twisted remains of its front gate, the dark sedan with the German woman inside was speeding down the treelined boulevard in front of the embassy. And then it turned a corner and was gone. What was happening? Debra asked herself as she watched the sedan speed off into the night. One thing was clear, Goebbels had regained his edge over them. He had to have been the one to have engineered the kidnapping. But why? Debra knew that she was probably supposed to believe that Goebbels had taken Geli to find out what she had told them about Phoenix. And if that was true, he would have her taken somewhere now and interrogated. And once he'd learned what he could, Goebbels would have no more use for her. And before the night was over Angelique Von Stahl would in all probability no longer be alive. But Debra was far from certain whether the kidnapping that she had just witnessed or any other part of Phoenix was real or just another trap and illusion created by forces that she didn't yet fully understand.

# CHAPTER
# TWENTY

Sheridan's first instinct was to freeze, to dig deep into the earth and hope that he and his people would not be seen, but in the next instant he found himself issuing the prearranged arm and body commands and he watched as each member of his squad melted away into the darkness at the edge of the forest. Even Ramón, the young man who had been at his side just a moment before, was suddenly gone, vanished into the darkness.

Sheridan began his own low crawl, moving toward the protection of the dense forest only a few dozen meters away, but before he could move even a single meter across the barren hillside, he heard a low fierce growling and looked up into the glowing yellow eyes of a huge guard dog, its teeth bared. It was crouching, pulling the power into its hind legs for the spring forward toward Sheridan's throat. There was no room for even the slightest mistake, Sheridan knew as he raised his weapon. The fierce animal sprang forward, lunging at him, and Sheridan fired at the same moment. Claws flailed at the flesh of Sheridan's arms, and he felt the lunging weight of the beast impact against his shoulder. He fired again and the animal's side split open and blood poured from the wound. The heavy lunging body went lifeless and collapsed onto the ground in front of him.

There was more gunfire then and Sheridan looked up to see two uniformed guards and a second vicious dog caught in a torrent of fire coming from the forest. One guard fell backward, hurtling over the side of the cliff, hundreds of meters to the hard-packed sand at the edge of the lake. The other guard sank to his knees, his automatic weapon firing hopelessly into the darkness. The final victim was the second guard dog, falling by the feet of its master.

There was a moment of silence, but in an instant Sheridan began issuing a new set of hand and arm instructions. They had to go in now. Any delay and it might be too late. The roar of the falls would have blocked out the sound of the gunfire, but surprise was their only real ally, and once the main garrison knew that two of their guards were missing, it would no longer be on their side.

The squad executed their preparations for the descent calmly and quickly. Within a few minutes two rope lines were set and the men began their way down the cliffside. Sheridan stayed at the top until the last moment, his automatic weapon at the ready, his eyes scanning the forest. Only when he was certain that his squad was safely on the beach did he sling his weapon over his shoulder and begin his descent.

The stone of the cliff was soft and it crumbled away several times under Sheridan's weight as he moved down it toward the beach, but he made it to the safety of the narrow crescent of sand that rimmed the edge of the lake.

His men had already loaded their equipment onto small inflatable rubber floats, and at Sheridan's silent command they began their way toward the long steel pier and the collection of warehouse buildings on the other side of the water.

Once his men were safely under way, Sheridan went to his float and placed his weapon, a Browning automatic rifle, on top of the other equipment loaded onto the black rubber raft. Then he slipped into the water next to it and tied the raft's lead rope to his waist and started across the dark lake toward the lights on the steel pier, less than five hundred meters away.

When he was within a hundred meters of the far shore, he could make out the shape of a guard standing above him, looking down into the water from the edge of the pier. Had the guard seen him?

Sheridan stopped his movement across the dark surface and began silently treading water. Finally the guard continued his rounds. Sheridan quickly moved his raft below the outer edge of the pier and tied it into one of the cement pilings that anchored the long steel structure into the shallow water.

He took his automatic weapon from the raft and began to wade his way toward shore. He looked again at his watch as he approached the shoreline. It wasn't quite time yet.

He eased himself behind the protection of one of the cement pillars. Then he removed his binoculars from the watertight pack at his hip and used them to survey the secret inland staging area.

Directly ahead lay a series of warehouses. Men were carrying long gray metal boxes from the warehouses down to the pier. Any lingering doubts that he might have had earlier were ended with the all-too-familiar sight of the boxes up close. They were precisely as he had seen them in the river valley in northwest Germany.

He shifted the focal point of his field glasses from the warehouses up the hillside that lay behind them, until a large headquarters building set deep into the forest appeared in his field of vision. There was movement in the building's second floor and Sheridan slowly moved the picture in his field glasses to where a figure was striding out onto the building's upper balcony. The figure stopped by the balcony's railing and looked down at the activity on the pier below him.

The figure was dressed in a black military uniform with a splash of red and gold on the lapels. The man was short and he moved with a slight limp but with great authority across the balcony. Could it be him? Goebbels, alive and in charge of this final mad attack that could push the world to the brink of annihilation?

Sheridan couldn't be certain, and as he attempted to focus his night field glasses, a second figure appeared on the balcony and blocked the picture that Sheridan held in his scope.

Sheridan recognized Gruening from dozens of briefings he'd had in London—the Fuehrer's bodyguard. It was said that no one could ever get to Hitler as long as Gruening was alive, and now, Sheridan thought, it appeared the same had become true for Goebbels.

Angrily Sheridan watched the two men walk back inside the upstairs room.

Sheridan looked again at his watch. It was nearly time now. And he began to push his way out from the base of the pier, moving as fast as he could in the knee-deep water. Suddenly he heard the shouts of men coming from the shoreline in front of him. The guards had seen him. He dropped his weapon into position and began to fire, but there were dozens of black-uniformed soldiers on the shore and some of them had opened fire before he had. Bullets rained into the surface of the water, dropping all around him.

He turned and ran back the way that he'd come, but there was another line of guards on the pier above him, and as he rushed at them, they began to fire at him as well. He was caught in a thick cross fire. He raised his rifle to make a final attempt to return fire when suddenly the entire night sky above the pier was lit with flames. A deep booming explosion of noise and concussion followed a moment later.

Sheridan was thrown violently backward onto the surface of the lake and then floated for a moment in shock, his mind a blank, staring up at the dark, moonlit sky, with a panorama of orange flames somewhere in the vast distance that surrounded him.

The pier was on fire and the warehouse behind it. The flames were spreading rapidly to the ships and the pontoon aircraft tied to the dock. There was another explosion and the airfield and the adjoining hangars went up in a great billow of smoke. Slowly Sheridan regained his feet. He watched while the pier crumbled into flames in front of him. The soldiers who had been firing their weapons only a moment before dropped like rag dolls into the water.

Sheridan turned back to shore then, more flames, more explosions, the warehouses, the forest, seemingly the very sky itself exploding and burning, bursting into great torrents of orange-and-yellow flames. The soldiers on the shoreline were running, some firing their weapons, others dropping to the ground from the concussion, still others caught by the flames.

Sheridan raised his rifle, firing into the fleeing guards. Then from nearly every side came even more explosions, rocking the ground beneath him, throwing up waves of dark water. Sheridan ran to the shoreline, his rifle at the ready across his chest. He could see the devastation in front of him. The entire compound was on fire, residual explosions going off every few seconds. The airfield, the ships and aircraft, the temporary warehouses, all roaring with flames. His team had done its job well, Sheridan thought.

Several of the long gray metal boxes stood on the shoreline. The dead and torn bodies of the soldiers who had been moving boxes to the ships when the explosions had begun lay draped over the casketlike boxes or lying next to them on the blood-drenched sand.

Sheridan knelt by one of the boxes. It had been blown open by the debris from the exploding pier and warehouses. Sheridan examined its contents. He knew at once that something was wrong. He looked closely at the black seeds that spilled out of the box's broken sides. There was no smell, nothing of the hideous stench that he had expected. He looked more closely—wood ash and coal dust, not the Phoenix microbes at all. He stood and used his rifle butt to smash open another container. He removed a handful of the black material from inside of it. He knew how dangerous that could be, but it was only more of the black ash and dust. What the hell was happening? He tried to understand, but there wasn't time.

Soldiers were running down from the main house, charging directly at him. Sheridan continued on, moving away from the hillside path. A soldier appeared in front of him. Sheridan fired his weapon and the black-uniformed figure dropped to the ground.

He pushed up the hillside, his destination the second-floor balcony of the headquarters building where he had seen the mysterious uniformed figure. But suddenly another soldier appeared, blocking his way. Sheridan fired his weapon once, cleanly, steadily, and the man dropped to the ground.

Sheridan was almost to the house now. He could see more soldiers pouring out of the barracks building behind it, headed for what remained of the pier and warehouses. He looked above, up at the balcony of the main house. The black-uniformed figure had returned to the balcony, his hands gripping its railing as he stared down at the chaos of fire and explosions and running men beneath him. A sudden burst of firelight revealed the figure's face. Goebbels.

It was true, Sheridan thought in a flash. Goebbels had been behind it all, all the deceptions, all the false leads and traps leading all the way back to the bunker in Berlin. And he had found him on the eve of what he had planned to be his greatest triumph, just hours before he unleashed Phoenix on the world. And he was within thirty meters of him—killing range.

Sheridan lifted his weapon. He had Goebbels' face perfectly in view. Without hesitating another moment, he pulled the trigger. A body hurled itself into the line of fire. The bullet struck the intervening figure's shoulder. The figure staggered backward with the blow, but still somehow managed to continue pulling Goebbels back away from the edge of the balcony and out of Sheridan's line of sight. As he did, Sheridan caught a hint of the figure's face, but even that moment was enough: Gruening again, the infamous bodyguard, Sheridan realized as the big man finished pulling Goebbels from the balcony and out of the range of Sheridan's weapon.

But nothing was going to stop him, not when he was this close, his target only moments away. He would get to him and he would end Phoenix whatever the consequences. And Sheridan felt his own will and determination moving him forward up the front steps of the headquarters building. Goebbels and Gruening and whatever else awaited him must be beaten, he told himself as he flew through the first-floor rooms to the central staircase.

Just as he reached the foot of the stairs, a man appeared on the landing above him—a fat man in a wrinkled gray suit. Sheridan recognized him in a flash: Morell, Hitler's personal physician. Morell pointed a Luger at him and fired, but just as he did, there was a series of rattling explosions from behind Sheridan and the fat man's face exploded in blood and he toppled forward over the railing and fell to the entry hall below, his head dashed open against the marble hallway.

Sheridan looked behind him to see Ramón, the barrel of his automatic weapon still smoking. Soldiers were appearing through the front door drawn by the gunfire. Bullets began flying around Sheridan.

He continued up the stairs as a hail of bullets exploded into the wall of the staircase where he had just been. He could see a hint of Ramón below him backing up toward the front door, his gun blazing at the soldiers closing in around him, making a final stand against overwhelming odds. Sheridan fired into the cluster of black-uniformed soldiers until he saw Ramón take a final hail of bullets and then collapse onto the floor of the entrance hall.

Seeing the young man's fallen body filled Sheridan with even more anger and determination. He must get to Goebbels, he told himself as he fired a final volley at the advancing soldiers and then turned and crossed the hallway and entered the upstairs bedroom.

Goebbels, dressed in a full Phoenix uniform of black and red, stood frozen in place at the center of the room staring at him, not ten meters away.

Sheridan raised his rifle to fire, but before he could, Gruening appeared as if from nowhere, a pistol in his hand. Gruening was Goebbels' last line of protection. And as Sheridan looked across the room directly into the big man's eyes, all he could see was the dark remorseless glow of a dangerous animal, but Gruening had seen him first and had been waiting for him and Sheridan knew that the big dangerous man had the enormous advantage now of making the first move. There would be no way for him to react effectively before the bodyguard did. The initial move would be Gruening's and Sheridan knew that it would be a deadly one.

Gruening fired his pistol. Sheridan could see its muzzle flash a bright fiery red-orange, then again.

It took Sheridan another stunned moment to realize that neither bullet was fired at him. They had been fired at Goebbels' face and then his chest.

Not understanding what he was seeing, but knowing that he had to act, Sheridan fired his own weapon at Gruening. The big man swung his body back toward him and his third shot was directed at Sheridan, but it came too late. Sheridan fired again and the big man dropped to the floor.

Sheridan sprang to Goebbels' body as it lay sprawled across the center of the room. He looked into the shocked and blood-spattered face, but there was no mistaking this time the man's identity. Joseph Goebbels was dead. Gruening had done his final job expertly. But why?

Sheridan's thoughts swam with questions and confusion. The boxes of phony Phoenix materials. Goebbels lying dead below him. Gruening, the feared bodyguard, turning on his master. None of it made any sense, but Sheridan could hear more soldiers climbing up the staircase toward the second floor and he knew that in another moment they would find him.

He ran to the bedroom door, nearly tripping over the two dead bodies beneath him. The first of the soldiers was at the head of the corridor. Sheridan raised his weapon and sprayed automatic fire into the soldier's face and chest. But there were more men behind him. Sheridan dashed into the corridor and ran down it away from the staircase, bullets flying around him. There was a back stairs. He started for it, but it was blocked by more onrushing guards.

The building was on fire, red-and-orange flames roaring up around a stained-glass window of a great black Phoenix rising from stained-glass flames that was mounted at the end of the cor-

261

ridor. He sprayed the stairs with bullets and then used his shoulder to break open the window.

He looked down at the white glass roof of a greenhouse, bursting with flames. Behind him the soldiers were quickly advancing down the corridor toward him.

Sheridan stepped out onto the window ledge and slung his weapon over his shoulder and leapt across space to the top of the greenhouse. One foot broke through the glass roof, but the other struck a solid piece of wooden supporting beam. He clutched out with both hands, grasping at pieces of broken timber, as he began to topple through the glass roof into the interior of the fiery greenhouse. His fingers managed to grip a piece of framing. The soldiers above him began to fire down at where he dangled halfway through the broken wood and glass roof. He tried to steady himself, but the framing gave way and he fell to the floor of the greenhouse. The fire roared around him. He forced his body to lie flat on the floor and roll in the dirt, smothering the flames that had clung to his uniform. Then he stood and ran through the rows of tropical plants to a rear entrance and out into the night.

He could see the forest directly ahead of him, and behind him he could hear more automatic-weapons fire as he ran to the wall of dense foliage and disappeared into it.

He ran through the underbrush looking up at the bright, nearly full moon for direction. He could no longer see the compound, but he could smell the smoke, and the entire sky above him was still lit with the orange-yellow light of the flames.

He ran for several hundred meters and then crept back to the very edge of the tropical forest. The dark lake loomed ahead of him, and across it he could see the inferno that had been the secret compound: the warehouses, the pier, the ships, the pontoon aircraft, the hangars, the headquarters building, all of it being consumed by great waves of flames. They had accomplished what they'd come for and yet Sheridan felt a confusion of thoughts and questions. Kneeling in the wet sand at the edge of the lake, he watched the compound burn into the night.

★   ★   ★

The telephone call that Debra had been expecting came into the embassy just before dawn. Lowry took it and he and Debra were in an embassy staff car within minutes.

On the northern edge of the city was a coastal road that led into the hills. Lowry turned the staff car up the mountainous road and drove high above the night lights of Buenos Aires. He stopped only when he saw a huddle of police cars parked at the edge of the mountain road.

Debra was the first out of the car and down the rocky incline that led off the side of the highway moving toward a small group of men in civilian clothes that were gathered around an object that lay at the base of the dirt hillside.

"British intelligence," she said as one of the men turned to try and stop her advance. Debra stepped forward then and looked down at the object lying in the dirt below them. It was a woman, her face smashed beyond recognition, her body a bloody tangle. Her long blond hair was matted with even more blood, her white linen suit soaked with crimson. Debra looked back up the steep hillside that rose above her. The body had fallen or more likely been pushed several hundred meters to this spot.

"Is she the one you reported having been kidnapped from the embassy earlier?" one of the policemen in plain clothes asked.

Lowry nodded, while Debra bent down and looked more closely. "She must have been taken by Goebbels' people. They needed to know how much she'd told us," Lowry said as he knelt next to Debra. "When she told them, they killed her. It's the only thing that explains it."

Debra nodded. She knew that was what they were meant to believe, and yet, the unrecognizable blood-spattered face was just too eerily reminiscent of two other bodies that they had been led to believe were something that they weren't. In Phoenix, she reminded herself, nothing ever seemed to be precisely what it appeared to be.

# CHAPTER
# TWENTY-ONE

Well, that ends it," Lowry said, moving forward in his chair. The Phoenix team was gathered around the conference table in the first-floor room at the British embassy in Buenos Aires. Sheridan, tired and unshaven after his return from the interior, was seated at the head of the long table. "Let me try to sum it up," Lowry continued. "I think we owe Command something final as soon as possible."

Sheridan nodded at him to go ahead.

"It's pretty clear now," Lowry began, "that Goebbels took up the leadership of Phoenix after Hitler packed it in. Hitler must have realized that Phoenix had little or no chance for success, something that Goebbels refused to see. Phoenix was powerful and deadly, all right, but the Nazis were never really able to manufacture it in any great quantities. What we saw in the river valley in Germany, and the other location in France, were only small experiments, probably left behind to frighten us. What they flew out of Camp 19, except for the few grams in the single crashed aircraft, were just those boxes of dirt and ashes that Major Sheridan found in Chile."

"Why?" Debra asked, unconvinced. "Why go to all that trouble to mount a major airlift of boxes full of ashes?"

"A trick, I suppose," Lowry said. "A gigantic well-orchestrated bluff. Goebbels probably had some kind of blackmail scheme in mind. That's all Phoenix every really was. Sail his ships right up into the San Diego or Los Angeles harbor and then enter into a negotiation that would give him some kind of a victory. And it might have worked, I suppose, as long as we believed that the threat from Phoenix was as real as it appeared. The mistake was the woman. She was thrown into the middle of the operation at the last moment, but she gambled that her best chance of long-range survival was to work with us, not them. So she waited for her chance and when it came she escaped.

"Goebbels ordered every remaining Nazi agent in South America to find her and get her back so that he could learn what she'd told us before they killed her, but by the time they finally found her, it was too late. She'd already told us enough that we were able to break through to the truth and end it. And if she hadn't managed to survive and reach Major Sheridan, we may never have gotten to any of this in time." Lowry took a deep breath then and sat back in his chair. "Thank God it's over," he said with finality.

"I'm not so certain," Sheridan said.

"I don't understand," Lowry responded angrily. "There are no loose ends. Goebbels is finally dead. There can't be any doubt about that this time. You saw the body yourself, Tom."

"He was murdered right before my eyes by his own bodyguard," Sheridan said.

"Final orders," Lowry answered. "Goebbels had probably instructed him that if he was in danger of being captured, Gruening was to shoot him before he could be taken prisoner."

Sheridan still looked unsatisfied. He stood up and walked to the window and looked out at the front of the embassy grounds. "I don't think Goebbels was that big of a fool," he said. "He wouldn't have mounted an operation of the size and complexity of Phoenix unless he believed that it had at least a reasonable chance of success."

"But you saw the boxes, Tom," Lowry protested. "There's nothing there but ash and dirt. The cleanup forces in Chile have confirmed that. They were never able to manufacture enough of their superweapon to use it to mount an attack of any real significance."

"I know," Sheridan said. "But what if the real supply is still somewhere else? Every way we turn in this operation there's another trap, another diversion. We have to be damn certain before we report to Command that it's ended."

"What if the real supply of the poison never left the transfer point near Puerto Nueve?" Debra said, pointing at the map on the conference table in front of them. "It's still the most logical launching area for an attack."

"But they were never even at Puerto Nueve," Lowry said. "According to everything the German woman gave us, the real transfer point for the material, when it was brought in from Europe, was five hundred miles to the south, halfway down the Argentine coast. There may even be something left there now," he continued. "But if their pattern remains consistent, it will probably look like Camp 19 all over again, all ashes and no clues."

Debra nodded her head. Lowry was probably right, but she felt the same doubt filling her that she had when she'd interrogated the German woman, some telltale misplaced fact or clue. If she could only remember what it had been that the German woman had said.

"What was the shipwreck at Puerto Nueve all about, then?" Sheridan asked thoughtfully. "Those were real Phoenix microbes on the beach there."

"That was just another decoy," Lowry said. "Goebbels needed to delay us, keep us busy, while he made the transfer from the landing area into Chile. So they planted some of the poison along the coast south of here, far away from the real transfer area. Puerto Nueve never was anything more than just another false lead. The maps, the flight plan that we took from the German woman, her testimony as to what she saw when she was flown in from Europe. It's all the same. It all leads to the same spot for the actual transfer point. Not Puerto Nueve at all, but five hundred miles from there halfway down the coast of Argentina."

"Through the rain," Debra said suddenly, finally remembering the disturbing part of the German woman's testimony. "She told us that she had seen the transfer point through the rain."

"Yes, I believe that's right," Lowry said. "She did say her view of the area was somewhat impaired by—"

"Don't you see?" Debra interrupted. "Through the rain. It was raining in Puerto Nueve when we inspected the wreck. A freak summer storm. It wasn't even raining in Buenos Aires only a couple of hundred kilometers away, and we can find out for certain, but I'll bet it didn't rain anywhere else along either the Argentine or Brazilian coast over the last ten days. It's not the season for it."

"I don't quite understand," Lowry said.

"I'm not sure of all of it," Debra said. "But I think she made a mistake. She wanted to lead us away from Puerto Nueve, but she mentioned the rain by accident. Her maps and her story about the Gulf of San Matías were the real diversion, and the actual transfer point was right down the coast from here some-where near Puerto Nueve, just as we suspected all along. And we're going to have to go down there now and find out what it is that she didn't want us to see, before we can report to Com-mand that Phoenix has truly ended."

★   ★   ★

Debra stood in the protected bow of the police launch and watched the jagged cliffs south of Puerto Nueve go by on the shoreline, while Sheridan stood above her at the helm, guiding the craft through the last of the blowing rain.

It was growing late and the day's storm was finally fading away and leaving behind a dramatic crimson-colored sky. But Debra knew that somewhere just ahead lay the bottleneck and the red stone hacienda that she had seen on her earlier trip down the coast. And she and Sheridan had no intention of turning back now.

And then suddenly a glow of light appeared out of the growing late afternoon darkness, high up on the cliff above the sea.

Debra pointed to it, but Sheridan had already seen the bank of lights glowing against the darkening sky and he cut the wheel of the launch, guiding the craft toward a tide-washed dock and boathouse that stood at the base of the cliff. Debra looked down the entrance to the bottleneck to where a long, narrow river channel ran back into the interior. The maps that they had for the areas showed several inlets and hidden bays that led off from the main channel. Could any of them hold a clue to Phoenix? But the launch was approaching now to within a  few meters of the boathouse, and Debra could see two men dressed as common la-borers standing on the raised wooden dock that extended out from it. Both men were holding rifles. She looked over at Sheridan, wondering if he would take the launch back out to sea, but his face was set hard and firm. And he swung the craft to the very edge of the dock and then called up to the two men in English. "We are Allied intelligence officers, here to see Count Heinreich."

The men said nothing, but only watched, their rifles at the ready across their chests, as Sheridan tied the launch into the dock.

The armed men began issuing orders in German, and one of them stepped forward and removed the .45 from Sheridan's holster. He started to protest, but then he stopped when he saw the other man's rifle barrel drop down, pointed level at his chest. Were they being taken prisoner? Debra stole a quick look at the radio mounted below the wheel of the launch. Lowry and the others were searching the coast to the south. She could probably reach them if she could just get to the radio, but she could see the men on the dock watching her. It would take only a single false move, and their rifles would be directed at her, she realized. She knew that she didn't dare try to contact Lowry.

She stepped carefully off the launch and onto the dock. As they started up the stone steps toward the sprawling hacienda at the top of the cliff, she thought of the handgun that she wore in a small flat holster beneath her uniform jacket. The guards hadn't even thought to search her. Would it become necessary to use her weapon? And if it did, would she have the skill and nerve to do it effectively? She had proven a great deal to herself at the harbor in Buenos Aires, but using a gun against another human being could be an entirely different matter.

As they reached the level ground at the top of the winding staircase, Debra looked above at the exterior of the large red stone house. The upper rooms of the hacienda were lit and Debra could see the shadows of figures moving against the window. But then the figures were gone, disappearing into the vast interior of the house. Debra felt a chill of fear pass through her.

Then the guards ushered them through a tropical garden dripping with the last of the day's rain and they moved into the interior of the house.

When they reached the grand central staircase that led to the hacienda's upper floors, Debra stopped. There was a light but unmistakable fragrance in the air. She looked over at Sheridan. He had smelled it as well. All the pieces of the Phoenix puzzle were coming together now, Debra realized in a flash, but she couldn't quite bring into focus the full pattern that they were taking.

Below the massive staircase was a vast dark sitting room. The room smelled of dampness and age. The furniture had once been grand, but was now old and threadbare. On the walls were great oil paintings of epic themes, ornately framed.

They were led the length of the room to an ancient sofa that stood near the door to the garden. From there, Debra could see out over the front of the estate to a view of the last of the storm blowing over the crimson surface of the late afternoon ocean.

The guards motioned for Sheridan to sit at the far end of the sofa near a great unlit stone fireplace.

A few minutes later a very old woman entered the room. The Countess Heinreich, Debra guessed, the count's mother. The woman was dressed in a very formal yellowing-white lace dress with a ruffled high collar that hid the aged woman's neck and chin. She was a picture from another century, Debra thought as the woman approached her.

Debra stood and extended her hand. The woman took it and Debra felt dried skin, cold and repellent like the flesh of an aged reptile. Debra was repulsed by the touch, but she was careful to show no emotion as she looked back into the woman's face. It was badly wrinkled with small, pale, almost lifeless gray eyes.

271

"Please forgive my servants. They are very concerned about our safety here," the countess said in German without waiting for introductions, and even as she spoke, the two armed men remained standing in the shadows of the room, with their rifles at the ready.

"Lieutenant Marks and I are Allied intelligence officers," Sheridan began, and the countess remained silent as she seated herself in a worn high-backed chair that stood across from Debra.

Debra nodded at her. "You may have heard. There's been a terrible accident just a few kilometers from here. A small ship was apparently lost against a reef and it spilled its cargo onto the beach, causing considerable damage. We've been looking into it."

"No, I have heard nothing," the countess said.

"The maps of this area," Debra continued, "show a series of bays and inlets just west of here that appear to be accessible only through the river channel that runs below your estate."

"The maps of the area are very poor," the countess said. "There is nothing of any importance."

"I'm sure you're right," Sheridan said, joining in. "But we would like to take a look."

"There is no need," the older woman said. "We maintain the docks below and the boathouse. We would know of anything."

"We were hoping that perhaps your son . . ." Sheridan began, but the countess cut him off abruptly.

"I'm afraid that is quite impossible," the woman said. "You see, he was involved in a very severe accident. He is still recuperating." She pointed an aged finger to the hacienda's upper floors.

"An accident?" Debra said.

"Yes, in his automobile," the countess said. "He was thrown through the windscreen." She touched the sides of her own face as she spoke. "He was badly hurt, terribly cut, his face, his arms, but the surgeons do such marvelous work now. Soon he will be almost as he was."

There it was. Debra could feel her fear finally mixing with a shocked understanding. She looked over at Sheridan, and Debra could see in his face that he knew the truth now as well.

The countess began to turn away, indicating that she desired the interview to be over. "You must forgive me, I'm very tired," she said.

"I'm sorry," Sheridan said, challenging her. "We are going to have to insist."

"Major . . . Sheridan, is it?" The frighteningly familiar voice spoke in German from the top of the staircase, and hearing it filled Debra with a flood of fear. She understood the truth now, and yet it was all so incredible, so difficult to accept. She turned toward the top of the staircase to see a man with short bone-white hair, dressed in a uniformlike black tunic and matching trousers. Around his shoulders he wore a long flowing cape of matching black fabric. The man appeared at a distance to be strikingly handsome, with classic hard-chiseled Germanic features. He stood looking back and forth between her and Sheridan. "We know all about the two of you. We have been watching you for weeks. And we cannot permit you to continue any further," the man said, and Debra could see the guards step from the shadows of the room and train the barrels of their rifles on both her and Sheridan.

"Count Heinreich," Sheridan said calmly, and the man nodded as he moved down the staircase toward them. "Or should I address you as your true self?" Sheridan added, looking directly into the man's artificially bright blue eyes. "The true ruler of Phoenix from its inception to this very moment, the Fuehrer of the Reich, Adolf Hitler."

# CHAPTER
# TWENTY-TWO

Hitler was alive and he was standing close enough to her at that very moment that Debra could almost touch him. They had the solution to the last of the Phoenix mysteries now; the only question that remained, she thought, looking at the two armed guards in the corner of the room, who watched her every movement, was if they would ever leave here alive to do anything about it? Anxiously Debra's hand went to the empty place around her neck, and she regretted more deeply than ever that at that very moment she wasn't wearing her parents' final gift to her. But she could feel the weight of the pistol under her uniform. She was going to have to use it, she told herself as the two armed guards moved into position behind her. Sheridan would do his part, but he was unarmed. And the first and crucial test would be hers alone. If they were going to get out of this alive, she was the one who was going to have to make the first very dangerous move. But not yet, she told herself. First, she had to be absolutely certain that they understood how all the pieces of the Phoenix puzzle fit together.

She watched then as the man in black moved slowly down the staircase, and she could see his face closely for the first time. What she saw horrified her. It was the eyes that took Debra's attention immediately. They were artificially bright, so blue, so brilliant, that she knew they could not be real, and she realized that was what caused the horribly bizarre quality of the rest of his face as well. None of it was real. It was like a veil of flesh, dropped down over the underlying network of broken and reset bones, the reconstruction of which had made the features too unnaturally straight and perfect. Even the white-blond hair was dyed and artificial. And the bright blue eyes, really small colored-glass lenses. The man's entire appearance was like a madman's distorted dream of Aryan perfection.

He stopped at the foot of the staircase and Debra looked across the room into his unnaturally bright eyes. She could now see the ragged red ridge lines running across his face where the pieces of flesh had been sewn together but then apparently not been given the time or care to heal properly. She remembered the countess' words of a car accident, but she knew the story was a lie. It was the work of a surgeon, an attempt to disguise his real identity.

"You understand why we cannot let you look any farther down the inland channel?" Hitler said to Sheridan, and then motioned with anxious, almost palsied hands for the countess to leave the room. She obeyed immediately, standing and scuttling down the dark hallway and out of sight.

"Because we will find a small fleet of ships," Sheridan said. "Loaded and prepared to depart at almost any moment. And those ships will be filled with enough poison to destroy a continent."

"Precisely," Hitler said as he moved into the living room and seated himself at the high-backed chair that the countess had occupied only a few moments before.

"You have always been the true master of Phoenix, haven't you?" Debra said, and Hitler moved his angry gaze to her as she continued. "You were only acting in Berlin, pretending to be sick and in despair, and to be contemplating suicide. When the truth was that all the time you were planning to escape from Germany, leaving behind the body of a double, just as Goebbels engineered his own disappearance. A double burned beyond recognition, but whose dental remains matched those in the official files of the Reich, because those official records had been changed years before and the double's records substituted for your own. We almost learned the truth of that in Berlin," Debra said, looking from Hitler's hideously distorted face back to Sheridan's. "We thought it was the Russians who stopped us before we could get to the truth, but we were wrong. It was agents of Phoenix, your own people. Then you were brought to a safe place far away from Germany. And while we and the rest of the world were given false leads to chase, your appearance was altered by facial surgery. Your new face was designed to match the identity that had been established for you out here years before by another man. A man using your actual dental and fingerprint records. So that when the time came for you to take his place, Count Heinreich could conveniently have an accident and you could step safely into his identity. The accident would even be one that required facial surgery to correct, and that would explain the change in his appearance. And I'm certain that the real Count Heinreich did have an accident, but I suspect that it was a fatal one. And now the real Count Heinreich is dead and you live in his place."

In the long tense silence that followed, all that Debra could hear was the sound of the last of the storm blowing away outside the stone walls of the hacienda, while Hitler's horribly scarred face grew red and strained and then finally, as if it would burst if he didn't speak, words exploded from him. "You are a Jew, are you not?" he said with hatred dripping from every syllable and then added, "a vile, foul Jewess."

"And you are the monster himself," Debra said.

"But aren't we missing someone?" Sheridan interrupted the angry exchange, and Hitler's body stiffened slightly as he hesitated over Sheridan's question, but before he could respond, a woman appeared at the head of the staircase. She was dressed in tight-fitting khaki slacks and a dark brown leather flight jacket. She walked slowly and coolly to the rail of the hacienda's grand central staircase. As she did, Debra confirmed what she too had suspected a few minutes earlier when she had smelled a hint of expensive perfumes and powders in the air. The woman was Angelique Von Stahl.

She hesitated for a moment and then came slowly down the staircase and into the room to sit directly across from Debra. As Debra looked across the room at her, she could see the two armed guards just visible in the shadows of the room behind her.

"I told you that it was too late." Geli smiled and lit a cigarette, wreathing her face in smoke.

"So many deaths," Debra said, her voice a mixture of sadness and pain.

"If you mean the woman in Buenos Aires," Geli said, "she was beautiful, but only a street whore."

"A life," Debra said angrily. "Just to protect your escape."

But Geli only waved her cigarette in the air to show that to her it mattered very little.

"It was all a charade, wasn't it?" Sheridan said, moving his own gaze from Hitler's hideously distorted face to Geli's sapphire-blue eyes. "A charade that you both played out not only to deceive us but to deceive Goebbels as well. He became the perfect decoy for us to chase and to waste our time following, because Goebbels himself never knew or even suspected that was what he had become. And the two of you planned it together from the very beginning, didn't you? In the end, even your precious Eva Braun became nothing more than a pawn to the great Phoenix operation."

"Yes," the blonde woman said. "We were separated briefly, and I wasn't told everything, only what I needed to know to play out my part. I even had my moments of fear and uncertainty. But I knew if I remained strong and survived that in the end I would be sent for and taken to safety."

"And that happened at the embassy in Buenos Aires," Debra said. "Once you had told us your story about the secret jungle base, your part in the masquerade was over. It wasn't Goebbels' men that came for you that night, but your own, men loyal to the two of you. And it wasn't a kidnapping at all, but an escape from our custody to freedom."

"Of course," Geli said. "I never really doubted." She looked at Hitler. "I was never deterred, although things were often not as they seemed. I knew ultimate victory would be ours and it now is."

"The two of you," Sheridan said, "with Morell's and Gruening's help, deceived Goebbels into believing that he had become the new master of Phoenix, but he was never anything more than an errand boy, and an elaborate diversion for your enemies to follow across nearly the entire continent, while the real preparations for Phoenix's final attack continued safely hidden here." Sheridan pointed back down the river channel that lay below the hacienda.

"He wanted to believe that he had become the new leader of the Reich," Geli said calmly. "And you and your people wanted to believe that you'd solved a great mystery. So we gave each of you what you wanted. You were given a wonderfully intricate mystery to solve, complete with all the clues and leads that you could possibly need. Two dead bodies, a secret base in Chile, my escape from the villains, their revenge on me, all melodramatic rubbish. With our help you unmasked Herr Goebbels." But then Geli stopped and looked directly at Debra, laughing at her as she spoke. "However, it was neither the right nor the real mystery."

"Only four people knew even part of the real truth," Debra answered her back. "The two of you, Gruening, and Morell; that was all that was required to execute the plan and its cover-up, and to deceive Goebbels, and only one man knew the entire truth." Debra turned to Hitler for a long moment, then returned her gaze to Geli and continued. "The rest of you were told only what you needed to know to play out your role in the overall plan. The pilot in Berlin, Kline, was killed by your people—Gruening probably—so that Morell could substitute you as Goebbels' pilot at the last moment and Goebbels would think that you were merely a fortuitous replacement. Earlier you'd had Goebbels' dental records removed from the official files so that we would become suspicious of the identity of the body that was supposed to be his, and we were prepared to believe you when you came to us later with your story that Goebbels was still alive."

"Yes, all of that." Geli smiled. "It wasn't as simple as you make it sound, though. There were many problems. The unfortunate Dr. Morell proved a great difficulty for me. He had his own dreams of glory and power, just as Herr Goebbels did. But we understand that both of them are no longer a problem for anyone. Thank you for removing these obstacles for us."

Debra continued. "The shipwreck and the damage at Puerto Nueve, that was a problem too, wasn't it? The shipwreck wasn't in your plans, but you had already ensured against a mistake of that kind by leading us into the interior and by giving us yet another false lead to follow on the central coast five hundred miles south of here. You knew that in an operation the size of

Phoenix there would be mistakes and that was why all these intricate diversions were devised in the first place."

"None of this is any longer important," Hitler said. As he spoke, Debra could see the armed guards that had been standing behind him step from the shadows and await their orders.

"Goebbels brought tons of the Phoenix microbes across the Atlantic to this very spot," Sheridan said hurriedly, pointing down to the river channel that ran below the hacienda. "And then using Morell, you tricked him into believing that they were being transferred to the location inside Chile and this base destroyed, but the authentic Phoenix containers stayed here, for the real attack, while Herr Goebbels continued on to his final destination with crates of ashes. Miss Von Stahl led us to the false Chilean base hundreds of miles from the true staging area. And when the deception had run its course, the final card was played. Goebbels, the grand decoy, was simply murdered by his own bodyguard, so that he couldn't be taken prisoner and the truth could come out. And we were left to believe that the threat had ended and that Phoenix was over, when it is just about to truly begin, isn't it?"

"Yes," Hitler said. With every word that he spoke, Debra's tension grew. She knew that she would have to act soon or it would be too late.

"Within a few days," Hitler said, "the first attacks will be made on the Florida coast; a few hours later, perhaps even along the Potomac, only a few miles from your precious capital. It will bring your country to its knees."

"The coastline is filled with Allied ships just waiting for you—" Sheridan started, but Hitler only laughed and cut him off.

"No, there is nothing," he said. "Only two frightened and powerless and nearly dead Allied agents."

"And you will command the attack yourself?" Sheridan asked.

"In the first ship," Hitler said.

"That's what this is really all about, isn't it?" Sheridan said, looking deep into Hitler's mad face and eyes. "You want to be personally responsible for defeating your great enemy, the United States. You want to ride triumphantly through the streets of Washington, D.C., and New York, just as you did through Paris."

"Yes," Hitler said. "And soon I will." Then he motioned to the guards standing behind him. The two armed men removed the rifles from their shoulders. Debra knew that she could delay no longer. She could sense Sheridan's confident tension next to her, ready to follow her lead. She had the only weapon; it was up to her to make the first move. And he seemed absolutely confident that she would do it well. Debra moved her hand into her uniform jacket. It was the moment of her life, she thought, but she felt strangely calm as she slowly let her hand close around the grip of the pistol.

Then Hitler caught the sight of her movement and his hand went for the pistol at his hip, but Debra's Webley was clear of its holster and pointed at him before he could unsnap the restraining flap.

Geli saw the small pistol in Debra's hand and she stood to block Debra's shot. As she did, the guard standing closest to her trained his weapon toward Debra and fired, but the bullet thumped hard into the center of Geli's back and pitched her body forward onto the table in front of her, knocking ashtrays and glassware into the air. She slumped to the floor and lay dead still. The guard turned his weapon on Debra, but he hesitated for a moment as Geli's falling body blocked his line of fire. In that moment Debra fired her weapon, splitting the guard's jaw with her first round. She dove forward as Hitler's weapon came free of its holster and he fired at the place on the antique couch where she had been only a split second before. The bullet tore into the aged fabric, turning it to dust.

At the same moment, Sheridan leapt forward off the couch, knocking the second guard to the floor. He wrestled the man's rifle from him, wrenching it from his arms and swinging its heavy wooden butt into his jaw and knocking him unconscious.

Debra fired a second shot wildly and then scrambled toward the door to the garden. She burst through it as a glass pane next to her exploded from a second round from Hitler's pistol. There was more gunfire, but Debra was through the door and into the garden.

Sheridan followed. Debra could hear the sounds of other running footsteps on the cobblestone. A figure blocked her way. It was another guard and he began to raise his rifle, but Sheridan fired first and the bullet drove the guard backward over the edge of the garden wall and he fell down the cliff to the rocks below.

They raced down the winding steps, Sheridan taking the lead. There were pursuers behind them and several more guards were cutting across the cliffside toward the winding stone steps in an attempt to cut off their escape. But they made it safely to the dock and the waiting launch. Sheridan quickly undid its line and leapt onto the deck. Debra was only a few steps behind him. He climbed onto the bridge of the launch and started its engine and then moved it ahead into the water of the bottleneck. There was more gunfire from the dock, but the launch was soon free of the shoreline.

Sheridan pushed the launch up to high speeds. Ahead he could see the mouth of the bottleneck and the open sea beyond. But suddenly a pair of ships moved through the opening, their big guns trained directly on his small unarmed launch.

The first gunboat opened fire immediately and bullets flew through the air and over the bow of the launch. Sheridan swung the craft inland back down the narrow channel.

Debra went to the radio mounted just below the helm and made contact with the communication linkup in Puerto Nueve, giving their location and requesting assistance over and over, but as often and hard as she tried, she couldn't be certain that she was being heard.

They were approaching the hacienda again. In the fading light, Sheridan could see a motor launch leaving the boathouse and heading inland. A man stood in the bow of the craft, his body outlined against the dark red sky, with a long black cape fluttering behind him. It was Hitler.

The German Fuehrer's boat cut across the fiery red water and continued down the narrow river channel that led back into the interior. Sheridan followed after it, taking his own small boat up to nearly unmanageable speeds, as the prow of the launch cut a sharp vee through the water, but the two gunboats continued closing on his craft from behind.

Another burst of gunfire exploded overhead and a volley of rounds sliced through the windscreen in front of Sheridan. His launch was flying across the surface of the water, moving furiously down the narrow channel, the rich thick forest a blur of green and brown on either side. A spray of white river water was kicking against the windscreen and whipping around Sheridan, nearly blinding him, and it was all that he could do to weave his craft safely down the tortuous bends of the channel and keep the launch ahead of him in view.

And then, suddenly, Hitler's craft was gone. Sheridan caught just a glimpse of its red stern lights cutting sharply to the starboard into what appeared to be a solid wall of forest.

Sheridan cut the wheel of his launch, using all of his strength and reflexes to turn the craft hard to starboard. The small launch tipped at a brutal angle, nearly capsizing. Debra clutched at the rail, river water pouring over her, while machine-gun fire from the chase ships that had closed to within fifty meters continued cutting through the air just overhead. A wall of jungle rose up in front of them. Sheridan braced for a crash, but at the last moment the jungle gave way and his craft began speeding down a dark narrow tunnel of thick foliage and then out into a small bay. Ahead, the last of the sun's rays were cutting through the gray storm-laden air, casting the waters of the bay an even deeper crimson than the river had been.

The bay was filled with ships lined up on the blood-red water, behind the single great shape of an enormous U-boat, the *Leviathan,* as big and as deadly and as frightening as the German woman had described it. Its great black steel hull was moving ominously across the turbulent fire-red bay directly toward Sheridan's launch and the exit to the secret harbor.

But as Hitler's launch came alongside, the *Leviathan* slowed to a stop. And Sheridan watched as Hitler moved from the launch to the metal hull of the great U-boat and began crossing toward the ship's conning tower, his long black cape billowing out behind him, like great dark wings. And then almost instantly the ship was under way again, slicing across the bay directly at Sheridan's speeding craft, but Sheridan didn't shift course or slow the launch even for a fraction of a moment. He held its course and speed steady, directing it at the sharp iron prow of the *Leviathan.*

Behind him the first of the gunboats emerged from the narrow tunnel of thick foliage into the bay and immediately opened fire again on Sheridan's launch.

Sheridan turned to Debra only for an instant and pointed at the reserve cans of gasoline stowed in the rear of the launch. She understood in an instant and went to them, opening both of them and tipping them over, flooding the launch's deck in gasoline. Then she opened the gas tank, ripping away the blue-and-white Argentine flag that flew from a short metal pole in the bow of the ship, doused it in gasoline, and pushed it into the tank.

Sheridan removed his cigarette lighter from his pocket and waved for Debra to jump, and she rushed to the side of the craft, bullets sailing over her head as she leapt into the water.

Sheridan turned back to the rapidly moving U-boat. It was rushing even faster now toward the prow of his launch. On the big ship's conning tower, Hitler had removed his pistol from its holster and was drawing aim on Sheridan.

He fired the pistol and Sheridan saw the bullet crack the windscreen in front of him. Hitler raised and aimed his pistol again. Sheridan looked directly into his madman's hideously distorted face as the two men sped directly at each other, closing at a furious speed. They locked eyes for a moment, neither giving any ground, Sheridan with his speeding launch, Hitler with his great hulking U-boat. Hitler was screaming at Sheridan in rage, firing his pistol wildly, his face filled with a frenzy of hatred. Sheridan fought with himself to stay cool and determined. He knew what he had to do and he knew there was only one moment in which to do it—the very last instant. And he waited, using all of his powers of discipline and courage, until the U-boat seemed inches from him, and then he flicked the lighter in his hand, tossing it flaming into the sea of gasoline in the bow of the launch and then he ran to the rail and leapt into the air. He saw only a flash of Hitler screaming in horror as his great iron ship hurtled forward into the prow of the speeding launch—and he tried to move from the bridge, but his long black cloak tangled in the conning tower's metal railing. There was another powerful jolting impact and then another as the first of the gunboats collided with the launch from the rear and the three ships came together in one final enormous explosion. An instant later Hitler's madly screaming figure ignited in flames, his body consumed in a fiery holocaust.

# EPILOGUE

Sheridan stopped the jeep at the crest of the forest road. He sat for a moment looking down at the spot where, two days before, the *Leviathan* had collided with his launch and then with the first of the trailing gunboats, creating a fiery explosion that had destroyed all three ships and blocked the only exit from the bay.

The help that Debra had called in had begun arriving soon thereafter. And Allied aircraft and naval ships from Buenos Aires had arrived and taken possession of the harbor. Most of the enemy personnel and the ships packed with Phoenix had surrendered to the Allied forces before morning. Only a few of the enemy had escaped back into the South American continent.

It was an Allied base now and it had been the center of an intense effort over the last few days. The *Leviathan* had been a command ship, not an attack or transport craft, and only a few boxes of Phoenix had been on board when it had gone down. It appeared that only one had broken open in the collision, and only a very small amount of its contents had actually spilled into the bay, but the results were still dramatic, and ships, aircraft, personnel, and equipment had poured into the area to help control the effects of even the small amount of the poison that had escaped into the harbor. Backfires had been set and earthmoving equipment had been brought in to build walls and dig deep wide ditches to control its spread. Men in protective gear were still working to contain the black ring of destruction that extended out from the harbor several kilometers into the surrounding forest.

Dr. Stevenson was in charge of the efforts and he had set up a small command post on the hill above the bay.

Sheridan sniffed at the air as he crossed from the road to the small tin shack that had become the center of the containment operation. It was Sheridan's nose that told him more than anything else that the threat was coming to an end. The air smelled clean and full of the salt air of the ocean.

"Looks good," Sheridan said as the shack opened and Stevenson appeared. He was wearing protective gear on his feet and legs, but like the other nearby workers, he wore no gas mask or breathing apparatus, as he had only the day before, another sign that the threat was nearly ended.

"Yes, it's going very well. Only a very small amount of the material got out into the water," Stevenson said, looking back down at the blackened bay. "No more than in the European locations or at the shipwreck at Puerto Nueve. It never reached the river." Stevenson pointed down at the narrow river channel that led out to the bottleneck and then to the open sea. "The rest of this," Stevenson said, pointing back at the harbor and the dying tropical foliage that surrounded it, "we've lost, but the important thing was that it not spread any farther. We don't think it has, or that it will in the future, but, of course, we can't be absolutely certain. The truth is we've never seen anything even remotely like this before and it may be that unleashing something as monstrous as Phoenix could have some kind of serious long-range implications, especially to the ecology of the area." Stevenson pointed back at the tropical forest that lay inland to the west and to the north of the harbor. "It might take years for that kind of harm to show up, maybe even a generation. We're going to have to study its effects thoroughly. At least for now, though, I think we were damn lucky."

Lucky. Sheridan smiled grimly to himself, remembering the bravery of all the people on two continents who had fought Phoenix and even for a moment permitting himself to think of his own and Debra's heroism. But Sheridan said nothing, only nodding at Stevenson's remark.

"I have to finish a few things," the elderly scientist said, and started past Sheridan.

The Allied agent stood for another moment looking down at the bay and the forest and then across the river channel at the red stone hacienda on the cliffside above it. Finally he turned back up the hill. He could see Debra crossing from one of the temporary barracks buildings that had been erected at the side of the road, to stand by his jeep.

"All set?" Sheridan called out to her, and Debra nodded, pointing at her gear piled into the backseat of the vehicle.

Sheridan hooked a long leg over the driver's seat and swung himself on board as Debra seated herself next to him in the passenger seat. Neither of them spoke as the jeep made its way down the narrow forest road, then toward the small airfield at the base of the hill.

When they reached the field Sheridan pulled the jeep to a stop. A C-147 transport stood at the edge of the airstrip. American soldiers wearing full protective gear were loading a last few gray metal boxes into the belly of the transport. Behind the large coffinlike boxes were stacked the wooden and metal treasure boxes that had been found in the sunken remains of the *Leviathan*. What remained of Phoenix and its destructive power belonged to the American government now and he could only hope that his own country would use it more wisely than their enemies had.

Sheridan removed Debra's duffel bag from the rear of the jeep and carried it across the windswept field toward the open lower cargo bay of the C-147. The tense, awkward silence between them continued as Debra followed along next to him. When they reached the open cargo hold, Sheridan stopped and turned to her. Debra stood across from him, fingering the golden Star of David that she wore at her throat, and when she noticed Sheridan looking at the small Jewish star, she explained. "A gift from my parents." She smiled with only a faint trace of sadness in her eyes. "Their last one to me before I left Germany."

"I never saw it before," Sheridan said.

Debra nodded. "I haven't worn it in a long time." She stopped then and smiled slightly. "But now I don't think I'll ever take it off. My present to me, a medal that I presented to myself for my heroism, just in case the generals forget."

"They just might," Sheridan said. "I don't think you can get a medal for something that didn't happen. And officially none of this did. Phoenix and everything connected to it is officially nonexistent and always will be."

"Everything including us?" Debra asked quietly and then waited tensely for Sheridan's answer. He stood for a moment saying nothing, only looking at her as the breeze lifted her soft red hair and ruffled it across her forehead and bright green eyes, until she swept it away with a brush of her hand.

"You'll like Washington," he said finally.

"Your government has asked for a complete debriefing on Phoenix," she said. "Then I'm hoping for a permanent liaison assignment."

Debra could sense the feeling of awkward angry parting that they'd known so many times beginning once more, but this time it would be the last. She couldn't go through it ever again. It hurt too much.

"I received orders to return to Berlin," Sheridan added then.

"I know," Debra said quietly, her words so soft that they were almost lost even in the light breeze of the runway.

"But I asked Harkins to join you in the States," Sheridan continued, and threw Debra's gear into the hold next to his own that he had loaded earlier. "If we can do what we did back there," he said, gesturing down toward the harbor, "there can't be a hell of a lot that together we can't do."

"No, there can't," Debra said, smiling as she looked back across the runway at him.

"America is a good place for new beginnings," Sheridan said, and went to her. They held each other for a long moment, until something behind him made Debra break the embrace. Sheridan turned back to see what it was.

American soldiers were lifting a wooden casket into the cargo bay of the large transport, placing it next to the gray metal boxes of Phoenix. The casket was unmarked and simple, but Sheridan knew its contents: the true final remains of Adolf Hitler.